Entangled Paths

Second Chance Romance

Decisions and Destiny
Book 2

Natasha Allen

Ink Siren
Publishing

To those who want their leading man to be a great cook, fix your car, warm your heart and make your panties melt...

This one's for you.

"If I had to choose between breathing or loving you, I would say 'I love you" with my last breath."

— Shannon Dermott

Trigger Warnings

This book contains content that might be troubling to some readers, including, but not limited to, depictions of and references to sexual content, depression, suicidal thoughts, alcoholism, mild emotional abuse. Please be mindful of these and other possible triggers and feel free to reach out to me on www.natashaallenauthor.com if you would like to discuss further.

Prologue

"Babe, I know I said I was going to cook the fish and stuff, but I just can't be bothered. So why don't I order us a pizza instead? We can go half and half, pick a movie, and just lounge on the couch tonight," I shout as I close the fridge door. Resting my hip against the counter, I look over and see Roman sitting on the couch, staring out the window.

My heart hurts. I hate seeing him like this. I really thought he'd be happier once he got out of the hospital. But it's almost as if he's gotten worse since he got discharged over three weeks ago. I drive him to the physical therapy sessions twice a week, but besides going to those, he won't leave the apartment and the only people he'll allow to visit are his dad, Olivia, and Serena. None of his cousins, no friends, not even any of his teammates. I've tried to entice and encourage him. Even suggested we try some workouts together. I made a board with various ideas of things he likes, seeing which we could turn into a hobby. I've said we should go on a road

9

trip, or maybe look into us doing some traveling, maybe heading over to Europe for a couple of months. But nothing seems to interest him. Not an inkling of excitement for anything.

I'm running out of options. What more can I do? I would do anything to take all this away from him. I wish it were me that had been in the accident. Not him. It wouldn't have been as bad if it had been me.

Finishing my water, I put the glass next to the sink and make my way over to him. Moving the plush throw, I take a seat and grab the hand of his uninjured arm, bringing it into my lap. He flinches and pulls it back to his chest. That flinch felt like a kick to the gut. He has never, ever flinched away from me. Hurt and pain ricochet through me.

Why would he do that? Maybe I should call the doctor. Maybe he's not managing the pain as well as he's making out. "Hey, baby, please. Let's just order a pizza, and relax," I offer softly before grabbing my phone to look up the pizza place. "So, shall we just get one big one or a smaller one each? I don't think I need any sides I don't—"

"No," Roman says, his voice cold and detached.

"What do you mean, no? You don't want to share one or you don't want a pizza? Would you like something else instead?" I ask.

Shaking his head slowly, he just continues to look vacantly out the window. Taking a deep breath, I'm just about to ask him to elaborate when he speaks again.

"No. I don't want pizza. I don't want to order. I don't want anything. I don't want this."

"What do you mean, you don't want this?"

"I can't do this anymore?"

"Do what?" Panic seeps through my voice as I try to rationalize what he's saying.

"Ruby, I just can't. I can't do this. I can't keep pretending everything is going to be okay. I can't keep acting as if things are normal, pointlessly chatting about what to have for dinner. I can't do it."

Tears sting the backs of my eyes and my stomach churns as I start to understand what he's saying, but I can't bring myself to believe it.

We have been together for years. We have plans for the future. Yes, I understand things are a nightmare at the moment. And yes, I know Roman is going through a horrible time, but surely he can't mean what I think he does.

"Look, let's just forget the pizza. I'll put something together for us. Today's been a tiring day and you're probably just drained from the physical therapy. We can just eat and have an early night. Tomorrow, if you're still feeling frustrated, we can start looking into therapy or something. Or maybe even mixing things up a bit. Maybe we should get out of Wisconsin for a while. I've seen a job I think would be perfect. It's not the highest paying job, and it's in New York, but we could start fresh. We could—"

"I said no," he shouts, finally turning to face me. "Don't you get it? I have nothing left. My career is over. My life, my dreams, they're fucking gone. I have nothing. Football was everything to me. It's gone. I'm not getting it back. I have nothing left," he stammers, his voice straining at the end. He's clenching his fists so tightly I can't tell if it's to stop the trembling of his arms or an attempt to control his anger and frustration.

How can he say he has nothing? How can he dismiss me,

dismiss his family and friends like this? We don't love him simply because he played football. We love him for him, for the man that he is. How can he just dismiss me, as if our entire relationship is based on him playing ball? Does he really think our relationship is that weak? That superficial? Does he really think like that?

"Don't say that." My voice cracks, physically demonstrating how my heart feels right this second. "You've got me. You've got your family. I know things are shit right now, but I promise they will get better." Tears roll down my cheeks as I plead with him to listen. He needs time to process, time to grieve, time to think about what he wants to do with his life. Time to rebuild both physically and emotionally, but I know he can do it. I know we can do it. Together. All we need is time.

"I can't, Ruby. It's over. I can't do this anymore. You need to leave. I'm sorry." Looking me in the eye, I can see a resolve there that scares me. I can tell this isn't something he's only just thought about. This isn't new. My heart physically breaks. Goosebumps explode across my whole body, and I have to wrap my arms around myself as I begin shaking.

"I'm sorry. One day, you'll thank me. You will find someone who can give you everything you want. Not some damaged, useless, washed-up failure like me. You deserve better, Ruby. Better than I can give you. If you want me to pack up your things, I can. Or we can arrange that I'll be out while you grab all your stuff."

The solemn, yet decided tone of the voice of the man I love, the man that from the moment we started dating back in high school, I knew I was going to be spending the rest of my life with. And hearing that he's done, that he wants out of our relationship is the most devastating thing I have ever heard. His eyes might show sorrow and heartbreak but his words clearly don't hold the same sentiment.

Leaning forward, he kisses me softly on my forehead before getting up and making his way to our bedroom. Rubbing his shoulder, and even despite the agonizing heartbreak I'm feeling, I momentarily wonder if his arm is giving him pain today. The sound of the door closing is one that I know will haunt me for years to come.

Frozen, I can't move. My chest tightens as I struggle to breathe. It's like I'm living a nightmare, but one I can't wake up from.

Never in a million years did I think today would end like this. Not even after the accident, when we found out he would have to go through several surgeries, or when they told him he wouldn't be able to play football anymore. Never once did I consider he would end things between us. We were a team. But that's not what he wants anymore. He wants to take the coward's way out, making me feel disposable. Like I never meant anything to him. How can the man who has meant the world to me treat me like I mean absolutely nothing to him?

And just like that, I sit there, sobs breaking out of me as the man I love, the man I thought I was going to marry, who would be the father of my children, the man I have been together with since we were fifteen years old, ends it.

I've always thought I was a strong woman—someone who would fight tooth and nail for everything—but how can I fight for something he clearly no longer wants?

Roman has broken my heart into a million pieces and I don't know how I will ever be able to put it back together again.

Chapter 1

Ruby

1 *2 years later*

"What do you mean you all flights are canceled?"

I tried my hardest to channel everything I learned on my last yoga retreat to help when I felt my temper fraying. And right now, as I stand in line with three hundred other passengers waiting for some kind of response from the American Airlines check-in staff, I realize there is nothing, no amount of deep breathing or mantra repetition, that will help.

"All departure flights have been canceled because of air traffic control. I'm afraid the earliest flights will be tomorrow. If you wish to be booked onto one of those, then you can make your way over to the sales desk. They can try to book you on the next available flight or exchange your ticket for another day. If you would like a refund, we can do that here."

I stop listening to the rest of the spiel that the check-in woman is announcing as, despite my frustration, I know it isn't the lady's fault. It still doesn't calm the annoyance that courses through me because I need to get on that flight. Nor does it stop the other passengers from shouting over one another, jostling me as they squeeze their way closer to the desk in an attempt to get themselves seen and heard by the one woman who's been left to deal with now a whole flight's worth of angry and grounded passengers who needed to be on that flight. Okay, I don't *need* to, but this holiday has been the lifeline that has gotten me through the last couple of weeks.

The collective moans and frustrated complaints from the hundreds of passengers around me sound like a swarm of bees, angry that the hive has been disturbed. The only thing uniting us is our collective annoyance and anger that we're all now stuck here with no fucking flights. Everyone is desperate and scrambling to find a solution.

My fingers tighten their grip on the handle of my suitcase as the press of bodies around me intensifies.

The air feels thicker as tensions continue to rise. I've never been one to have an issue with crowds, yet suddenly, I feel overwhelmed and just want to get the hell out of this pressure cooker.

I grab my phone out of my handbag, wanting to see if there is anyway I could salvage this mess when I spot a message from my best friend, Serena.

Miss you, babe! Let me know when you land. I can't wait until you get back. Rhett said everything is all set up and ready for you at the house when you arrive. But if you need anything while you're there, just drop one of us a message. Love you. XX

. . .

Goddamn it. I really need this holiday. I need to get out of the city so I can shut the world out and relax. The plan was to spend some alone time in Virginia Beach at one of Serena's fiancé Rhett's properties. Then, on the way back I was going to stop off to see my parents back in Philly, having a day or two back in my childhood home with the warmth and comfort of my old bedroom and my mother's delicious home cooking. By then I was hopeful that I'd have a clearer head and an answer of what to do.

I've taken time off work, but besides my parents and Serena and Rhett, no one else knew that I was going away. Especially not Julian. Which, considering he's the brother of my best friend's fiancé and the two of them have a completely broken and fractured relationship, has made the whole situation even more awkward and difficult. I just needed a break. I don't know how much more I can take. His mood swings, the drinking. I feel like I'm running out of excuses. I don't even know who I'm making the excuses for anymore. Is it for his benefit? Or my own?

I've lost count of the number of nights I've fallen asleep, silently crying as I try to hold on to the hope, to the memories of the good times. That's the thing. The good times are so good. When Julian's in a good mood, when he's sober, he's got such amazing qualities. He makes me laugh. He's adventurous, spontaneous, and like an Energizer Bunny, he just can't sit still. Yet all of that goes out the window when he's drinking. Especially as he can't seem to just have one or two drinks. No, he always goes hard and takes things to the extremes. Then we either argue and he gets mean, or he storms out and leaves. The next day, he's either dealing with a hangover, or he just has another drink so he doesn't have to deal with it all.

We've only been together for about eleven months, give or take, and they haven't all been bad. That's why it's such a struggle for me to work out what to do. Whether I should carry on fighting for this or if I should cut my losses. That's what this trip is for. To allow me the time and space to think. No distractions, no stress. Just the freedom to dig deep and think about what's best for me. For my life. For my future.

I still feel bad that I asked Rhett not to let Julian find out that I was planning on staying at one of his houses. It was never my intention to potentially add even more fuel to their already turbulent relationship. They already don't talk as it is, so I know it's unlikely Rhett would have gone to him to bring it up, but I still just felt I needed to stress the point that I didn't want Julian finding out. I know I could have just as easily stayed in a hotel or an Airbnb, but I didn't want to be around people and as soon as I told Serena I wanted to get away, she jumped on the suggestion that I should stay at one of her fiancé's places. And given that Rhett is a millionaire both from his familial background as well as the wealth he has amassed on his own, there is no way it is going to be some ramshackle hut, so it's the obvious choice. That's why I needed to get the fuck out of here.

Scrolling through my phone, I look and see if there is any way I can find another way to get there. The next train isn't until this evening but there's no way I'm sitting on a coach for hours. I check the car hire companies, but they're all fucking sold out. Everything.

Fuck, fuck, fuck.

I move to a quiet area and sit and search for a solution to fix this damn problem.

Around thirty minutes later, the battery on my cell is dropping and I'm not any closer to finding a way out of here. It's looking like I'm going to have no choice but to grab a cab and head back home. Letting out a loud huff as I look up at the ceiling, I'm frustrated that out of all the days this had to happen, it would of course be today. Why? Why did this have to happen? Just then, my phone rings. Looking down, I see Serena's name flashing on the screen.

"Hey, I've just seen the news saying flights have been grounded. I'm gonna take a guess that it also includes yours?" Serena asks apprehensively.

"Yup. Because why, oh why, couldn't I have luck on my side just this once?" I say with a sigh.

I hear some rustling followed by some murmuring in the background, then the clicks of a keyboard.

"Hmm, yeah, I can't find anything. How the hell is there nothing going out?"

"Are you checking on a laptop or something? Why did you take work with you on your engagement trip?" I ask, though part of me isn't surprised. My best friend is a successful lawyer and a bit of a workaholic. She hasn't gone on vacation in years because she's been busy running her law firm, so I guess isn't that far-fetched that she's taken her laptop with her on the surprise trip her fiancé has taken her on. I'm curious how she got it though because I'd helped Rhett with organizing the proposal he'd done at her dad's house, and packed a suitcase for her as he was whisking her off to Paris straight after she said yes. I swear if she made him go back to New York just to get her laptop, she really needs help. And needs to learn when to switch off.

"Haha, it's actually Rhett's. He's currently trying to see if any of the private airfields are flying out."

"Woah, woah, no. Nope. Tell him no. There is no need for anything extreme like that. That's just silly. Besides, you're both doing me a big enough favor, letting me stay in one of Rhett's properties." I can still hear her typing away. "Serena, are you listening to me?"

"Yes. I'm listening. And that offer wasn't actually my idea, by the way. That was Rhett's," she amends.

My heart warms slightly that my best friend is engaged to a man who really is continuing to do everything to support her. I couldn't be happier for her. For both of them. I'd be even happier if I was on my flight right now though.

"Well, tell him thank you for the offer, but I'll come up with something. Or I'll just head back home." My shoulders slump and I can feel the backs of my eyes begin to sting at just the thought of not being able to get away.

"I do have another idea. It's one I'm pretty sure is the easiest option, but I'm not sure you're going to like it." Though the tone of her voice is cheerful, her words feel ominous.

Between Serena and me, there have been hundreds of times when the words 'you're not going to like this' have been uttered over the years. Yet usually it's been me saying them. Why do I now feel like this is some sort of punishment for all the times she's gone along with things I've said.

Taking a deep breath, I prepare myself for whatever lunacy or haphazard suggestion she's about to come out with.

Chapter 2

Ruby

"No. No, no, no, no, no. That isn't a good idea, that's a stupid one. Why on earth would you think asking Roman to drive me from New York to Virginia Beach to be a good idea? In what world could you have that thought pop into your head and go, 'Yeah, that sounds like a brilliant plan?' Are you drunk? I know they love their wine in France. Have you been trying to compete with the locals?"

Now, I love my girl to death, she's my best friend. The sister I never had. We were inseparable from kindergarten all the way until Serena went away for college. We've been on countless vacations together. Hell, we'd even split our Christmas days and ended the day either at her house or mine. My dad used to joke that we were each other's shadows. Where you'd find one of us, the other wasn't far behind. And despite all the laughter, heartbreaks, drunken nights, and regrettable decisions, this has to be the dumbest idea she has ever come out with.

"Hey, no need for any cheek. And for your information, no, I haven't had a drink yet. But I'm sure I will when we go out for dinner later. That doesn't matter, though."

"Yes, it matters. At least if you were drunk, then it would be some sort of explanation why you would put forward an idea like that."

My eyes hurt from how much I am rolling them. If I wasn't already so irritated, I would actually find it funny. But right now, laughing is the last thing I want to do.

"Listen, I get that you're overwhelmed and frustrated right now, but it's really not that much of a ridiculous solution to your problem."

"Ha. Yeah, because anyone would think when you're stuck and annoyed and have no good options, a great idea is to call your ex up and drive together for like six or seven hours. Yeah, I'm sure most people would think that's a brilliant idea," I rumble.

Seriously, it sounds even more ludicrous when saying it out loud.

"Well, first I wasn't exactly expecting you to call him, so that is one thing you can check off your irritated list," she says with a chuckle, one I find really unassuming.

"So that doesn't change the stupidity of the idea. Besides, I think you've missed two gigantic problems."

"Oh really? And what are they?"

"I get Roman is your brother, but he's still my ex. And yes, I know we don't have the same animosity or awkward tension that we used to have. Nevertheless, it's not like we're friends."

"Well, you're both friendly to one another. It's not like

you two haven't spent time together over the years. We've had more than a handful of family barbecues, get togethers, birthday parties, and holiday get-togethers, and you've been to all of them with Roman being there and the two of you we're amicable."

"Yeah, *amicable*. Not best buds stuck together in a tin can on wheels for hours alone with one other."

"Tin can." She laughs at that. "Plus, you guys seemed fine at Dad's when Rhett proposed."

I keep my mouth shut, as I don't want to think about the conversation Roman had with me when he followed me into the kitchen that day. Shaking my head, I focus back on trying to get my girl to understand why this not only wouldn't work logically, but also logistically.

"Listen, we might be polite to one another when there are other people around, but we both know this is completely different. And if—and this is a huge *if*—we would ignore the fact that the two of us would be alone in a car, driving for multiple hours, feeling awkward as hell, it just wouldn't work logistically. Roman is in Franklin Park. That's like two hours away. So there's no way that he's going to drive up to New York, then drive me to Virginia Beach," I say breathlessly.

There's a moment of silence from Serena, and I lift my phone, checking to make sure my battery hasn't died. "Yo, Serena, you still there?" I ask.

"Yeah, sorry, I am listening, just sorting something out. Alright, so let me explain how I can counter your two points."

I blow out a huff as I can hear in her voice that she's gone into full lawyer mode right now. Why didn't I think about the fact that arguing with a successful lawyer is about as fair as playing ball with a Larry O'Brien trophy winner?

"Regarding your point about spending time together in the car, now I get that. Yes, it's not ideal. I'm sure it's not exactly peaking at the top of your list of things that you would ideally like to be doing today. However, he isn't a stranger. If you said to him you didn't want to talk for the entire journey and just put your headphones on or sleep or whatever, we both know he'd respect that. I know he's apologized for his behavior and how he dealt with things after the accident, but honestly, I think you could almost get him to do anything for you."

I take a seat on my suitcase, stretching my back against the cold wall inside the terminal. I know she's right. In his own way, Roman has been apologizing pretty much every time I've seen him over the past ten years. And that's the thing. I forgave him. Yes, it hurt, especially the first year after the breakup, but eventually, the pain and sadness eased. I started dating again; I had two long-term relationships. Okay neither of those panned out, but I still put myself out there, moved on. I got me back. I don't feel like there is still anything for Roman to feel sorry about. It's done. In the past. We were young. He got into a really dark place and now we're both out, on the other side.

"But I don't need him to apologize or make up for anything. And if he felt compelled to—especially being stuck in a car together—that'll just end up making me feel even more awkward."

"Yeah, I get that, but I can promise you he wouldn't do

anything to make you feel like that. Because if he did, I'd be on the first flight back to the States, and boy, would I tell him to run for cover."

I can't help but laugh. Although he is her brother, I know she's always had my back. I remember when I called her, crying hysterically after he broke up with me. She didn't talk to him for weeks. She was so disappointed in him and what he'd done. It was only a little while later, when he went to the doctor and apparently broke down that they found out the extent of his depression. When she told me, my heart broke for him, and while it made some of his behavior and choices make a bit more sense, it still didn't take away my hurt. It was, however, what kick-started them to rebuild their sibling relationship. And I'm glad it did. I knew Roman would have needed all the help and support around him back then.

"Now, onto your other argument. Well, that one is null and void," she states.

"How so?"

"Roman isn't currently in Philadelphia. He's actually been staying at my apartment for the past week. I'd had some repairs booked in, and when I'd planned them, I obviously hadn't known that Rhett was going to propose and whisk me off to France. So Roman had offered to stay at mine for a couple of days while the work was going on, which then turned out to be a double blessing as Rhett then asked him if he could look at his Plymouth Cuda as he wants some custom work done to it. So they agreed Roman would fly up and stay at my place, then he'd drive Rhett's car back when he heads home. He's literally planning on driving back, anyway. And I know it wouldn't be a problem for him to do a slight detour and first drop you to Virginia Beach before he heads back home."

Seriously? What are the odds? And damn, she hasn't given me room to argue, has she? "Alright. but for all you know, he's not planning on leaving for a couple of days. He might have plans, places to go, people to meet."

My face scrunches as I cringe. Even I know just how ridiculous I sound right now. "Babe, you can hear yourself right now, can't you?" Serena points out, laughing.

"Yeah, yeah, I know. But still. He probably won't be thrilled that he has to cut his trip short, pick me up, drive me to Rhett's beach house, drop me off, then drive all the way back."

Running my hand along the back of my neck, I try to relieve some of the tension.

"Listen, I know I'm joking and laughing and I'm sure it's the least helpful thing right now. If you really don't want to get a ride with Roman, that's fine. I understand. But you're stuck at the airport, flights are canceled, and I'm sure you're tired, hungry, and fed up. So I understand that the thought of getting in the car with your ex and driving for seven hours doesn't sound too appealing. But I know how much you not only want this, but need this little getaway. I know I haven't been the best friend recently. I can imagine there's a lot more to what's going on with you and Julian than you've told me. He isn't my favorite person, but still, I want you to know I'm always here to listen if you want to talk. I promise we will have a proper catch up. You can come and stay with me, we'll order takeout, watch our favorite movies, do facials, the lot. In the meantime, I think you should go this trip, have the time and space to think and relax, and do anything you want, even if that's just staying in bed all day. Let Roman drop you off, relax in the sun, then you can just go from there. What do you think?"

Closing my eyes, I take deep breaths in and out through my nose. She's right. Everything she said is right. Yes, it's not ideal that out of everyone to be asking for help, it's my ex-boyfriend. But it's not the absolute worst thing in the world. And I really need this trip. "Fine. You win. I'll give Roman a call, explain my solution, and see if he's willing to do me this massive favor. I don't think I have his number. Can you send it to me, please?"

"I'm already a step ahead of you, babe," she says with a sing-song lilt to her tone that has me slightly wary.

"Okay, and how is that? What have you done?"

"Well, when you first called, I had you on speakerphone, so Rhett heard the first part. He called Roman"

"And what did he say?"

"He's already on his way."

Surprisingly, I feel a little lighter. Like a weight has been lifted.

"Thank you for helping me. And coming up with a solution. Even if it's a bit of a mad one." This time, we both laugh.

"It's not a problem. You know if I was there, I'd have to do it myself. And I know my brother isn't the ideal replacement for me, but I guess he's the next best thing. Alright, let me call him now. And by the way, he still has the same number. Hasn't changed it since high school. Wonder if you remember it, especially considering how often you used to call it," she says with a cackle.

We say our goodbyes and I grab my headphones from my handbag and put on my favorite playlist. Today really hasn't gone how I expected it to. I guess one good thing is that once I get to the beach house, there'll be no more surprises popping off.

Chapter 3

Roman

My sister's name lights up as my phone rings in the cradle on the dashboard. "I was wondering when you were going to call to ask for an update," I say with a smile.

"Roman, you're so, so funny. Don't mess with me right now. So are you still at my apartment or are you in a cab on the way to Rhett's? I told Ruby this wouldn't be a problem, so don't tell me I've unknowingly lied to my best friend."

"Woah, calm down. There's no need to jump the gun. I picked up Rhett's car and am just about to drive to JFK now. Calm down," I reassure Serena.

I get it. She's in her fixer mode. And when it comes to family or friends, she takes things to another level. I won't deny it, I was shocked as hell when my phone rang, and my sister's fiancé, Rhett, told me about Ruby's predicament. I know Ruby has moved on and is happy in a relationship, and I remember laughing when I heard it was with Rhett's brother. How funny is it that she'd dated me, and my sister is

29

her best friend, then ended up dating the brother of her best friend's partner? It's like she has a soft spot for brothers. But there's a part of me that still feels like I'm being punished. Haunted by the way I treated Ruby all those years ago. She didn't deserve to be in the crossfire of my breakdown. I've spent so many years hating that I not only broke up with her, but also the way in which I did it. It's weird because there are certain blocks of time after the accident that I don't remember. Not because of any kind of head trauma, but mentally, I think I blocked it out. Those times when I felt like I couldn't take anymore; when the darkness engulfed me. It was only after I'd started going to therapy that bits and pieces would come back. Like vivid dreams. But they weren't dreams. I knew they were real. And the one that has replayed on a loop is from when I told Ruby it was over. A shiver runs down my back and I shake my head to focus on the traffic in front of me.

I can't think about that right now. Not without losing my temper at myself. All I know is that I still want to, and will do anything to help Ruby. And maybe one day I'll feel like I've done enough penance to make up for how I treated her.

"Thanks, Ro. Sorry for snapping. I just feel helpless. I wish there was more I could do."

"Yo, I get it. But you really gotta chill. I'm on my way to pick her up, and I'll drop her to the address Rhett gave me. He also gave me a number for the housekeeper, to call them when we're nearby. So it's all good. Besides, you're stressing like this is some super important trip or work emergency. Rub's is just going away for a mini vacay. So just chill. I got this."

"I know, and I appreciate you doing this for me. But you

don't get it. She really needs this trip. She needs it more than ever."

"What do you mean? Is she okay? Is everything alright?" I ask as unease slithers through me and the steering wheel creaks while my grip tightens around it.

Serena sighs, and it does nothing to reassure my mind now racing with a handful of possibilities of what could be going on.

"It's not my place to say anything."

"I'm your brother. She's your best friend and my ex. If she's in any kind of danger or trouble, you need to tell me," I quipped sternly. Despite anything that happened in the past, my sister should know that I always have, and always will care and concern for Ruby.

"No, no, it's not like that. Well, not exactly. There's nothing for you to worry about. I promise. If I felt Ruby was in any kind of danger, trust me, you'd know. Especially as you'd have to call Rhett to post my bail."

"So what is it, then?"

"I won't go into details with you. I don't have permission from Ruby, and I don't think she'd be happy with me talking to her ex about her, even if said ex is my brother. But I also can't give you any details because she hasn't gone into anything specific with me. I just know things aren't great between her and Julian."

"How so?" I ask apprehensively. I won't lie, there's a part of me that doesn't mind the idea of Ruby ending things with her guy, not that I'd ever tell anyone. But the whole secrecy thing and her not sharing with Serena what's going on has me a little worried.

"Well, after Rhett and Julian's dad died like four months

ago from his brain tumor, I think it hit Julian harder than we thought. Or not necessarily harder, but he seemed to struggle with his grief more. And from the bits and pieces Ruby's said, it is causing a big strain on their relationship. That's why she wanted to get away, to have some time to think. And I guess work out what she wants to do. She also doesn't want Julian finding out where she's planning on staying. Rhett nor I would tell him anything—you already know his relationship with his brother is fractured. Anyway, I just want you to understand why this is so important."

I struggle to unpick the emotions ricocheting through me. I feel bad Ruby is going through all of this. I'm fucking raging that this asshole has pushed her to where she needs to get away. They haven't even been together for that long, so surely this should be the honeymoon phase. "Listen, I get it. It's shit that Ruby is going through a tough time. And don't worry, when I pick her up, I promise I won't mention that you've said anything to me."

"Thanks, Ro. I mean it. You're the best brother I could ever ask for."

"I'm your only bro." I huff a laugh. "But like I said, I got this."

"Perfect. Do you want me to call her and tell her?"

"No, no, it's fine. I'll do it."

"Sweet, alright, I love you. Drive safe and send me a text when you guys get to Virginia Beach. I don't care what time it is, okay?"

"Sure, sis. Love you."

"Bye,"

When I pull up at the red light, I bring up Ruby's number and press dial. I wasn't expecting the weird feeling

I've got in my stomach. It's not as if we've spoken recently. The only phone exchanges we've really had are birthday and holiday texts, but those don't really count, so it's almost like a sense of déjà vu as I call her for the first time in like ten years.

"Hey, Roman,"

"Hiya, so the traffic isn't looking too bad, so I should be there in about forty minutes."

"Thank you. Are you sure you're okay with doing this? I feel really terrible." Her voice is almost unrecognizable. She sounds so sad, and I hate it.

"Of course. It's not a problem. I'll let you know when I pull up outside of departures?"

"Thanks again, Roman. I guess I'll see you soon."

"See you soon, Rubes."

Hanging up, I fucking hate how sad Ruby sounds. That girl does not deserve this. And that son of a bitch is a stupid asshole for driving her away. I know better than anyone that he is making the biggest mistake of his life driving Ruby away. I know because I made that same mistake ten years ago.

Chapter 4

Ruby

Although I'd usually stay away from the excessive sugar, I couldn't help myself. I grabbed a large French vanilla swirl iced coffee from Dunkin Donuts along with a sourdough breakfast sandwich. I realize I should pick up a bottle of water for the journey and, still feeling bad about this whole situation, I grab Ro a glazed chocolate stick and a butter pecan swirl iced coffee.

The tension in the departure area is as high as ever, with more and more people arriving and finding out there are no flights going out. Fuck, I really need to get out of here.

Putting the donuts and water in my bag, I somehow balance my half-finished drink and Roman's full one in one hand, my carry-on in the other, and make my way outside. Taking a seat on a bench in the sun, I grab my sunglasses from my tote and slide them on before sitting back, luxuriating in the sun's warmth as it beams down on my face. It feels so bizarre that I'm sitting here and waiting for Roman to come and pick me up. Especially considering the number of times he used to in the past.

I've just finished getting a manicure and pedicure at my mom's salon. What eighteen-year-old wouldn't wish they had a mom who has her own beauty salon? Who wouldn't love to change up their nail color every two weeks? Since Serena and I first got interested in hair, makeup, and all things beauty, I've dragged her along with me. Although, now we only get to go to appointments together when she's back visiting home. Even though I'm stoked she's at Columbia, I can't help but miss her. Especially as we used to spend pretty much every day together. It still feels like I'm missing a limb.

Shaking off the sadness of missing my best friend, I grab my cell to see if Roman has texted. I'm in the process of messaging him to ask how long he will be when I hear the loud beep of a car horn. Looking up, I see his green Jeep pulling up in front of the salon.

Roman reaches over and opens the passenger door. Climbing in, I smell the tropical scent of his air freshener hanging from his rearview mirror and his Hugo Boss after-shave that I gave him for his birthday. Leaning over, he rests his hand on my thigh and pulls me in for a kiss. His full, pillow-soft lips feel just as good now as they did the first time he kissed me when we first started dating three years ago. "Hey, babe." The sound of his deep and sexy voice always sends a thrill through me.

"Hiya. I was just about to message you to ask how long you were going to be."

"Yeah, I thought coach was going to make me stay for

extra training today as practice really didn't go great, but we have to come in earlier tomorrow and do double sessions in the weight room until he says otherwise," he says with a slight huff as he rolls his eyes.

Looking over, my eyes are instinctively drawn to his full and luscious lips that have me instinctively running my tongue over my own as he backs out of the parking space.

"Aww, my poor baby will need some extra care and attention from me. Why don't we quickly stop at Walgreens and stock up on ice packs and that vanilla and coconut body oil you like me to use for your massages?"

He glances over at me, biting his bottom lip in the sexy way that he does. "See, this is why you're the best girlfriend. True wifey material right there."

The sound of a loud horn breaks me from my daydream. And just like that memory, I look through the dark tint of my sunglasses to see Roman pull up in a flashy-looking vintage car. Shyness and nerves wash over me, and there is a slight tremor in my hands. I'm not sure why I suddenly feel nervous. Before I send everything I'm trying to carry flying, a large, warm hand covers mine and grabs the handle of my carry-on. I hadn't even realized Roman had gotten out of the car.

"Looks like you're double parked on your drinks there, Rubes. You know we could have stopped to get you another one?" he says with a laugh.

I push my sunglasses up onto the crown of my head, spilling none of the drinks on me. And, as I turn to face Roman properly, I'm hit by the intense green hue of his eyes.

"Ha, well for your information, I didn't double park. You see this one?" I hold up my iced coffee and shake it in his direction.

"Yeah, what about it?" Roman replies.

"Well, this one is mine. I knew it wouldn't have been a good idea to get a jug of margarita, despite how desperately I could do with a cocktail right now. So instead I went with the biggest coffee I could get my hands on, hoping to get both a caffeine high and a sugar rush. And I thought you probably would want something. Especially as I'm sure Serena demanded you leave instantly to make your way here ASAP."

I hand him his iced coffee and watch as he takes a large sip through the straw. His brows raise in surprise.

"Well, I'll be dammed. I don't remember the last time I had this flavor."

He takes another sip, grabbing the paper bag that has the chocolate stick and hand it to him. Letting go of my carry-on, he takes the bag between two fingers, then picks up my case again and walks over to the car.

Roman opens the passenger door for me before walking around to the back of the car and placing my bag in the trunk. Climbing in, I place my handbag down in the footwell and have to stifle the laugh that's bubbling in my chest from watching how Roman enthusiastically continues to gulp down on his drink as he makes his way to the driver's side.

"I have to say, I didn't think it was possible, but you surprise me, Ruby. Wouldn't have expected you to remember my order after all these years. But damn, I swear either my teeth have gotten more sensitive, or they've made it sweeter than it used to be."

This time, I do laugh.

"It doesn't seem to bother you that much. Look how much you've already drunk," I challenge, pointing to his half-empty cup in the drinks holder as he fastens his seatbelt.

"Say what you want. But there's nothing better than the sweet taste of nostalgia."

Despite his tone not being flirty—maybe it's because of his choice of words—I can feel a blush creep over my cheeks. The air feels thicker as tension builds within the confines of the car.

Roman sets up the navigation and I grab my phone out of my tote to give my hands something to do and distract my mind from why I suddenly I'm feeling uncomfortably warm.

"So, it's saying with the current traffic, we should get there in about six and a half hours. If you want, I can just drive and only stop when we need to refuel or use the bathroom. Or we can break it up and stop first in Wilmington, then maybe Ocean City to grab a bite to eat, have a bit of a stretch, then carry on. Which would you prefer?"

"I really don't mind. Why don't we just see how it goes?"

I know that's not really a helpful answer, but my head is spinning with all kinds of thoughts about this whole situation and I can't focus properly. Turning my head slightly, I look over at Roman, who's watching me. He nods in silent agreement, then starts the engine to begin our long drive.

We travel the first half hour in silence. Neither Roman nor I make any attempt to speak. For me, it's mainly because I can't quite get a grasp on my emotions. Yes, I still feel annoyed and frustrated that, because of the issues with air traffic control grounding all the flights, I've ended up being in a car with my ex for several hours. Although, I also feel grateful that my best friend came up with the ridiculous idea and is enabling me to still actually get away. And yeah, it might not be ideal that it's Roman of all people helping, but I still appreciate it, nonetheless. But what's really ruffled me is that I don't get why I'm feeling awkward in a shy kinda way. It makes no sense. Roman isn't a damn stranger. Yet I can feel my cheeks blush slightly every time I sense him looking over. And why the fuck do I keep hearing those words he spoke on repeat in my head? *"Say what you want. But there's nothing better than the sweet taste of nostalgia."*

Who even says shit like that? I bet he was trying to be funny and it's just completely gone over my head. Yeah, I'm sure that's it. With the Pandora's box of other shit I'm currently dealing with, I'm probably misunderstanding half the stuff that's going on around me. My brain has been otherwise engaged with deciding the fate of my future.

I guess the one good thing about this whole canceled flight/train wreck/driving craziness that's happened is that for the first time in days, I haven't had a moment to stress or overanalyze the situation with Julian and what I should do about it.

The sound of Roman clearing his throat shakes me out of my thoughts.

"Were you as surprised as I was that Serena and Rhett extended their vacation? I think this is the longest my sister hasn't worked since before college," he says with a light chuckle.

"Yes, and no. Yes, because like you, I know how much of a workaholic Serena is. Although, I wouldn't be surprised if she's been staying on top of emails and checking in with the associates every other day." I smile, as I would bet that both

Serena and Rhett have been checking in with work while being away.

"But I'm also not surprised. She's in Paris—the city of love—with her fiancé. And after everything they went through, I'm sure the two of them want to stay in their little romantic bubble as long as possible."

"Yeah, I get what you're saying. But please don't put the thought of romance and my sister in my head. To me, they're just stuffing their faces with pastries and drinking endless bottles of wine before passing out and sleeping through 'til lunch. Then repeating it all over again."

I cannot contain the belly laugh that burst out of me. "You do realize how utterly ludicrous that is, right? There's no way you can convince yourself that all they are doing is eating croissants and sipping Pinot Noir?" I ask, still chuckling.

"Of course I can. As that's all they're doing. Okay, maybe also trying out a selection of cheeses. The French love their cheese, right?" Taking my sunglasses off, I wipe away the tears of laughter. There is nothing funnier than seeing a big brother try to convince himself that his sister is some sort of virginal saint. He would die if he knew even a quarter of the things Serena has told me about what her and Rhett have gotten up to. I wonder how much of our drive I can make him squirm for. Suddenly, I feel a lot more relaxed and excited for the next few hours.

Chapter 5

Roman

I look over at Ruby for the hundredth time. It's not like I haven't seen her over the years—hell, she's even invited me to her birthday celebrations in the past and I went. But being in the car with her is different.

It took me almost two years after I ended things for me to reach out and properly apologize to her. After the accident, I was in such a dark place. I just couldn't think rationally. I hurt, so I pushed away the people closest to me. I pushed away the woman I loved. Then my darkest day happened. I still look back at that time and am terrified at how close I was to ending things. I almost don't recognize the person I became back then. How could I have felt that death was the only option? I was scared. Scared of myself. Terrified that I'd sunk so low, reached such depths to the point that I felt like there was no other solution as I sat there thinking of ways to end it. But as I sat there and ran through which possible way I could go through with it, I realized that, as much as I felt miserable and helpless and like things would never get better, the fear of actually going through with it scared me beyond anything I've ever felt before.

After that dark day, realizing that total fear, truly acknowledging that I'd convinced myself that there was no other option, the way I thought that was it... *that* was the moment I knew I needed help. On top of that, knowing what my actions would do to my family, how it'd destroy and hurt the ones I love the most, I knew I had to do something. That's when I finally asked for help. My doctor referred me to a therapist and that's when I started twice weekly sessions.

When I started opening up, it was like the floodgates had burst open. And I learned that to heal, I needed to build myself back up. Re-stabilise my foundation, brick by brick. So, that's what I did.

Once I was finally in a better place, I reached out to Ruby to apologize. I could have done it over the phone, but I asked her to meet in person as I wanted her to see the sincerity in my face. She deserved that. She deserved way more than that, but I knew it was the bare minimum I could do.

She accepted my apology and we've been cordial ever since. Or at least in this weird new normal of her being my sister's best friend. But despite us having 'moved on,' there was one thing I could never deny or escape, and that was knowing how I truly fucked things up with her. She will forever be 'the one that got away,' and it was all my doing.

I couldn't seem to find what I'd had with Ruby in any of my other relationships, all of which never ended up lasting more than a month or two and Ruby had moved on and was now taken. Even if they are going through a rough patch at the moment, it doesn't un-ring that bell. I can't rewrite history. So with that, I feel it's best to just follow her lead with how we interact on this journey.

"Alright. I'm being serious. No more. No brother ever needs to hear or think about that," I tell her, unable to think about what my sister is getting up to in Paris.

"I see that side of you hasn't changed." She chuckles.

"What do you mean?"

"Don't you remember how bad you were in high school? The second you caught wind of a guy being interested in Serena, you'd find out everything you could about him. Then you'd grill him about what his intentions were and acted like we were in eighteenth-century England or something. All that was missing was you offering to duel at dawn," she remarks with a wide smile.

"What? I wasn't that bad."

"Yes you were, and you know it. That's why once Serena and I worked out what you were up to, we'd spread fake rumors. We'd say that one guy was interested in her when in reality it would be someone else. Then she'd go on secret dates with the guy you had no idea about."

"What?" I quip trying to keep my concentration on the road.

"You heard me. Didn't you never wonder why you didn't hear about the dates with the supposed guys she was into?"

"Well... I... uh."

"I bet you just thought they were too scared of you. Am I right?" Her amusement is cute, but also irritating.

With one hand on the steering wheel, I rest my other elbow on the door and scratch my jaw. I don't wanna tell her she's right. "Man, I can't believe the two of you did that and you never told me," I tell her in genuine bewilderment.

"Hey, you may have been the quarterback and the most popular guy in the entire school with everyone desperate to be your minion, but Serena has and will always be my ride-or-die. Sorry to burst your bubble, but my girl was always number one and I will take her secrets to the grave."

The smile that beams off her is the same one she used to have. Like when her parents got her and Serena tickets to their favorite band. Or when one of her many crazy ideas would go exactly as she planned. Man, she even had that smile when I'd found her in the stands after we won a football game.

"Well, I guess there are worse things than having a ride-or-die best friend."

"Exactly."

We ease into more light conversations, most of which center on her telling me all the clever and sneaky shit she used to get up to with my sister. Most of it right under my damn nose. Like how on one occasion, they spent weeks plotting so they could go to this art exhibit, when in reality, they'd saved their allowances so they could spend the day pretending they were famous, shopping, and eating out.

"Wait, how far away did you guys do this? Did you leave the state?"

"Don't laugh, but we didn't really think it through. We were only like fourteen and just wanted to make people think we were rich and famous. We probably should have picked somewhere to do it besides the mall."

"You mean the mall the two of you used to hang out at most weekends?" Now I can't stop laughing and roll down the window to get some fresh air.

"Listen, we thought it was a great idea. But we both realized how stupid we must have looked," she says with a shake of her head as she puts her hands over her face in embarrassment.

"You gotta admit it's kinda funny that Serena is now engaged to someone who is basically the exact type of person you guys were pretending to be."

"Yeah. To be honest, I never would have imagined her to end up with someone like Rhett."

I glance over at her. "Yeah? What makes you say that?"

"Well, think about it. On paper, the two of them are so different. And I don't mean it in relation to money or stuff like that. We both know she was financially stable and secure before he came on the scene." I nod in agreement, my eyes gliding over the tops of the full and luscious trees as we drive past them before flicking on the indicator to change lanes. That's one thing I was really proud of my sister for. She's always been independent.

"But Rhett is someone who's been in the papers and magazines almost all of his adult life. The only time Serena doesn't mind being in the public eye is when she wants to shine the spotlight on one of her cases. Serena gets more excited when she can get something on sale than when she's gifted something fancy. Her wardrobe is filled with clothes most women would die for, but most of the time, she'd pick out cut-off shorts, a flannel shirt, and boots."

Out of the corner of my eye I see her push her hair behind her ear and shift slightly in her seat before continuing.

"Serena is the only woman I know who will get a manicure, then immediately have her hands dirty and greased up while helping you guys in the garage. I honestly thought nothing would develop between the two of them at the beginning, but I was wrong. I guess I presumed I knew the kinda man he was based on things I'd read online. A cold, albeit mysterious, bachelor who was the epitome of nepotism. But then I noticed all the little things he did for her. Like, come on. Remember when we were younger and all the guys you used to be convinced weren't good enough; the ones you tried to scare off as you didn't feel like they were a good fit, a good match for your sister?"

I'm surprised at the warm feeling that seeps through me at her mention of the past. Our past and when we were younger and still together.

"Yeah, I get what you're saying. If you'd put a line up together of different guys and I had to guess which one she was with, he'd have probably been the last I picked. But as long as he's good to her and keeps her happy, I'm happy for her."

I look over and see Ruby staring out the window. I kind of want to address the elephant in the room, but I don't want her to shut down and go quiet again. Fuck it, I wanna know.

"So, I know you're in a relationship with his brother. I think Serena told me his name, but I can't remember. Are him and Rhett similar?"

Her laugh is dry and humorless, and I can see out the corner of my eye that she's rubbing her palms up and down her thighs in a nervous fidget.

"His name is Julian, and let's just say he's the polar opposite of Rhett." I nod and wait for her to continue as I pump the breaks in the slowing traffic.

"Are we really gonna do this? Have this conversation?

I'm sure Serena gave you some indication of what's going on. Won't this make our drive really awkward?"

"You don't have to talk about anything you don't feel comfortable with. The only thing she told me was that you were going away to have a mini break for yourself. Now I don't need to be a rocket scientist to understand that maybe you've got some stuff going on and need some space. Otherwise, I'd imagine your boyfriend would join you." I pause but she doesn't say anything. "Listen, I don't wanna make you talk about anything you don't want to. But I'll have you know, I've become a good listener. Or at least a better one. So if you wanna talk, I'm all ears. And I promise I won't make it awkward."

Chapter 6

Ruby

If anyone would have told me a few years ago that I'd be in a car with Roman and that the topic of conversation would be my current boyfriend—or better said, this issue I'm having with him—I'd have laughed in their face. When he first mentioned Julian, I thought, *oh god no, where is this going?* But as I sit and think about it, maybe it wouldn't be the worst thing in the world. Maybe talking to a guy and hearing the opinion from a male perspective might help.

I pull one leg up so I'm sitting on it and rest the other on the edge of the seat so I can get comfy and lean my head on it, looking at Roman. "Where do you want me to start?"

"Wherever you want. But it might be easier to go from the beginning so I have a better chance at understanding it all."

I take a deep, steadying breath before I speak. "I first met Julian on the night of my birthday. We hit it off, and I guess from there everything went pretty fast. We started dating. I enjoyed his playful nature and how he was always up for a laugh or the way he'd take me out to the best bars and restaurants. He was always fun." I glance over and see Roman nodding along as he both listens and concentrates. "Dating felt like a show, a big event, we'd end up somewhere flashy, always busy, popular places, and what was even more obvious was that there was almost always alcohol involved. Now I'm all for having a drink, say after a long day's work, a glass or two of wine with dinner, or even going out with friends. There's nothing wrong with that. But with Julian, it was something more. At first, I just thought maybe he's a bit of a party boy, one who hadn't been in a relationship for a while and didn't know how to rein it in. But I couldn't keep denying the truth and started suspecting that he had a drinking problem. Not necessarily that he always needed a drink, but more so that he used it as a crutch."

It's surprising how good it feels to let this out. "I knew that he was going through a lot since finding out his dad was dying. So, for a while, I guess I just justified it. The sicker his dad got, the more Julian seemed to struggle. Which then led to him needing to blow off steam more and more; so more drinking, more partying. I tried to suggest we both go on a cleanse. I guess it was my way of trying to get him to detox or something. But he wasn't interested."

Reaching down, I take the bottle of water from my bag and take a quick sip.

"I know it sounds like it's all been bad, but it hasn't. When he's in a good mood, things are great. He has these moments where he's really kind and sweet and he makes me feel so special and cared for."

This is weird because the more I talk, the more I realize

how much I've held onto those moments. Like I'm clinging on to them as if they are some sort of rare artifact.

"Can I ask a question?" Roman asks, his voice soft and light. "The times that are good, do they usually coincide with when he's not drinking?"

I don't even need to think about it. I know the answer. "Yeah. And I think that's one of the things I've found so frustrating. That version of Julian is truly is amazing. And it's the side no one else seems to see. Not his family, not his friends, no one. Just me. It's like that's the real him. The other version is the façade, a character he puts out to the rest of the world. But he's too scared or not confident enough to let others see the kind and soft side of him. So instead, when he steps out the door, he hides it behind the mask of the loud, obnoxious, spoiled party boy. Yet that's the one I can't handle being in a relationship with anymore."

My fingers continue tapping and fidgeting on my knee, and it's like I can't sit still. I feel like I'm on a never ending seesaw, dipping from high to low. Every time I feel like I've reached some sort of resolve, I'm then drawn in the other direction as I either reminisce or regret. I think this is also why I've not fully opened up to Serena about everything. I mean, I know she doesn't like Julian, but beyond that, I know that if I really open up and admit the state of how things really are, then I can't keep shying away from it. Gently pressing on my temples, I try to ease the pressure that's beginning to build.

I can feel Roman's eyes on me but can't bring myself to look at him. Shame creeps up through me. I can't help it. I never would've pictured myself as that woman. The one who makes excuses for their partner. But the thing is, when you're in the cocoon and confines of a relationship, you can't see it for what it is.

"I just don't know if I'm holding on to something that's there, or the idea, the fantasy of a relationship that I'm just so desperate to be in. That's what I can't seem to wrap my head around."

I pick at my cuticles as tears begin to sting the backs of my eyes. Goddammit, why is this so hard? Why am I in this situation? Roman's voice, that's still soft and calm, brings me back to focus.

"Do you feel if, let's say, he got help for his drinking or didn't drink at all that all the issues the two of you have would go away?"

It's weird because a part of me wants to jump in and say of course. Of course all those problems would go away and everything would all be fine. But would they really?

In the last few weeks, I've been analyzing absolutely everything about our relationship. For example, when Julian says 'I love you,' does he actually mean it? I remember when he first said it, only about two months in. And although I was a little taken aback, I thought it was sweet. Especially when he told me he's never said it to anyone before. But the more I think about it, the more I question if he actually means it. Because surely, when you love someone, you don't just tell them, you show them. Your actions define and validate your words. It's not a placeholder, not a bandage you can stick on. But I can't say I believe what he says. And in all honesty, what has it meant when I've said it back to him? I've never had that besotted, unyielding type of love for him. Have I not been just as guilty of perpetuating this lie between us? Returning words that maybe I don't mean, or at least not the real depths of them? Almost as if the more I say them, the more I try to make myself believe it.

I just really don't want to be alone. I've always felt happier, more complete when I'm in a relationship. Sharing my life, making memories, building something together with someone makes me complete. Otherwise, I'm just half a person. My partner is the one that makes me whole. That's why I don't like the idea of just walking away, even if it would be easier to do so. Because if I do then I feel like I'd be not only giving up on that person but also on myself.

"I honestly don't know. I want to say yes, but I don't think I believe it. Not honestly. Not deep down. But in the same breath, it doesn't mean it can't happen. That with the right help and support it wouldn't be unobtainable." My sigh is loud and clearly telling of how frustrated I feel. The confines of this car and the open and honest intensity of our conversation have me feeling so unbelievably vulnerable. So exposed. And with that, the first tears begin to fall down my cheeks. I try to wipe them away, so Roman doesn't see them, but it's no use.

Roman reaches over to the glove box and hands me some tissue and I wipe my face dry, embarrassment prickling my skin. There he was saying it wouldn't get awkward and here I am crying. There's no place for me to hide in here, so I do the next best thing and put my sunglasses back on. As the song in the background ends and changes into another, I do my best to get my emotions back on track.

I peek out of the corner of my eyes through the safety of my glasses, and see Roman continue to focus on the road ahead. My breathing evens out, but I can still feel my nose slightly running.

As if he could read my mind, he passes me another tissue and gives my knee a quick squeeze as he speaks. "Last week, I met my cousin Anthony after work. We went to Ryder's. You know the bar I'm talking about?"

"Yeah," I reply, my voice croaking slightly.

"So I've gone there countless times during the day for lunch, but I don't remember the last time I went there after work. Anyway, I don't know if you've been back since they've redone it. It doesn't look massively different, but they've added a pool table in one corner, and they have this small stage as well. Trying to bring in more of the evening crowd. Apparently, they do open mic nights, stand ups, and all that shit. Well, we were at the bar, having a beer, waiting for our food to arrive. And trust it to be my luck that it was the one night a month they do karaoke." His exaggerated head shake is comical.

"So, did you end up asking to have your food to go?" I know he hates karaoke.

"Nope. Because the story gets wilder."

My curiosity piqued.

"Remember, I said Anthony was with me?"

"Yeah. Why do I have the feeling the drama is involving him?"

"That's because you know him and what he's like," he says with a chuckle, before continuing, "The first guy that goes up has a guitar with him and I think he was picturing himself performing in a sellout crowd, instead of the thirty people there. Then a couple went up and sang a song together, and I'm telling you, it was like they were doing some weird kinda foreplay with each other. It was some seriously awkward shit." I shake my head and grin. When I look over at him, his whole body shivers at the memory.

"Anyway, next was a table of four women. Every one of them going up to do a number. Anthony had been watching their table pretty much from the minute they walked in and had his eyes set on one in particular. The one that ended up being the last one to sing. She goes up just as our food arrives and I focus on eating, but he's giving her all of his attention. When her song finishes, he orders a drink for everyone at their table but tells the barman he'll take them over to them himself."

Biting my lip eagerly, I await what I can just tell is going to be something ridiculous.

"He goes over, does his thing. I'm watching as I eat and notice all the women now glaring at him. I don't know what's been said but the next thing I know, every one of them chucks the drink he's just got them on him."

"What? Why?" I shriek with a nervous giggle.

"He then comes back to the bar, drenched. I have tears running down my face from how much I'm laughing. The barman hands him a towel to dry himself, and he explains that, apparently, the one he had his eye on... well turns out he'd hooked up with her last year. Not only was it bad that he didn't remember, but after that night, he ghosted her. And not just that, but when he snuck out, apparently he let the cat out, and the cat was a house cat who ended up getting run over."

My eyes widen in disbelief. "You've gotta be shitting me. I... I... Yeah, I don't know what to say to that. Geez, that poor woman. If that had been me, I'd have done a hell of a lot worse than just throwing my drink on him."

Roman nods his head, knowing too well that I'd have gone psycho on Anthony's ass. For the next hour he continues to keep the mood light, and we chat about all sorts. I'm grateful he doesn't mention the crying earlier. After about two more hours of driving, we stop to grab a bite to eat.

Once we're back on the road, I recline my seat a little as I'm so full up from the Philly cheesesteak and shake we ate, and we listen to The Fugees album playing in the background.

I'm awoken by the sound of Roman talking. He's on speakerphone and I recognize the sound of his dad's voice on the other end. He says his goodbyes and ends the call as I pull myself and my seat back up. The day turned to early evening, and the sun has just set; the sky awash with shades of orange and pink.

"Hey. How long was I asleep for?"

"Almost two hours."

"Oh, shit. Sorry."

"Don't be. You clearly needed the rest. And on the plus side, we should arrive in about forty-five minutes."

"You okay?" I ask, feeling bad for being asleep so long, but also sensing something has shifted in his mood.

Turning in my seat so I can face him, I watch as he rubs a hand over his face and checks his mirrors before concentrating on the road ahead again. "I want to ask you a question, but I know I shouldn't. It's not my place or my business to. But I've been running it over and over in my head the whole time you slept."

"So ask me. If I don't wanna answer, I'll tell you."

"Fuck. Alright. Why? After all the stuff you told me about Julian and everything going on between the two of you, why have you put up with it? You know you deserve so much more."

I'm touched and a little taken aback by that last bit. Roman's said before that he wished the best for me but there's something calming, almost like a soothing balm to my soul hearing him say those words out loud. I guess I'm not surprised by his question though. I think it's one of those scenarios where when you're on the outside looking in, things seem so straightforward. So simple. Yet for me, it couldn't be any further from simple. I wonder if I hadn't turned into a blubbering mess, he might have brought it up earlier.

"Hmm, well, I guess there's kinda two answers to that question. And in a way, they're connected. At the core, I don't want to be alone. I want to have my person. My other half. I want the romance, the wedding, kids, building a life, a future together. A future where my partner and I grow old together. I want it more than anything." The air in the car feels thick with tension as the silence worms its way through me and I have to swallow down the ball of unease that leaves a sour taste in my mouth.

"And I guess the reason I've clung on, tried seeing the best and doing everything I can to see if a future like that would be possible with Julian, is because the last time I pictured that life..." Taking a breath to refocus my thoughts. "That future? That dream? It all got snatched away from me, and I accepted it was over far too easily, telling myself that the relationship had run its course." This hurts to admit out loud to him, of all people. But he's the one who asked. "So I guess now, especially as I'm getting older, I feel like I need to fight. Make sure I give and do everything I can instead of accepting defeat too soon."

"Ruby" he whispers so quietly I can barely hear it. But his face winces as I see the realization sink in on just how much his actions all those years ago still play a part in my life and my lack of faith in myself.

Silence stretches between us, and I know he understands the weight of my words. He knows what happened between us. It was like a poisoned dagger to my heart. And even though I forgave him and moved on, it didn't alter the fact that his actions changed me. Changed the way I acted in relationships. After Roman ended things, I had to completely rewire my head, my heart, and what I hoped would be my destiny.

Chapter 7

Ruby

"You mentioned there are two reasons. What's the other?" The strain in his voice is as clear as day.

"Well... so... like I said, the reasons are connected. I feel like I have to fight. Have to hold on. I want that dream, that future so much. More than anything. And the thing is, I know you're not gonna like this, what happened between us, the way..." I shift in my seat and start playing with my hair nervously. Although I know there's nothing wrong with me being honest about this, it doesn't take away from the fact that these still aren't easy words to say.

"I want you to know that when you reached out after... when you apologized and I said I forgave you, I meant it. I still mean it. When you opened up about what you'd been going through and where your mental state was, it broke my heart. I wished I'd been able to do something to fix it."

"But, Rubes, like I said then, there was nothing anyone could do. Only I could work through it once I was ready."

Glancing over at his still handsomely chiseled face, I can't help but wonder what life would have been like if things had gone differently. If we hadn't broken up. Would we have managed to get through it all together? Gotten married and have a couple of kids by now? It's insane just how different both of our lives could be right now.

"I know. And I'm so glad you found your way through it. It amazes me just how far you've come. How much you've grown. But you have to understand when you ended it, when you told me you were finished... there was no discussion. No fighting for it" my voice quivers slightly and I breathe through my nose to try and get a handle on my emotions. "For me, it felt like if you could switch off your feelings for me so suddenly, then that meant one of two things. You either didn't love me enough, or you never truly did," I mutter, tucking my hair behind my ears in a silly attempt to stop my uncomfortable fidgeting.

"No, Rubes—"

I stick out my hand, needing him to stop. I've started this, and now I need to finish it. "That's what I felt. It was like a switch had been flipped and I couldn't see things any other way. And from that, I guess I started feeling that maybe I'm not good enough. And no, this isn't me feeling sorry for myself or wanting compliments or anything. But when the person who was your first love, the one you'd have done anything for, no longer wants you, it's like a searing burn to your skin." Biting down on my lip, I take a second to compose myself. Needing to get the words out despite how hard they are to admit. "At first, it hurts. The pain is so uncomfortable it makes you cry. The burn continues, intensifies as it spreads deeper. And even when the top heals, the scar runs way deeper than anyone could know. The reminder is forever imprinted on you and you can never get away from it."

My mouth is dry, so I pick up my water and take a large gulp. So much so that I feel a little lightheaded. "I... Ruby. I'm so sorry. I..."

"Roman, it's fine. I just wanted—"

"Please." The sorrow in his voice makes me feel terrible. "I know there's nothing I can say to undo the past. If I could, I would have done so every day since. You know that I would never want to intentionally hurt you. But that's exactly what I did. I hate that I was so fucked up that I broke something in the last person in the world I'd ever want to hurt. Rubes, does my sister know all this?" His mouth is turned down slightly and his eyes are blinking rapidly.

"No. I mean, she knew how much I struggled. But she's your sister. And especially back then, from what you told me, you were at your lowest. So the last thing I wanted to do was make things any worse. Plus, I knew it was a difficult situation for her. She was stuck between a rock and a hard place. As time went on, I put myself out in the dating world again, but none of those relationships panned out. I guess I'd carried all the issues from our failed relationship and latched them onto the next ones. Where I never truly dealt with it, I never allowed myself to start any type of relationship with a healthy and clean slate."

It's so dark outside now that it's hard to make out his expression. "I think when she gets back from her trip, you should tell her. It might help her understand why you do and feel things the way you do. How you're hesitant with some choices that in her mind may be simple, then adamant with others, where she'd presume you'd react or think differently. The two of you have been best friends for so long. I know she'd hate to be left in the dark and we both know she'll always be there to listen and support you."

I know he's right. I just don't know if it's really going to make that much of a difference. Knowing Serena, she'll end up beating herself up for not having seen any signs earlier. I know she just wants the best for me. And for me to be happy and in love and have a caring and loving partner. The last thing she'd want is for me to hold onto a relationship that is toxic and endlessly up and down, simply because I don't want to be alone. I've just gotten so used to letting people believe that I'm fine. That there isn't a shitstorm currently going on. But that's the thing. I've been so good at hiding it.

"Yeah, maybe. We'll see."

The GPS announces that we are almost there.

"Can you call the housekeeper and let her know we won't be long," he asks.

I switch my phone back on that I'd turned off in the effort of trying to preserve the last bit of battery and pull up the contact Rhett sent me. The lady offers to meet us at the house, but I decline since it's late, so she gives me the codes to access the electronic keypad entry and tells me to call her if I need anything during my stay. When I hang up, despite the long journey, I feel super alert.

Roman reaches out of the car window to enter the security code at the front gate before driving down the short drive that leads to the sprawling seafront house. Though 'house' seems too small of a word. I remember Serena telling me it's like 9,800 square feet.

Warm lighting emanates from various rooms across the three levels, which makes it look magical against the crisp white of the building's exterior. We pull up in front of one of the three closed garage doors.

The second I step out of the car, the warm ocean breeze skates across my face, making me smile instantly. I can hear the waves crashing nearby and cannot wait to see what I know will be an amazing sunrise view tomorrow.

"Why don't you open up the front door and I'll grab your bag?" I'm so excited to get in the house that I don't even notice I left my handbag in the car until Roman nudges my arm and hands it to me. Despite it being the most innocent of gestures, my skin still feels warm at the exact point where he touched and I have to shake my head at the silly warm feeling I get from it.

Focusing back on what's in front of me, I can feel knots of tension and stress slowly melt away with each step I take into the house.

I'm in awe as I look around at my home for the next few days. The split staircase creates an arch that leads into the heart of the property. Walking further in, I'm amazed at how everything is interconnected. Each section leads into the next. A baby grand piano sits in one room with enough seating for about twenty people who can all watch a movie on the biggest TV I've ever seen. There is a 1940s-style bar with gold and black panels and fixtures that looks outlandish next to the warm neutral tones of creams, whites, and dove gray in the rest of the room.

I continue my tour to the stunning kitchen that's fitted

with everything a chef could ask for, including a vast island that seats six. Opening the fridge, it's freshly stocked and even has homemade meals that just need to be heated. "Hey Roman, are you hungry?" I shout, realizing I don't know where he is.

After a couple of seconds, he appears with my suitcase.

"Yeah, I could do with some food. Let me go find a bathroom, then I can help."

"No, it's fine. The least I can do after you did all the driving is heat some food. There's a tray of lasagna here. I could put it in the oven and maybe throw together a quick salad?"

"Sounds good to me. Damn, this place is enormous. And I swear my sister said this was one of his smaller places. Man, I still can't believe this is going to become her new normal. Anyway, I'm sure there are probably about eight bathrooms here, so I'm gonna go find one."

Watching as he walks away, his head craning, looking at his surroundings, I can't help but smile. This is the longest time we've spent in each other's company since we broke up and I'd expected it to feel awkward and maybe a little uncomfortable but that's not been the case so far. Instead, it's like I've been transported back in time with how Roman would always be the one person that makes me feel safe and most at ease.

I spend the next five minutes working out how to turn the oven on and finally manage it just as Roman re-enters. I put the lasagna in, then get a start on the salad. Roman helps and I can't help but notice how much more domesticated he's become. Back in the day, he would take every shortcut possible, like picking up pre-cut fruit and veg at the supermarket because he didn't like the hassle of chopping.

With the salad ready and the lasagna needing a bit more time, we take a tour of the house. Bless him, Roman carries my suitcase up for me, even if it's not a heavy one and I could have easily managed carrying it myself. Once again reminding me that the chivalrous way he always used to be with me is still deeply part of who he is. I guess some things really never change and I can't help but like that it hasn't.

There are five bedrooms and a home office with floor-to-ceiling windows looking out at the ocean. Even though the place is palatial, I really like that it still has a warm, cozy feel to it. Once we're done looking around, we make our way back to the kitchen where I dish us each a plate, then head to the wine fridge to grab a bottle.

"Do you want one?" I ask after I pour myself a crisp glass of white wine.

"I'd prefer a beer, but I think it's best if I didn't. I still need to drive back."

Shit. I didn't even think about that. I don't know why, but I'm suddenly not as keen at the thought of staying here alone tonight. I put the bottle back in the cooler, then head back to the fridge and grab two bottles of water and put them by our plates. Then, without looking back, I get a beer, open it, then hand it to Roman. My eyes momentarily widen at the electric shock type feeling I get when my hand briefly brushes against his before picking up my wineglass and taking a seat at the top end of the island. Only then do I look up and see the confused expression on his face as he takes his seat.

"Listen, you've already done a crazy amount of driving

today. Plus, it's late. It would be ludicrous for you to get back behind the wheel. I was lucky enough to have a nap today and even I'm exhausted, so god knows how tired you must be. You're more than welcome to stay the weekend, then head back. It still gives me the week to enjoy my alone time. Or if you've got plans this weekend, then at least stay tonight so you get a full night's sleep before driving again. It's the least I can do. Think of it as a way of saying thank you for being a lifesaver and helping me out today. And come on, who wouldn't want to wake up right by the ocean? What's the worst that could happen?"

Chapter 8

Roman

I can't work out if this is the best or worst offer I've ever had. Yeah, I won't lie. I wasn't exactly excited at the thought of driving for the next three or four hours, especially at night and with how tired I'm already feeling. But my gut is telling me this isn't a good idea and I don't know why. Maybe it's because I still haven't processed everything she said earlier in the car. I don't even know how I'm going to untangle that revelation that to this day, my actions, my words, and behavior still have such an impact on Ruby and her life. I never could've imagined that it would still be effecting her. I'd presumed she'd long since moved past all that and feel like shit that it's still causing her pain.

My stomach rumbles. Looking at the beer, then the plate Rub's set, then back up at her to see her smiling as she digs in, I decide to at least stay the night. Taking a big swig from the bottle and salute her with it.

"I'll stay. Thank you. I guess it's good I have my bag in

the trunk from staying at Serena's. At least you won't have to deal with a funky-smelling hobo in the morning."

Her laugh is loud and carefree. "Yeah right. Roman Parker, you may have changed over the years, but one thing you have never done and never will do is dress like a hobo or not look after yourself. You have never left the house without a shower, lotion, and your pearly whites sparkling. Not even when you were a teenager. So there's no way you'd step foot outside without doing those now."

It's funny because I don't know if I'm more surprised that she remembers or how much I like that she actually does. There's something comforting, almost sweet about that fact that despite all the time that's past, there are just some things that stick with you. But at the same time, as much as it sets something off deep within that she remembers my little habits, I can't help but feel a pang of sadness alongside that, yes we may have had great memories in the past, but that's it. The past. I only wish it could also be now, in the present.

"So, how's your dad doing?" Ruby asks. "I have to say when Rhett did the surprise engagement at your house and your dad was barbecuing, I forgot how good of a pit master he is. I don't care what anyone says, home cooks are always so much better with flavors than any of the fancy, super-expensive restaurants."

"You're not wrong there. But yeah, he's good. You know what he's like, always busy." I chuckle, because she was around so often when we were kids, I think he counted her as an additional daughter. "How about you? How are your mom and dad doing? Sometimes I see your mom around town and every time I've driven past her salon, it always looks busy. But I don't remember the last time I saw your dad."

Her parents still live in the house she grew up in, only about ten minutes from me. Yet, even though we live in the same town, we rarely cross paths. There was a time when her mom felt like a surrogate one for me. I even used to buy her flowers on Mother's Day. She sure as hell deserved them more than the woman who birthed me and my sisters who, after a couple of years, decided motherhood wasn't for her and just upped and left all of us. Leaving my dad to pick up the pieces and raise the three of us single-handedly. Ruby's voice brings me out of my head, which I'm grateful for, since I always feel like shit when I think back on that.

"Dad's doing great. He got tenure, what like ten years ago? And apparently his classes have had the highest number of enrollments for the past couple of years." She huffs a small laugh. "Who knew there was suddenly the uptake interest in picking history as your major?" Getting up she takes her plate to the sink as I finish the last few bites still on mine.

Sitting back down, Ruby continues, "So, yeah, things are going well for him. And Mom is also going amazingly. Business has been going so well that she's hired a full team and she only does certain appointments with some of her favorite customers. I've told her she should expand and open up at least one more location, if not more. Yet every time I tell her, she always says the same thing back to me. '*When I came over to America, I had nothing. I got a job in a salon and worked my way up. Now I have my own salon that makes me money and I hardly have to work. I'm living the American dream, my ljepotice.*'" I choke as I laugh at how accurate

Ruby's impression of her mom is. Even down to the perfect way she mimicked the accent.

"Well, I'm sure you're very proud of her. And if she ever expanded, she'd definitely be set for success. Especially with you helping her, right? Isn't that kinda part of your work?" I ask as I take my plate to the sink.

Ruby refills her wine glass, so I do the washing up. I'm sure there's a dishwasher somewhere in this kitchen, but I'll have finished clearing up all this by the time I've located it and worked out how to turn the darn thing on.

"Not quite." Her amusement easily seen on her face. "My actual job title is Pre-Sales Consultant, and I've got my blogging site. So, there may be certain things I could help Mom with, but not everything. Although, I love the idea of working with start-ups or doing expansions on small businesses. But that's never going to happen. Anyway, what was I saying? Oh yeah, so my mom and dad are both doing really good."

I'm a little confused by her sudden rush to change topics, and why she thinks working in a different field is unlikely to happen. But I don't wanna push her since she clearly doesn't wanna talk about it.

"Do you want another beer?" she asks.

"Yeah. Sure. Why not?"

She takes another bottle out of the fridge, opens it, then hands it to me, pointing out to the decked balcony. I nod my agreement and we head outside. Even with the light ocean breeze, the air still feels warm enough to sit out in.

"So, how's work going for you? And can I just say I still think it's amazing that you work with your dad?"

There's a part of me that can't quite wrap my head

around the fact that we're having this small talk, updating each other on our lives, when back in the day we used to know everything about one another. It's bizarre.

"Yeah. It's crazy. Obviously, you know I never thought things would turn out the way they did. Never thought I'd have any other career than football. But I guess everything happens for a reason. And now... now, I honestly couldn't imagine doing anything else."

Taking a drink of my beer, I lean back in the deckchair. "I guess, where I grew up basically in Dad's shop, always around, thinking I'm helping him and fixing cars, when in reality I was probably just getting in his way. It's not that crazy to think that I've now been working there for ten years. Dad pointed out the other day that I've been working there longer now than I played ball. Which is wild." My chest feels tight, just like it does every time I think back at how different my life could have been if it hadn't been for that accident.

I can feel Ruby's eyes on me, and as much as I want to just ignore what I'll guess is a look of pity, I won't be rude and dismissive. Looking up, I see her eyes aren't filled with the expression I expect. Instead, those green hazel eyes are filled with empathy, as is her small soft smile. Our eyes lock as we both ignore the elephant in the room. The fact that if I hadn't have been in that accident, my life would be completely different. I'd have been playing pro ball and likely been approaching the end of my professional career. We'd still be together and probably married and have a bunch of kids. Yet, none of that happened. I break our gaze as I look out to the dark shore ahead, needing to focus on something other than her face.

"Anyway, like I said, I can't imagine doing anything else. It took me a couple of years 'til I felt comfortable with the customers, as all too often they would just irritate the shit out of me, and I'd end up snapping at them. So at the beginning, I just kept my head down and focused on the cars. But I've grown used to it. Used to them."

"Well, that's good. And besides, don't be too hard on yourself, you've always struggled to warm to people quickly," she says with a teasing tone, which has me turning to face her, my eyes wide in disbelief at her accusation.

"That's not true. I'm normally good with people. Well, most of the time. As long as they aren't assholes." She coughs and chuckles at me and I can't help but have a sense of déjà vu from when we were younger and I used to make her laugh either at myself or the things I'd say all the time. She has her head back and her hand on her stomach. And just like it often was back then, I'm lost by her amusement. I really don't understand why she finds this so funny. It's not like I'm terrible with people.

"Why are you laughing? It's the truth."

She takes a minute to pull herself together before she can finally speak. "I'm sorry Roman, but that is complete BS. It's cute that you think otherwise. But can you seriously not remember how you were in high school and college? Whenever someone new came around, they were always scared of you. Always convinced you didn't like them. Or you had some issue with them. Your nickname was *The Iceman,* for heaven's sake. And whenever I brought it up, you'd just say there was nothing wrong with them, but you just didn't see them bringing anything to the table."

"Well, most of the time I was right. They didn't." I huff.

Shaking her head, she giggles at my futile attempt at justifying myself. Yet even I can hear how childish my words sound.

"I think I'm an excellent judge of character. Maybe I have like a sixth sense or something," I say with a smile.

As I finish my drink, the wind seems to pick up, and it's a little chillier. "Do you want my sweater?" I ask, leaning forward, ready to take it off and give it to her, knowing she must be feeling the cold through her thin, long-sleeved shirt.

"No thanks, it's fine. It's getting late, so I'm gonna call it a night." I nod in agreement, and we head back inside.

As Ruby throws my bottle in the trash and rinses out her glass, I run out to the car and grab my bag. When I'm back inside, I make sure all the doors and windows are tightly locked up.

Switching off all the lights downstairs, I follow Ruby upstairs thinking she must be in her room. But as I go to step into one of the guest bedrooms, Ruby's hand gently takes my wrist. I pause, looking down at where we touch as explosions of electricity travel up my arm, her proximity stealing my breath.

"Thank you, Roman. Thank you for helping me today. I really don't know what I'd have done otherwise. You didn't have to, and it really means a lot that you did." Her voice is soft and filled with sincerity.

I do my best to try not to show just how good it feels having her touch me. Not wanting to give away just how much I know I'm going to struggle being under the same roof as her. Being this close, but unable to hold her, touch her, kiss her. Having my fingers run through her hair as my nose fills with the sweet coconut scent of the shampoo she used to always use. Having my mind flooded with memories of all the times I had her in my arms, the way her soft skin felt beneath my lips, remembering just how good she tasted.

"Like I said, it really was no biggie," even I can hear the gravely tone in my voice, I hope Ruby didn't notice.

"Well, it was to me. So, thanks."

I'm frozen in place as she reaches up on her tiptoes and gives me a quick kiss on the cheek. Though it only lasted a millisecond, it feels like her warm lips have branded my skin, leaving behind a tattoo, imprinted on me for eternity.

"Goodnight," she whispers, then walks to her room without looking back. Seeing the soft round curves of her ass and remembering just how good it felt holding it, gripping it, eating it, I know will be the focus of my dreams tonight.

"Night. Sleep well," I murmur almost to myself.

Chapter 9

Roman

"So do you want to watch a movie or just wanna chill? I got a couple of new albums the other day I think you might like," I ask Ruby as I toss the ball in my hands.

She takes the pillow off the couch in my room, places it on the floor, and sits in front of the couch instead of on it. She does it every time, and I never get why.

"Well, the last four times you've put a movie on when I've come round, you've fallen asleep. Then you complain when I don't tell you what happened. So I say we're better off with some music," she says in a playful, teasing tone. It's not that I mean to be so tired. I'm just always exhausted after a long training session. Surely, after dating for four months, she should be used to it and know it's not in any way a reflection on her. It's just my body is exhausted.

I pick up the CDs from my desk, flicking through them before finally picking one and put it in the sound system. When I turn, she's stretching her long, lean legs out in front of

74

her, her yellow sundress glowing against her skin. My eyes catch on the way it rides up her thighs every time she moves, and I can feel my dick twitch as I imagine it riding higher and higher. When we have moments like this, together and alone, I can't help how much I want her. But there's no way I'm gonna show it. The last thing I would ever do is force any woman to do anything. And even though I'm ashamed to admit it, when we first started dating, Ruby was hanging out with my sister. I'd been by Serena's door and just happen to overhear them talking and found out that Ruby's still a virgin. So I need to get my head on straight and think with my head, not my cock.

I take a seat next to her and after a little while, Ruby climbs onto my lap. Her fingers play with my braids as she kisses me softly, sending an excited shiver through me from head to toe and only makes me want her even more. My hands grip her hips and I don't know if she's even aware that she's grinding against me. I'm as hard as rock and can feel the precum already begin to drip out of the tip. There's no way she doesn't feel it. It takes everything in me not to hurry this up, push things further, because inside I feel like an animal, ready to ravish her. But I need to stay in control, so I keep my hands on her hips and let her take the lead, swallowing her moans as we continue to kiss. I can feel the heat coming off her pussy and I—

Why the fuck am I thinking back to the night Ruby allowed me to take her virginity? Where the fuck did that come from?

I change the water in the shower to ice cold and blast myself before getting out to dry myself off. Once I'm moisturized and have secured my silk durag, I finally climb into bed. I thought I was going to crash the second I got into bed, yet now, my head feels wired.

I'm still processing the things Ruby opened up about in the car. Knowing just how damaging my actions were and selfishly, I kinda wish I didn't. I wouldn't feel as riddled with guilt, though I know I'm completely and utterly deserving of it.

The other thing that's gotten me all worked up is just being in her proximity. Having so much time to reacquaint myself with every contour of her face and now, to be hit with that long-forgotten memory of are first time together—so young and naïve; unaware of everything that would eventually happen—I don't know what to do with it all. I can't work out whether to just push it down and bury it where I know it belongs, or try to make sense of it.

I readjust the pillow on the bed for the tenth time in only a handful of minutes, unable to get comfortable. Though it's not because of the bed. My discomfort comes from within. Indecisions swirl through me and I know it would be better, more sensible, to leave in the morning. Yet, I can't deny how tempted I am to stay the whole weekend. I just can't tell if that feeling in my gut is telling me to stay or to go.

Chapter 10

Ruby

To say that I slept like a log would be an understatement. I'm pretty sure I was out for the count the second my head hit the pillow. I don't think I even moved because I swear I've woken up in the same position I fell asleep in.

Climbing out of the comfy bed, I make my way to the bathroom as my bladder feels like it's about to burst, then wash my face and brush my teeth before I unpack my case.

The sun is already shining through the curtains and before I pick out what to wear for the day, I wanna check to see how warm it is. I open the balcony doors and am hit with a warm wall of air. The sun beats down on my skin and it feels amazing.

As I pad out onto the balcony, the beautiful, glistening pool below instantly catches my eye. Even though the beach is only about two hundred yards away, there's just something about the pool that's calling for me to jump in.

Deciding I'm going to do a couple of laps before making

some breakfast, I grab a bikini to change into before taking a towel from the bathroom. I don't know if they have specific pool towels, but I'm not risking not having one when I get out.

Letting out a contented sigh, I luxuriate at just how warm the sun already feels against my skin. At a guess, I'd say it's still early morning, with where the sun currently sits in the sky. I should have checked the clock inside, but I was just too desperate to get in the water. Plus, there's something freeing with not knowing the time, being somewhat away and distant from technology, and the general rules and restraints of time and daily structure.

I throw my towel onto the sun lounger and take the first few steps into the pool as my mouth draws up into the biggest smile. The temperature is perfect. I feel like *Goldilocks,* as it's not too hot and not too cold. It's just right.

Before reaching the bottom step, I dive into the water, sending a prayer of thanks to Rhett for accommodating me, and his housekeeper for setting everything up, ready for me to enjoy.

The first few laps I do with some pace. I can feel the burn in my arms and legs. I like that I'm pushing my body, my chest rising and falling rapidly beneath the water in a breathless state. Once I finally feel that I've pushed myself enough, I ease up, simply enjoying the feeling of weightlessness in the water and the sun on my skin. I forgot how much I enjoy swimming. I used to do it a lot when I was younger. It also reminds me that Serena told me Rhett not only used to swim, but apparently was really good at it. A pang of guilt runs through me as I realize that, because of my relationship with Julian and the animosity the brothers have with one another, I really haven't had the chance to properly get to know the man my best friend is going to marry. Hell, if he'd have been anyone else, I'd have not only compiled a complete dossier on him, but I'd have definitely interjected myself more, making sure the guy is legit in every way. But I guess despite all the things that've happened in the past with the two of them, and considering how everything has now turned out, my girl's got one of the rare good guys.

Not wanting to dwell on any of those things—especially Julian and our relationship just yet—I focus on the water.

It's true what they say about swimming and being in a body of water, the way it taps into the deep recesses of your brain and setting off the feeling of being in the womb. The way the water's buoyancy provides a weightlessness and feels like you're in this supportive bubble. One that embraces you and protects you from the world. It's something I've always felt and connected with. Like your body and mind correlate into a meditative and dreamlike state.

The last time I felt like this, felt so connected to the water was ironically when I went with my mom back to her hometown in Croatia after Roman and I broke up. We were there for a month. It was just the thing I needed, spending time with cousins and other family members I hadn't seen in years. Even though the house was very basic, run down, and showed the wares of decades of my family living there, the pool was the only thing that had been updated.

Each and every day, I woke not knowing how to deal with my emotions with the heaviness of my heartbreak. The only thing I did know was that being in the water was the one place I could wash away all the stress. All the hurt.

Where the endless questions that were running through my head would quieten down.

Swimming in that pool every day was my escape, while also having my mom there to hold and comfort me at night when I cried. Then at the end of the month when my mom flew back, I decided to see some more of Europe. So after Croatia, I went to Austria, then Italy, Spain, France, England, and finished in Ireland before finally flying back.

I can honestly say it was one of the best decisions I've ever made. Those three months abroad helped reset me, allowing myself to sit and deal with my emotions. Like when I'd burst into tears while I was on the train, I didn't care, since I knew I'd never see the people around me ever again.

As I went from city to city, I really had to put myself out there. Not knowing anyone, I had the choice of either sitting there alone and sad in places I'd always dreamed of visiting, or go out, explore, and meet like-minded people. So that's what I did. There are a couple of people I met that I'm still in contact with now, all these years later. It definitely was not just a trip I'd seriously needed, but one that I'm forever grateful that I went on. I guess that's why when I'd first realized I needed space, I knew I needed to get away somewhere. So, coming here was more realistic than getting the time off to fly abroad.

The sun keeps getting warmer, and despite being in the water, I still feel hot. Diving under the cool water feels nice and soothing against my face.

Breaking back up through the surface, I'm hit by the loud calls of the birds flocking above me. My eyes are momentarily blinded by the sun as they attempt to focus on the lush full trees that are softly swaying in the breeze. I float on my back, letting my feet lightly kick out like a floating water angel. That thought has me smiling as I close my eyes, hoping that the weather stays just like this for the rest of my time here.

I don't know how long I've been in the water. It must be some time, as my fingers have gone pruney. Right on cue, my stomach rumbles, so I swim back to the stairs and get out. I've worked up an appetite and am dying for a coffee. With all the things that I saw in the fridge last night, I think the biggest struggle I will have is deciding what to eat.

Chapter 11

Roman

Damn, I don't remember the last time I had such an awful night's sleep. How is it I feel even more tired now than I did before I got into bed? It took me a good few hours to get my racing mind to simmer down and felt like there was an emotional pinball game going on in my brain. Regrets, memories, feelings of anger, frustration, and annoyance endlessly bouncing around. I tried every technique my therapist had given me over the years, like the box breathing, thinking of song lyrics, imagining I'm walking through a particular landmark and noting all the surrounding things. Yet nothing worked, no matter what I tried.

Everything always found a way of relating to the woman sleeping across the hall from me. Why does this somehow feel worse than waking up hungover? My few experiences with extreme drunkenness resulted in passing out, waking with a sore head, and dehydration. At least that I could fix with Tylenol, some electrolytes, and loads of carbs. This however, I don't know how to fix. How can I fix the past? I get that I can't, but dammit, I want to.

When I ended things with Ruby and fully recovered, physically and mentally, I knew I had been an asshole.

As if it wasn't bad enough that I'd been in a car accident that had ended my football career plus led to multiple surgeries and months of physical therapy, all of which sent me into a deep and dark depression, during which I ended my relationship with Ruby. The fallout of that, as well as the already dark place I was in mentally, made me spiral to the point that I became suicidal. It was the darkest point in my life. I was in so much pain, and so upset that I let that pain out on those closest to me. I didn't need anyone to point that out. I was fully aware I'd broken the heart of the girl I loved and had always pictured to be at my side. But I guess one thing I never really discussed with anyone—well, no one besides my therapist—was the real reason I'd done it. Yes, I'd been in a really dark place and it's clear now that I needed help way before I'd asked for it. Still, ending our relationship hadn't been a sudden thought.

I'd started thinking about it the second I woke up from my first surgery. When they told me I'd never play again. That my football career, the dreams and life I'd always pictured I'd have, were over. I was so angry. I hated myself. I hated the drunk driver who was never prosecuted. And hated that the reason I'd been behind the wheel was because Ruby and I had an argument. Something so stupid and small. She'd wanted me to sit and talk it out, but I wanted to cool off. Get some air. So I went for a drive that would forever change my life. I hated that if I'd just listened to her; if I hadn't been such an asshole, none of this would have happened. Disgust and self-hatred seeped into me like a venomous poison.

Then, on one of the countless nights I couldn't sleep and was hating the world, I kept thinking about why I left. Why had I walked away instead of acting like an adult and talking things through? Was it because I was just like my mom? That, when things got too hard, the easiest option was to simply walk away. Once that thought planted itself in my head, it continued to fester and grew bigger and bigger. And the kindness, love, and care Ruby was giving me felt so undeserving.

So what started as a fleeting thought—letting Ruby go—was the final nail in the coffin. I had to do it. And like an injured soldier in battle, I severed a part of me in the hopes the rest would survive. It was never that I didn't love her or no longer cared for her. On the contrary. It was that I knew I didn't deserve her, knew I wasn't worthy of being the man she gave her heart to. And I guess my head had been so fucked up, I couldn't see that not only had I never explained the reason to her, but I never gave her a chance to talk about why I'd done it. I was too much of a coward.

But even in the years that followed, and knowing I'd hurt her, I never could have comprehended the extent of that hurt; the depths of damage my actions had on her. How what I did affected not just her outlook, but also how she responds; what she believes she should put up with. I just can't believe it. That's what kept me up most of the night. The last time I checked the time on my phone, it was around half past three in the morning. Even when I did finally fall asleep, my dreams were so fucked up, always ending with Ruby's heartbroken face staring back at me. I kept waking up in a cold sweat.

My skin itches, probably from the dried sweat still stuck to it. Knowing that there's no chance of me falling back asleep, I get my ass up out of bed and into the shower. I set the water to ice cold and, after the initial shock, embrace the feeling of washing the remnants of last night away.

Getting out of the shower, I finish getting ready and grab a pair of basketball shorts. While pulling my t-shirt over my head, I realize I've not heard any noises coming from Ruby's room or anywhere else and assume she's still asleep. I'm definitely going to be needing coffee to get through the day, and I might as well see if there's anything I can use to make breakfast.

Making my way downstairs, being quiet to not wake her up, I find the pod coffee machine in the kitchen with a quiet thanks to the universe.

While the machine works its magic, I walk over to the fridge and notice the back door is wide open. Instantly, alarm and worry run through me. I'm one hundred percent sure I locked everything up last night, and Ruby told me the housekeeper won't be back until Monday.

My fists clench and my heart beats faster. Adrenaline races through me as I walk to the door to check. My feet move me so fast I'm almost running by the time I get outside. And that's when I spot her. Ruby, on her back, swimming in the water. Reaching behind my head, I interlock my fingers, pressing down the tension that's starting to build at the base of my skull. I know it's not a migraine. No. It's like the throbbing from my hard cock has managed to migrate to my actual head. Plus I'd feel really inappropriate reaching down and touching myself, so this is the best I can do without feeling like I'm crossing a line. My eyes catalog every inch of her. *Fuck*, she looks so damn hot in a dark green bikini that looks like it was made for her. Water trails over her skin like silk as she moves. My fingers twitch, eager to feel her soft skin.

Fuck, fuck, fuck. I shake my head and quickly make my way back into the kitchen. What is wrong with me? Just standing there, staring at her like some sort of pervy creep. It's not like I haven't seen her naked before. My hands have caressed every inch of her body. My tongue and mouth have tasted the sweet delicacy of her essence. My cock has felt her mold herself around me. I could recite, recall, and describe every minute detail of her. So, why on earth am I fighting myself to not go back and have another look? Shit. It's got to be the lack of sleep and my messed up head fucking with me.

I need to keep busy, so I take a sip of my coffee, open up the fridge, and see what I can use to make breakfast. Grabbing the ingredients, I throw them in a skillet while I wait for the oven to warm up. Washing the fruit, I then mix them in a bowl and squeeze in some honey I found in the pantry. Reaching up to the cupboard, I grab a bowl and whisk up the eggs. I pour them into the skillet, then put it into the oven, setting the timer for twenty minutes

As I'm washing my hands I spot movement from the corner of my eye as Ruby walks through the door, wrapping herself in a towel. A deep groan vibrates out of my throat and Ruby's eyes shoot up in surprise. Droplets of water run down her chest, disappearing into the material of her bikini. My cock thickens, which is the last thing I need right now. Especially as my shorts hide nothing. I subtly press myself into the counter, then clear my throat, finally speaking.

"Morning." My voice is still croaky from it being morning and still not having spoken, on top of that fact I'm struggling not to think back on how I was watching her in the water. It takes everything to keep my focus on her eyes.

"Morning," she says cheerfully as she gathers her hair and twists it to the back of her head. "I hadn't expected to see you yet. Figured you'd still be sleeping."

Her eyes scan the kitchen, seeming to light up when they catch sight of my cup of coffee.

"Nah. This is already way later than I usually wake up."

She nods, making her way over to the coffee machine. Seconds later, the machine whirls to life.

"Mmmm, smells good."

"I... yeah, I woke up hungry. Thought I'd get a start on breakfast. I didn't realize you were already awake." I'm still pushing myself into the counter as, despite my best efforts, I've still got a semi. Luckily for me, Ruby hasn't noticed my odd behavior.

She chats for several minutes, telling me about how well she slept and that she was desperate to get in the pool and go for a swim. I don't mention the fact that I saw her gliding through the water. Now that I finally have my cock back in check, I check to see how much longer is left on the oven timer.

"I can leave you a plate if you want? I'll leave it in the oven so it can stay warm. Then you don't have to rush getting changed or anything."

"How long till it's finished?" she asks.

"Ten minutes. But like I said, I can just leave you a plate."

"No, no. I'm gonna jump in the shower really quick and I'll be right back."

She takes a sip of her coffee, and I'm guessing she forgot how hot it still is as she curses and shakes her head, muttering to herself before dashing up the stairs.

I've just plated up and taken a seat when Ruby reappears. Damn, she really was fast. This time, she's wearing denim shorts, a plain white t-shirt, and has a blue and white striped shirt in her hand. But it's not just the clothes she's got on that I notice. It's what she isn't wearing. A bra.

Oh, fuck.

I have to tear my gaze away from the outline of her nipples. I used to love that she often wouldn't wear a bra. Tell me what twenty-year-old wouldn't. But right now, I feel like someone up there really has it in for me. Once again, I need to keep myself busy, so I dig into my breakfast. I don't think I've ever concentrated so hard on a plate of food in my life. I'm so engrossed and focused that it takes me a second to realize she's talking.

"I just can't believe how lucky we got with the weather. Like, I knew the chances were good as I've been monitoring the forecast, but there's just something so much more enjoyable about the sun when you're by the beach. I was thinking of taking a walk into town. Maybe see if there's a path or something along the beach and hoping there'll be a market. I know last night you weren't sure if you wanted to stay for the weekend, so I thought, why don't you come and join me? Then when we get back, you can see if you want to stay another night. If not, then at least you won't be driving and potentially get stuck in traffic in this heat. What do you think? Sound good to you?"

I've always thought it was stupid in movies when they depict an angel and devil on someone's shoulder. Yet right now I couldn't feel any more torn. My head is telling me I should go. Head back home. Leave her in peace. But another part of me is screaming for me to stay. I know which one I should listen to. However, just like many other times in my life, I don't listen to the sensible, logical side.

"Yeah. Sure. Sounds good."

I quickly finish the rest of my plate and am about to clear it away when Ruby says she'll do it since I cooked.

"Alright. Cool. I'm gonna change and finish getting ready."

I make my way out of the kitchen without a further glance at her. There's literally no need for me to shower, as I just had one less than an hour ago. But I sure as hell need to cool down.

I strip off my clothes the second I get into the room and walk straight into the shower. The icy cold water blasts into me, yet it does nothing to cool my heated skin. All I can think about is the luscious body of the woman downstairs. And what's worse is, she isn't a fantasy. I know what she feels like. I know the softness of her skin, how it feels to have her body wrapped around mine. I know what her moans sound like. Know how she tastes.

My cock is rock hard, but I won't touch it. I *can't*. It would feel like a violation to her. And that's the mantra I tell myself again and again until I've finally cooled down.

Once I'm finally ready, I head downstairs to find Ruby waiting. Luckily, she's put a flowy shirt on and slides on her sunglasses before grabbing her purse.

"Perfect. Let's go."

Chapter 12

Ruby

I can't believe how much I've enjoyed myself today. After leaving the house, we found a path down to the beach and walked along the sandy shore to the Marina Bay area.

Rhett warned me that this beach house was apparently the least secluded of his properties, and didn't have the same level of privacy as most of the others. Yet, as we walked, we only passed a handful of people. There had been a moment when we'd first set off that Roman seemed a little quiet, and I suddenly wasn't sure if my suggestion of him joining me had been a good idea or not. He'd acted weird at breakfast, but I thought maybe he was still a little tired.

Luckily, after a couple of minutes of walking, he seemed to relax a little and we chatted about everything and nothing. Once we got into town, I begged him to play a little game with me—to pretend we are tourists. I got him to agree, but he drew the line at talking with an accent. It didn't stop me, however, as I exaggerated my mom's Croatian accent. And as much as Roman kept rolling his eyes at my theatrics, I didn't miss the way he broke into a smile and shook his head when he thought I wasn't looking.

We found a huge market and I'm pretty sure I dragged him to every stall. Even though we tried loads of the samples that the various vendors were offering, all that walking only made us hungrier. So we found a cute little Italian place tucked away in the marina's corner.

"Man, I knew I should have gone with the spaghetti alle vongole. Look. That looks and smells delicious," I whisper across the table, nodding my head at the couple next to us whose food has just arrived.

"I guess that's one thing that hasn't changed," Roman says with a grin. My brows crease as I take a sip of water because I'm confused by his comment.

"What do you mean?" I ask.

Looking me straight in the eyes with a grin on his face, he taps his fingers on the table.

"I don't think I ever remember being with you in a restaurant or really anywhere that serves food, and you not always making a comment on someone else's dish. I don't even think it's the case that you're even wanting what that other person has. I reckon it's just the case that as soon as you order your food, you're ready to eat instantly, so your eyes just snag on whatever you see around you. 'Cause as soon as you get your food, you're so focused on that, you never comment on any other plate."

I shake my head at his statement as I grab a piece of bread from the basket and dip it in the olive oil and balsamic vinegar. Despite me continuing to shake my head as I chew, I can't quite look him in the eye. Because one, I know I'll probably laugh, but two, deep down, I know he's right. "I'd say the biggest mistake I make with food, at least when eating out, is that I get so excited that I always order way more than I can actually eat. But remember, it's not like you didn't benefit from that. Just think how many extra dishes you used to get when I couldn't finish my meals." The overly sweet tone of my voice only amplifies the silly grin on my face.

"Touché. I'll give you that." He laughs.

I amuse myself by people watching and we have the perfect view since our table is right by the large floor-to-ceiling windows.

I've always found it a small victory whenever I've been able to make Roman actually laugh because he hardly does. His general demeanor is this stoic, unbothered enigma. Even when he's happy and enjoying himself, you get the feeling he's holding back. And he's been like that since I first met him. That victory had me enjoying my meal even more once it arrived. The food is superb and just like always, I ordered way too much. Wiping my mouth with a napkin, I take a sip of my white wine and can feel a set of eyes on me. Looking up, I find Roman staring at me with one brow lifted and his head tilted slightly.

"What?" I ask.

This time he raises both brows, then looks down at his plate. Following his line of sight, I realize I've pushed the rest of my food onto his. My eyes widen in embarrassment and feel my cheeks warm. I don't know how, but it must have been my subconscious that slipped back into old habits. I know this isn't that big of a deal, but it feels awkward. Less than twenty-four hours in each other's company and I've slipped back into that old familiarity. I'm waiting for the silly, teasing comment that I'm sure is on the tip of his tongue, yet he says nothing. He just carries on eating and I appreciate it.

Once he's finished, the waiter comes to clear the plates and asks if we would like any dessert. We both respond at the same time.

"No."

"Yes."

Roman rolls his eyes. Obviously, I said yes. I'd already seen that they have a pistachio cake with sour cherry and dark chocolate ice cream when I read the menu earlier. Telling the waiter what I'd like, I also add on a coffee, which Roman also orders. As the waiter starts to walk away, I call out to him, "Can we get another spoon for the dessert? We'll share it." I smile at Roman, knowing it's ridiculous to order a dessert when I couldn't finish my mains, but come on, it's cake.

Just as he opens his mouth to respond, his cell rings. Reaching into his pocket, he pulls it out and answers with a smirk. "Well, well, well. Look who it is. The lady of leisure. The globetrotter. I should feel lucky I get to say hello. Or should I say bonjour?" Roman says, holding the phone in front of him. The sound of my best friend's voice comes blaring through the speaker, causing him to quickly turn down the volume. From the way he's holding his cell, I'm guessing she's video called him.

"Oh, give it a rest. And let's be honest, that's probably the only French word you still remember from school," Serena argues back. I laugh as the two of them go back and forth. Just then, the waiter brings the dessert to the table.

"Thank you," I say before diving into the mouthwatering dish before me.

"Wait. Ro, where are you? Are you still with Ruby? That's what I was calling you about. I can't get hold of her and I was getting worried."

I've already plowed through half of the slice of cake and scoop of ice cream when Roman passes me his phone.

"There you are. I tried calling you last night, but it went straight to voicemail. I waited until I thought you'd be up but still couldn't get through." I can hear the genuine concern in her voice, and I feel bad.

"Aww, babe, I'm sorry. I wasn't ignoring you. My cell died just as we arrived, and I hadn't put it on charge. But as you can see, there's no need for you to worry. I'm alive and well and enjoying my..." I can't finish what I'm saying because I watch Roman eat the rest of the dessert.

"What? You said it was to share," he says with a Cheshire cat grin plastered across his face.

"Share, yes, not finish it," I exclaim.

"Well, considering you already ate half, it was clearly intended that I have the other half," he counters.

The sound of a throat clearing reminds me the Serena is still on the phone. When my eyes focus on the screen, I see a knowing smile on her face. Curiosity shines in her eyes. I've seen that expression way too many times before and know it's usually never because of a reason I'd like.

"I can see you guys are busy. I'll leave you to both eat in peace. Maybe you should order another plate. Sounds like there wasn't quite enough there. Just remember to charge your cell at some point when you get back just so I know you're alright."

"I promise. Love you, babe."

"Love you too."

. . .

If someone would have told me a couple of years ago that I'd have had one of the best Saturdays I've had in weeks with my ex, I'd have laughed them out of the room. But today really has been so much fun. Damn, it would have been near perfect if I'd have actually gotten more of the dessert I ordered," I tease as we slowly stroll back along the beach to the house.

"How many times do I need to tell you? Having half *is* sharing. And don't think I didn't notice that you ate that slice of cake from the back," Roman says, side eyeing me.

"What on earth does that mean?"

"You started eating from the thickest part. It was a triangular slice of cake, and you were working your way in from the widest bit. Who on earth does that?"

We're walking so closely beside one another I can't help but feel like I'm being transported back to the past. I can feel myself fighting the urge to reach out and hold his hand. Or lean against his shoulder, resting my head as my lips go to kiss his neck. It's been four times that our fingers have briefly touched. Four. The fact that I'm counting them, am so aware of how often we touch, makes me feel like one of those teen fans that's in close proximity to their idol, where every look, every small and slight touch holds such great significance.

"It's not that weird," I mutter.

"Yeah, it is. And when you think about it, you still had more than I did. So, you really don't have a reason to be sour."

My eyes widen, and my feet come to a stop at the

audacity of his words. Turning my head, I see he also stopped and has the most devilish grin on his face.

"You really know the way to wind a woman up and make her regret saying how much she enjoyed herself today," I respond with an over-the-top huff, then continue walking on.

The sound of his deep chuckle carries over the light sea breeze, and I'm so glad he can't see my face as I'm struggling to bite back my smile. When we get back to the house, I'm in desperate need of a shower. I didn't wash my hair after my swim this morning and I know if I don't remove the chlorine soon, I'm going to be needing hair masks for a week.

"Oh, I realized I never asked, but will you be heading back home tonight, or will you be staying until tomorrow?"

"I thought I'd head back tomorrow if that's okay. One more day by the beach will make next week easier."

Excitement bubbles through me. I find myself transfixed by the way his Adam's apple moves as he talks, and my eyes follow a drop of sweat that's slowing making its way down his temple the light glistening against it, making it look like a drop of liquid gold. It dips down his throat before disappearing into the collar of his top, and he must feel my gaze on him because he turns and looks me straight in the eye. I go to speak, say something to get me out of this hypnotic state but no words come out. My mouth feels dry as my mind goes back to memories of feeling the sweat dripping down his body as he played with mine. Licking my lips, I focus back on what he said. And despite that momentary erotic bubble I just felt myself in, I'm also genuinely happy that he's going to be staying. I'm happier about it than I dare to admit. Nodding at him, I give him a genuine smile.

"Yeah, that sounds like a good plan. I'm gonna jump in

the shower, then we can see if there are a few things to put together a little charcuterie board for dinner. I don't feel like cooking tonight."

Roman sinks his teeth into his lip, and I have to shake my head as my eyes focus on his mouth. What the fuck was that?

"Yeah, we have a little while still to think about dinner. I can always cook if you're not up for it."

I think on it for a moment before coming up with a suggestion. "I know. Let me have my shower, then when we can either make a grazing board or order some takeout. Let's have your last night here be a relaxing one."

"Great. Let's do that. I'm gonna do a couple of laps."

I take a deep gulp, as once again the most inappropriate thoughts begin to flood my mind. If I already felt myself getting hot and flustered at seeing a drop of sweat on him, how the fuck am I going to handle seeing him in swim shorts? Seeing his bare chest again. I wonder if he's still got those sexy washboard abs like he used to. Or has his body changed since he no longer plays ball? Fuck, I really need to pull myself together. There's no way I can let him see or guess the type of thoughts of him and his body that are running through my mind.

Giving him a parting nod, I make my way upstairs and remember to put my cell on charge.

My shower took longer than expected as halfway through deep conditioning and detangling, I ran the bath, then got into the tub and soaked in the relaxing hot water. I'm pretty sure I dozed off for a bit, as the next thing I knew, the water was lukewarm. Finally getting out, I lather myself in lotion and some aloe vera gel as I definitely caught the sun today. Grabbing the buttery soft lounge set I'd packed, I put it on and check my phone. Irritation runs through me when I see all the notifications. But that feeling quickly turns to worry when I see there are twenty missed calls from Julian.

An array of god-awful things pop into my mind. I'd told him I needed some space. That I needed time to get away and think things through. I'm ashamed to admit that I intentionally did it when he'd already been drinking. Just because I knew he wouldn't think much of it. It wouldn't really bother or affect him. Then the next time I brought it up, he seemed to have a vague recollection but thought I was going to a fitness retreat. And I didn't correct him. Well, not exactly. None of that was a lie. Yet, I still knew it was misleading of me.

I don't bother checking the messages he sent. Just seeing that many missed calls from him in the last twenty-four hours has me pulling up his contact and pressing the dial button. My heart pounds against my chest as I wait for him to answer. When he finally does, I hear music playing faintly in the background.

"Hey. I've just seen your missed calls. Are you okay?"

"So you do remember me. I think that's it you. Do. Tried calling you. Didn't answer. Don't like why." His words are slurred, and I squeeze my eyes shut as it becomes crystal clear that, once again, he's drunk. Climbing on the bed, I sit cross-legged and put him on speakerphone. Resting my head in my hands, I rub my temples.

"You are you still there, Red?" he shouts, his voice booming across the room.

"Yes, I'm still here. Julian..." I pause, taking a deep breath before continuing, "I told you I was going away. That I needed some time and space."

"I know, but we could have gone away together. I've got a couple of friends that have headed down to Miami. There where we could go. That boat they're staying on is amazing. It's fun. You don't like having fun. You need to relax more. You're always too serious."

I don't know if it's anger, frustration, or resentment I'm feeling the most right now. How dare he? How dare he disrespect the boundary I'd set? But no, he couldn't even respect that. Calling me, clearly drunk. Then not only that, but to suggest we go to a damn party boat in Miami where I'm sure all his friends will probably be as reckless and careless as he is.

"Julian, you can't honestly be suggesting this. I told you I needed some space. Told you I needed some time alone to think—" I'm interrupted by a knock on my door. But before I have the chance to respond, Roman's voice carries through.

"Heya, I heard your voice, so just wanted to quickly check and ask if you've decided whether we should do that grazing board or if you wanted takeout instead before I quickly jump in the shower."

My brain momentarily freezes when I hear the cold, angry tone of Julian's voice, reminding me that I've still got him on speakerphone.

"Who the fuck was that, Ruby?"

Chapter 13

Ruby

I try to brush it off as nothing. "Listen, I said that I needed some time and—" Once again I'm cut off, but this time it's by the beeping noise as Julian requests to FaceTime. I know that if I don't accept it, he'll just keep doing it. So I answer, pushing myself back so I'm leaning against the headboard with the phone held out in front of me. The look on his face is one I've only seen once before, and that was the day he turned up at my apartment unexpectedly after his fight with Rhett when he got fired. Pure rage. While I can see the glassiness in his eyes from the alcohol, I can also see the anger in them. Even through the screen, his fury is palpable.

"I said who the fuck was that? I'm not going to fucking ask you again," he shouts, and both the volume and tone of his voice sends a chill down my spine.

We've had our fair share of arguments, especially when he's had a drink or is hungover, but there's something now that feels different.

"Julian, I will not talk to you if you keep swearing at me. I really don't want to get into this while you're drunk. I shouldn't need to get into any of this. And if you'd have respected me and my wishes of just having some space, you wouldn't have called and we wouldn't be on the phone arguing right now."

A dull pain builds behind my eyes and I know I've got a nasty headache coming on. After a few moments of silence, he speaks again.

"What's behind you?" he spits, like a whip.

I jerk my head forward, looking at him in confusion. If I thought he looked angry before, that was nothing compared to his expression now.

"I fucking said what the fuck is behind you? Answer the damn fucking question, *Ruby*." His anger seems to sober him up as, unlike before, his words aren't slurred. I look behind me. "What are you talking about? I don't see anything."

"Above you. Above your damn head. What the fuck is that?"

I crane my neck to see what he's going on about. But the only thing there is a painting. "I know that fucking painting. I know that one along with the three others I'd bid on and won three years ago for my stupid brother. He wanted to bid on them anonymously, but I wanted to go to the auction, so I went as his proxy. So, unless you're somewhere that has a carbon copy of the exact painting Rhett owns, which I know he's got sitting in one of his fucking houses, tell me right now where the fuck you are and who the fuck you're with," he shrieks.

Taking a deep, steadying breath, I try to pull myself together to explain things. "Julian, listen. I didn't do this out of malice or as some sort of game. After everything that has gone on in the last couple of weeks..." I let out a breath as my throat tightens. "These past couple of weeks things feel like they've been getting collectively worse. I couldn't—can't—talk to you. You wouldn't listen. So I felt it would be best for me to have some time alone. Some space so I can think things through and work out what to do." I rush through my words as his eyes spear me through the screen. I feel like I'm on trial. Like a witness, taking to the stand.

"I didn't want to just get out of my apartment. I wanted to get out of the city, go somewhere I didn't know anyone, and work through everything that's going through my head. I was talking to Serena about it and I'm guessing she told Rhett, who then offered the use of one of his homes."

I don't miss the head shake and sneer when I mention my best friend's name. A burst of anger detonates through me, but I know now isn't the time to go on a tirade about his unjustified disdain for her.

"And given how bad things are between you and your brother, I asked him to keep it quiet and make sure no one knew I'd be here. That wasn't to be vindictive. I just didn't want to add any more fuel to the fire between you and your brother. All I wanted to do was get away." I really don't want to get into all of this with him, but I force myself to tell him the whole story. "Then yesterday, I don't know if you heard, but all flights out of New York were canceled because of air traffic control." His eyes narrow, but I can't tell if his anger has dissipated.

"Anyway, I didn't know what to do, but I was still adamant about getting away. I spoke to Serena, and it turned out her brother had been staying at her apartment and was going to be collecting one of Rhett's cars and take it back to his auto shop to do some work on it, so he offered to drive me. We got in late, and I didn't think it was safe for him to drive another stint at night after that already long drive. So he stayed in one of the other rooms."

I don't mention our day out today because, even though it was harmless, Julian's current facial expression is far from it. If looks could kill, I'd currently be dead.

"Serena's brother? As in your ex? The one that *left* you and broke your heart? He tossed you to the curb once he'd had enough of you." Though he speaks slowly, every word hits like a bullet.

My eyes blur as they fill with unshed tears.

"Damn, maybe that useless, washed-up quarterback had one thing right. You really aren't good enough." I gasp at the cruelty of his words. But I can see he's only just beginning.

"Man, I was so wrong about you. I thought you were different, but you're just like everyone else. A liar. You lie and exaggerate all the time. You used me. Was this all some sort of game? Make your ex jealous?"

"No," I shout, as the first tears fall down my cheeks.

"Yeah, I think you did. You found me—a rich popular guy from one of the most successful families in the country—and knew you could get your claws in. Make him jealous that I could take you to all the fancy places, every exclusive party."

"Julian, no. That isn't true." This is insanity. How is he spinning this false narrative?

"You did. It's so fucking clear now. You never took my side. Not with your stupid friend, not even having my back when my own fucking brother fired me. How dare you? Do you know how lucky you were I even gave you the time of day? That I even gave you a chance and thought you were different? Do you know how many stunning women throw themselves at me all the time? And I had to keep turning them down 'cause I thought you were something special. Something different. When clearly, you're not."

"That's not true. You're the one that's been pushing me away because of your drinking problem and your partying," I sob.

"Bull shit. I don't have a drinking problem. And if I did, the only reason I'd have one is because of you" Julian yells.

Sobs break out of me as he continues to list every flaw and fault in me that he's clearly felt for some time, but kept to himself. Until now.

"You're a liar, you're fake, you're a stuck up, selfish social climber that was never really there for me. I defended you to my mother when she said to keep an eye on you. When she questioned your intentions. Your motives. I should have fucking listened to her. Well, I am now. You will never, ever get a single thing from me ever again. You were never good enough, and you never will be. I am done with you and never want to see your face again," he shouts before hanging up, not even giving me the chance to respond and tell him how wrong he is.

I'm frozen like a statue as tears spill uncontrollably from my eyes. I feel numb and in shock. I can't believe what has just happened. I can't believe the words that came out of his mouth. A commotion outside my door catches my attention, but it sounds muffled. My head feels like it's underwater, as the loud pulsing of my heart is like a drum in my ears. The phone drops out of my hands with how hard my fingers tremble as every mean statement Julian uttered flashes like a neon sign before my eyes. How could he be so cruel? So evil? How could he be so heartless? I can understand that he'd have been annoyed, angry even, that I hadn't told him everything; that I withheld the fact that I was staying at one of the homes his brother owns. I can even understand the annoyance and frustration that Roman is here. But none of that—nothing—justifies that torrent of abuse he's just given me.

I know now that there isn't a thing worth saving. Nothing worth fighting for. Not if he thinks those things about me. There is no going back. Never. We are well and truly done. Yet, the hurt I feel right now is palpable. I can't unhear the words he said.

My sobs grow louder and my hands cover my ears as I try to block out everything he said, but it's no use. My body gives in, and I collapse down on the bed, squeezing myself into a tight ball.

My tears soak the sheets beneath my face, and I find it hard to catch my breath. My head feels like it's about to explode as a flood of endless sobs, cries, and tears break out of me. Everything hits me harder than I ever could have imagined, and I completely break down.

Chapter 14

Roman

White-hot, blinding rage curses through me. I don't think I've ever felt anger like this before. My grip on the door handle to Ruby's room is so tight, I'm surprised I haven't broken it off.

When I first came to her door, it was only to ask her if she'd decided on what she was in the mood for with dinner. I was about to go for a shower after my swim when I heard her voice. At first I thought she was maybe on the phone with my sister, but then I heard that son of a bitch. Heard every damn word that came out of his bitch-ass mouth. If he'd been behind this door, I'd have kicked it down, then smashed his face in. The more bullshit he said, the angrier I got. This guy really doesn't know Ruby, because if he did, he'd know she was the polar opposite of every vicious, degrading thing he said about her. I can't even let myself repeat the things he said in my head right now as the sound of her sobs through the door is one of the most heartbreaking things I've ever heard. As quietly as I can, I lean back against the door and slide down until I'm sitting on the floor. I'm so torn as part of me wants to knock and ask her to let me in, but I know she won't. And I feel like me being sat here is some kind of invasion of her privacy. Yet I can't bring myself to leave.

I don't know how long I sit here until her loud sobs subside, but I can still hear her choked cries. I would do anything to get that pathetic jackass on the phone and rip him to shreds. I know Serena already doesn't like him and she will hate him even more when she finds out about this. But one thing I know for sure is that no one hates that man more than I do right now.

I've never been an overly violent or aggressive person. Even when I used to play football, I never let my emotions or frustrations take over and always knew that I had to channel that anger, turn it into something productive. Now, though? Now, I'm just picturing how good it would feel as my fist smashes into his face. Let's see what kinda shit he's willing to say to my face. He sure as shit wouldn't have the balls to utter a word. He'd be on his knees crying like a baby, begging me to stop as I let my fury out with my fists. Land a couple of kicks too.

Has he always been like this? Surely not. There's no way Ruby would have put up with this kinda bullshit on a regular basis. I know from what she told me, things hadn't been good between her and that asshole. But not like this. Not to this extent. I know for a fact that my sister can't have known he's spoken to her like this. Otherwise, she'd have whopped his ass herself if she knew. If he has, though, if he's spoken to Ruby like this before, why has she allowed it? Why has she put up with it? Then her words from yesterday in the car hit me like a battering ram.

"At the core, I don't want to be alone. I want to have my person. My other half. I want the romance, the wedding, kids, building a life, a future together. A future where my partner and I grow old together. I want it more than anything. And I guess the reason I've clung on, tried seeing the best and doing everything I can to see if a future like that would be possible with Julian, is because the last time I pictured that life, that future, that dream got dashed away from me."

Fuck. Fuck. Fuck. Please, God, don't tell me this is the kinda stuff she was referring to. No. It just can't. I hang my head in shame as I realize that in all likelihood I play a large part in why she didn't leave his punkass the first time he showed signs of who he really was. If she didn't have those unwarranted, deep-rooted feelings that my actions gave her, she'd never put up with any of this. I actually feel sick to my stomach. She doesn't deserve this. No one does, but especially not Ruby. She's dealt with enough of my shit in the past.

I press my ear against the door but I can't hear a thing. I'm hoping she's fallen asleep. Or more likely, passed out from emotional exhaustion. I slowly and quietly get up and head to the room I slept in last night. Changing out of my boxers, I quickly jump in the shower, and put on some joggers and a sweatshirt before making my way downstairs. I need a beer to help calm my nerves.

I grab my phone that I'd left on the counter while I swam and see that it's 5:45 pm. From what I remember, they are six hours ahead in Paris. So it'll be coming up to midnight over there. I know it's late, but I've gotta call Serena and tell her about what has happened. With my phone and beer in hand, I head to the deck so I don't accidentally wake Ruby up if she hears me talking. Doesn't matter that the house is huge, and she's a whole floor above, I don't wanna risk it. Turning the chair so I can see both the house and the beach, I dial my sister's number.

"Heya, Ro. You okay?" my sister asks, her voice quiet, almost at a whisper.

"Yeah. I mean no. I... listen I need to talk to you about something. I know it's late, but I wouldn't call if I didn't feel I had to."

"What's going on? What's wrong? Is Dad okay? Is it Olivia or the girls?" she asks in a frantic panic.

"No. It's none of them. They are all fine. No one is in danger or anything like that," I reassure her, then quickly continue. "Listen, so you know Ruby and I went for lunch today?"

"Yeah. Is she okay?"

"After we ate, we walked around for a bit, then headed back to the house. I went for a swim, and she went to shower."

I hear some rustling in the background and her *"Mmmm"* as she follows what I'm saying.

"After my swim, I was about to get changed and stuff when I heard her talking in her room. I thought she was maybe on the phone to you or something, so I knocked on the door and asked if she's decided about dinner, but she then went quiet. Then I heard a man's voice. I wasn't sure who it was at first, but then she said his name. I realized I could hear her talking to Julian."

"Hold on, Ro, I'm putting you on speaker as Rhett's beside me. Okay, carry on."

"Well, he flipped out that I was here. And he worked out she's staying at Rhett's house. Something about a painting."

"Fuck," Rhett murmurs.

"Oh, god. What happened?" Serena asks, the fear and unease evident in her voice.

"Sis, as God is my witness, if that man was in front of me right now it would take an army to get my hands off of his throat."

Serena gasps and I know she understands how fucking angry I am.

"First, he laid into her about staying here. Then went on saying that she isn't good enough, how even I tossed her to the curb. He yelled at her, calling her a liar, a user, that she only got with him to make me jealous."

"You're fucking kidding me," she shrieks.

"Then said that she didn't have his back during some fight he'd had with Rhett or something. Called her a social climber, said even his mom warned him about Ruby. And that she used him to get things and to go to fancy places. The fucking jackass was screaming at her down the phone, talking to her like trash. He ended it by saying she will get nothing from him again, she never was and never will be good enough, that he's done with her and never wants to see her face again."

My knuckles crack at how tight I'm gripping the bottle of beer.

"That stupid motherfucking asshole. Who the fuck does he think he is? How dare he? Not good enough? *Not good enough?* He doesn't even deserve the shit on the bottom of her shoes. He's such a stuck up, self-centered, entitled fuck-face," she shouts. And she's completely right.

"Roman?" Rhett's voice comes through as my sister continues to cuss Julian out. This must be so weird for him as in the end, this is his brother we're talking about, but I don't give a shit.

"Yeah," I answer.

"Where's Ruby right now? I know asking if she's okay is a stupid question, but how's she doing?"

"She's... man she really broke down. I sat on the other side of her door and could hear her just break. She was sobbing for ages. I think she eventually passed out, so I waited until I couldn't hear anything anymore before coming downstairs and called you."

I can hear my sister crying. And I get it. Ruby and her are like sisters.

"Listen, Roman, I'm gonna call a contact of mine. I've used him a couple of times for security at events and during some hostile negotiations. I'm gonna ask him to put someone on my brother's tail. Make sure he doesn't make his way down to Virginia Beach. And if he tries, then I'll leave the security guys instructions to stop him even leaving New York."

I take a deep breath as I process everything.

"Also, as we're all the way over here, I'm gonna also give the guy your number. So if he can't reach me, then he'll be able to get a hold of you. Do you also want me to have someone watch the house? I don't think my asshole brother would try anything, but then I also didn't think he'd treat

Ruby this bad. Do you think she'd feel more relaxed if there was someone nearby? Especially in these next few days, where she'll be in the house alone?"

My head feels like it's going to explode. I still can't believe that this has all gone down. The only good thing that's happened is my respect and appreciation for Rhett has seriously shot up. He really is a decent guy. Even if he's only offering all this help because Ruby is Serena's best friend. It just shows how much he loves my sister and will do anything and everything for her.

"Thanks, Rhett. I really appreciate that. Regarding having someone come and stay or just be nearby, well, that's what I was gonna talk to you about, sis."

"Alright, why don't I leave you to talk to your sister and I'll go get on the phone and call my guy."

"Sure. And Rhett, thanks again."

"No problem."

"Ro. I just can't believe this. My hands are shaking with how damn angry I am," Serena says as she cries.

"I know. Trust me, I was more angry listening to that than I was when I woke up after the accident and the doctor told me I'd never play professionally again."

I take a swig of beer before asking her what she thinks with what I'm about to suggest.

"So one thing I can tell you for sure is that there's no way Ruby can stay here alone. She just can't. And where you're so far away, and I'm already here, I think it's best if I continue to stay. I want to make sure she's alright. Or at least as okay as she can be. The house is big enough that if she wants to be alone, she can do her own thing and won't feel like I'm hovering. And there is no way in hell I would let anyone get to her. They'll have to go through me, and I would break their legs if they even tried. I'll make sure she eats, and if she wants company, we can chill. But sis, I just can't leave her like this."

My voice is strained and my throat tightens as I'm filled with all kinds of emotions. We both stay silent for a minute, and I know my sister understands how important this is to me. Then she finally speaks. "I agree. I know you wouldn't let anything happen to her. I also agree with Rhett. I can't see that asshole even trying to make his way down to you guys. But yeah, I think you staying is the right idea. However, I need you to promise me something."

"What's that?"

"Please do everything at her pace. She's gonna be feeling really emotional and vulnerable right now. So just don't push her to open up or socialise or anything like that too hard. I can only imagine the wounds his words have created. And given the past between the two of you, I feel like there's a chance that, if you do too much, she will either retreat into herself more or lash out. I don't want either of those things to happen, okay?"

There is the tiniest part of me that bristles with annoyance that she even feels the need to warn me on how to behave. Especially regarding Ruby. But then, at the same time, I get it. She loves her. They are best friends. She saw how Ruby was after everything happened between the two of us, and has probably also seen first-hand how Ruby has dealt with other breakups she's had over the years. So I know, in the end, she's the one likely to know how these next steps will go.

"I understand. And I promise you, I won't push her or

irritate her. I will just be around and can help with anything she needs."

"Good. Honestly Ro, I'm so glad you're there. I think if you weren't, I'd have gotten Rhett to get us on the next flight back."

"I know, sis. I know."

We continue chatting for a couple more minutes and she lets me know that she'll text Ruby, not wanting to risk waking her by calling. After we say our goodbyes, and I reassure her I'll keep her updated, I call my dad, letting him know what's happened and that I'll need to take a couple of days off to stay here with Ruby. Even my dad, who is always calm and collected, lost his cool when I told him all the shit that was said. For him, Ruby has always been one of the family, and he cares for her a great deal. That's why it meant a lot when he said I could take all the time I needed.

After hanging up with him, I slowly sip on my beer, seeing the sun has now set. Even though the view out to the ocean is a pretty one, I feel nothing but darkness but wishing I had the power to fix everything and make it all alright.

Once I finish my beer, I head inside in search of something to make for Ruby in case she's hungry when she wakes up. Searching through the pantry I find some peanut butter and Nutella. I always used to find it weird when she'd made this combo, but she once told me that her mom used to make it for her when she was little. Apparently, if she'd hurt herself, her mom would make her this sandwich and the mix of the peanut butter and Nutella would magically make the pain go away. So that's what I do, putting it on a tray with a banana and bottle of water. I find a pad of paper and a pen, and write a little note for her before adding it to the tray.

I made you a little snack in case you were hungry. P.S. The pain you feel today is that strength you feel tomorrow.

I leave the tray outside her door and slip the note under and into her room, knowing she's more likely to spot it first.

Chapter 15

Ruby

They say that once you reach a certain level of pain you go into this shock-like state. Where the agony no longer hurts. You don't feel it, don't notice it even. That's the best way I can describe what I'm going through right now. The pounding throbs I felt between my temples is just a continual dull ache now. My tears no longer flow as uncomfortably as they had. Yet when the odd one escapes, I can feel the burning path it leaves behind.

I still can't believe just how horrible Julian was to me. That was the worst he has ever treated me. Yes, we'd had some terrible arguments in the past—ones that some would have already found too much, too toxic—but he's never gone that low. Last night wasn't just below the belt. It was straight-up cruel.

Never in my life could I ever imagine saying such god-awful things to someone, especially someone I'm in a relationship with and supposedly care about.

As I drifted in and out of sleep, I kept getting flashbacks

of the venomous names he called me. So, I buried myself deeper into the bed, wrapping the duvet tighter around me, attempting to block it all out. However, it was all pointless, leaving me to toss and turn.

I must have passed out eventually, because I woke up struggling to understand why this was hurting so much. This had been my shortest relationship, yet it was such a physical and mental blow, like being hit by a dump truck. I wondered if the pain stemmed from his cruelty or my desperate need to love and be loved. My limbs feel like lead, weighing me down, anchoring me in the cocoon of my bed. I've avoided looking at myself in the mirror. Which has been easy as the only times I've gotten out of bed has been to use the bathroom.

One of the times I got up, I noticed three pieces of paper pushed under the door. I recognize Roman's handwriting instantly.

I made you a snack in case you were hungry.
P.S. The pain you feel today is the strength you feel tomorrow.

That last sentence hits me hard. I'm sure there's truth to that statement, but right now I don't feel any stronger than I did yesterday. Quite the opposite, really.

I've made something fresh but that'll still keep. I know you probably don't feel like eating, but please, if you can, have a little something. P.S. We too, like trees, can shake off our dead leaves and begin again.

There's something kind of beautiful about that last bit. Even if the only part I can relate to is the death part. Or rather, me feeling like death. As I open the last letter, I notice this one is a little longer.

I think I need to try a different approach. I've made you three things. One thing I know you'll enjoy eating, the other you may be tempted to try, and the last one, well, you'll definitely react to it. P.S. Don't let someone who isn't worth your love make you forget how much you are worth.

Tears prick my eyes. I put the notes on the dresser and unlock my door. As I open it, I find a tray on the floor with three plates, all of which are covered with foil. I pick up the tray then close the door again, bringing it to bed. Curiously, I unwrap the first plate that has a stack of bacon on it. The smokey aroma instantly fills the room, making my mouth water. I grab a piece and am surprised they are still warm. He can't have left it that long ago. Uncovering the next one, my eyes narrow, trying to decipher what it is. Bringing it closer, I realize it's a pancake. Or what I think is Roman's attempt at some sort of pancake art. I honestly do not know what on earth he has tried to depict. Especially as I'm guessing he added fresh blueberries to the batter, which have burst and made this already unique-looking thing appear more like some scary alien blob-like creature. I honestly don't think I've ever seen anything that looks as unappealing. My lips twitch and I have to bite back a smile.

Thank god Roman has other talents because food art

definitely isn't one of them. Despite how unappetizing it looks, I push myself to break off a piece to try. And to my surprise, it actually tastes really good.

Finally, I uncover the last plate. At first, it's a little anti-climactic. It's just a sandwich. But as I take a bite, I'm instantly transported to my childhood. Goosebumps explode across my skin as I'm awash with both nostalgia and emotion. How did he know? After all these years, he remembered *this*? I am overwhelmed. Not only that Roman remembered, but also made me this—my comfort meal—but also with the urge to be back at my parents' house, where I could fall into my mom's arms and have her convince me that everything will eventually be alright. I manage to eat about half of my food as my tears continue to silently fall, then I place the tray on the floor before falling back asleep.

It must be early afternoon when I next wake and I finally decide to turn my phone back on. I'd switched it off after the call with Julian because I just couldn't face hearing or dealing with anyone. There's a part of me that's surprised there's nothing from Julian. No further rants or any kind of apology. I don't know why, but I guess somewhere deep down there'd been a flicker of hope that he would have sobered up, realized just how awful he'd been, then apologize. Not that it would have altered the situation between us, but it would show even the slightest bit of humanity.

Pushing that thought aside because I'm tired of crying, I read through the messages. Most of them are from Serena, so I'm guessing Roman told her.

I haven't really thought about the fact that Roman was

essentially a witness, albeit on the other side of the door, and shame hits me hard. It would have been mortifying to have anyone hear all that, but the fact that my ex did somehow feels ten times worse. I don't even want to know what he said when he told Serena.

After reading her worried texts, I message back promising to call her. I will, I'm just not quite ready yet. I decide to take a bath and feel a little better after relaxing in the hot water and putting some clean clothes on.

That evening, I'm back in bed when Roman slips a note under the door. There's a part of me that's surprised that he's stayed. I wouldn't have blamed him if he'd have left already. It's not as if I've been good company. I guess I'm just a little shocked. He's already done so much for me, and him continuing to stay, just being close and making sure I'm not alone unlocks something within me I thought I'd long buried.

I'm overwhelmed by it. Not only by the fact that he's chosen to stay but also the way he hasn't tried to be overbearing. Hasn't been hovering. He's just let me know in his own way that he's here. For me. In whichever way is needed. Right on queue, my tummy rumbles. I do really appreciate that he's still here and keeps bringing me trays of food. I just don't want him to see me like this. I'm not quite ready for company and real interaction just yet. I wait a couple of minutes, hoping he's back downstairs before I open the door, collect the tray, and pick up the note.

There's something about these notes that feels so special. Maybe it's because they remind me of the little Post-It's he used to leave in my bag and locker in high school. I remember all the girls used to be so jealous. Their boyfriends would barely remember to keep a seat free next to them in the lunch-room, whereas Roman would do the cutest little things that always managed to put a smile on my face. It's also the way that through these messages, he's letting me know that he's still here, still cares, while at the same time giving me space and just letting me deal and process everything on my own timeline.

I see my creativity managed to get you to eat. Good. I'm glad. And no, I won't tell you what that pancake was actually meant to be. You'll just have to keep guessing. This time I've gone classic with burri-tos. P.S. Don't be afraid to start over. It's a brand new opportunity to rebuild what you truly want.

I dig into my meal and, after I'm done, tear out a piece of paper from my notebook and scribble down two words before placing the finished tray back outside my door along with the note.

Thank you x

For the first time since everything happened, I fall asleep without tossing and turning, without tears soaking my pillow, or feeling like I'm drowning.

When I awake the following day, I decide it's time to leave this room and get some fresh air.

When I finally emerge, I find Roman in the kitchen,

music playing in the background, and something cooking on the stove.

"Jesus, Rubes. Do you moonlight as a ninja on your days off? You scared the life out of me," he says as he catches his breath, looking at me startled as he jumps back in surprise.

I have to roll my lips as he stares at me with wide eyes and his hand on his chest.

"Sorry. I wasn't even trying to be quiet." My voice has a slight croak to it, and I realize it's because I haven't spoken in like three days.

Roman must notice my voice too as his eyes immediately soften, and he gives me the softest smile. I don't know if it's because I probably look like a drowned rat in comparison to him. He looks great, standing there in his gray joggers that look like they were designed to just make any woman weak at the knees. Embarrassment creeps through me, and I let out a deep breath when he turns and carries on cooking. It's funny seeing him so domesticated. I feel like I'm looking into a life, a dynamic that I'd always wished and hoped for but could never have imagined witnessing.

Looking around, I see that he's got a fresh cup of coffee, so I take a cup from the cupboard and make myself one.

I don't really know what to do or say. There's no way I'm ready to talk about what happened, but I can't think of anything else to say. At the same time, I love the feeling of having someone around. No. Not just someone. Roman. He feels safe. Comforting. And right now his presence feels like that worn sweatshirt that you've had for years and always put on when you're feeling at your lowest and most vulnerable.

So I just take a seat at the kitchen island and slowly sip

my coffee. I appreciate that when he dishes up our food and also takes a seat, he doesn't ask questions. Roman makes small talk easily and surprisingly, even in the moments of silence, it isn't uncomfortable. When we finish eating, I offer to do the washing up, but he proudly says that he's not only discovered where the dishwasher is but also how to run it.

I'm just about to tell him I'm going to sit outside for a while when he calls my name. "Ruby. I don't wanna bring anything up or make you uncomfortable or anything. But I did wanna let you know that I'm gonna be staying here with you until you leave to head back."

My brows rise in surprise. I'm not surprised that he's going to continue to stay here. He's already been here for basically half the trip, I guess I hadn't expected him to bring it up given that we've both danced around talking about anything too heavy.

"Those are Serena's orders. She made it explicitly clear that either I stay, or she flies back from Paris, since she doesn't want you to be alone. And I guessed that you wouldn't want her to cut her trip short. So, I'm afraid you're stuck with me." He says this with a proud smile.

Dipping my head, I try to hide my smile. That is so like her. I can imagine her lecturing him for hours until he finally gave in to her demands. There's a massive part of me that wants to point out that it's completely unnecessary. I'm grown enough that I don't need a sitter. But I like the thought of having someone here with me. To be completely honest, if we hadn't had such an enjoyable time the other day, I'd have probably made a big fuss and said no. I don't need a watcher, especially not my ex. But given how understanding he's been, I really don't mind him staying.

"Okay. If you're sure it won't put you out too much?" I ask.

I'm surprised to see his whole body relax when I agree. As if he's been expecting a real pushback from me.

"Nah, it's fine. I promise, it's not a problem."

Giving him a small smile and nod, I take my coffee and sit out on the terrace for a while.

I take the time to enjoy the quietness and calming sounds of the ocean in the distance and just let myself process everything. Reflecting, I fully admit to myself just how far back these issues started between us. I acknowledge that I've been suppressing the magnitude of the problems between us simply because I was desperate not to be alone.

My mind muddles through the waves of emotions. I don't know how long I've been sat out here, but the next thing I know, Roman's bringing me a plate full of nibbles.

He doesn't say a word. Just sits here with me. It's not uncomfortable or awkward. On the contrary. His silent and steadfast presence feels like a powerful ball of energy. With each passing minute, I feel a level of strength continue to grow. A resonating belief within myself that even if it might take a while, I not only can, but will get through this.

I don't know how long we're both sat here but after some time he rises from his seat and tells me he's gonna go for a run in the home gym. I watch as he heads off to work out and I sit outside for a little while longer before heading inside to find some fresh sheets for the bed, and taking a nap.

When I wake, I finally FaceTime Serena. I don't know how, but I manage to get through most of it without completely breaking down. She says how sorry she is, and she wishes there was something she could do. When I remind her that she's already helped, especially by forcing Roman to stay so I'm not alone, she gives me a slightly puzzled look. I guess he wasn't supposed to tell me she was making him stay.

Just before I ask her how her trip is going, Rhett pops his head onto the screen and also apologizes. I honestly don't know what to say without getting more emotional, so I just say thank you, then spend the next ten minutes peppering Serena on all the things they've gotten up to. After our call, I head downstairs and find Roman at the front door with bags of Chinese takeout. He's ordered way too much, but I still enjoy it. We sit and eat, again not going into anything too deep, then eventually each head to our respective rooms and go to bed.

For the next two days, we do the same. Roman continues cooking all our meals, we eat together, then go our separate ways. I know he was initially giving me space and allowing me to just do things at my own pace, not wanting to over-crowd me. But I can't help the longing I now feel. Those small moments we spend together I'm beginning to realize are my favorite parts of the day. It's what I look forward to most. At the same time, I need to stay focused. Not allow myself to get caught up in it. My biggest aim, what I really need to focus on is myself. So, I spend lots of time thinking, writing things down in my notebook, and working through everything.

On the following day, we continue this routine, but by that late afternoon, I slowly feel a bit more myself and decide it's my turn to make dinner. I fancy something comforting, so end up making a baked chicken pie. After I put it in the over and have the veg simmering on the stove, I go to look for Roman to let him know. I call out his name but get no response. Making my way upstairs, I'm about to knock on his door but find it's wide open, and he isn't in there. Then I remember he's been in the gym a couple times since we've been here, so I head down to the basement to see if he's there.

The second I open the door, I spot him on the treadmill with his back to me. He's only wearing a pair of basketball shorts and beads of sweat trickle down the rippling muscles on his back. The deep caramel hue of his skin glistens from the exertion of his fast and steady pace. Each twitch and movement from his muscles is spellbinding, almost hypnotic. Shaking my head out of the weird trance I seem to get caught in, I raise my hand and knock on the open door. "You okay?" he asks as he pants for breath while turning off the machine.

My mouth goes dry as he turns towards me. He may have had to stop playing football over ten years ago, but he's definitely been looking after his body just as well now as he had back then. The six-pack and chiseled Adonis belt can attest to that.

"I... I was just looking for you. I made dinner. It should be ready in about thirty minutes," I say in a rush.

"Sweet. I'm gonna do some stretches to cool down, then quickly jump in the shower. So I'll be ready by then."

"No need to rush. It'll stay warm."

I give him a quick smile, then hastily make my way back up to the kitchen. Not wanting my mind to go in a direction it has no right or reason to be going, I keep myself busy in the kitchen. Luckily, I distract myself enough that by the time dinner's ready and Roman joins me in the kitchen, the only thing I'm thinking about is eating.

"I was thinking, if you want, do you feel up for watching a movie? I looked earlier and there's pretty much every new release on there," Roman asks as he sits to eat. "Yeah, sure. Why not? But only if I get to pick the movie."

Chapter 16

Roman

I stretch my legs out onto the footstool as we watch the second movie of the night. When I suggested a movie, I think I was just riding the high that Ruby seemed a little better. Then I panicked that maybe I'd done the one thing Serena told me not to: rushed and pushed for something she wasn't ready for. Even though it only took a few seconds for her to answer, it felt like much longer. When she'd agreed, I looked deep into her eyes to make sure there was no hesitancy or her seeming uncomfortable with my suggestion.

I won't lie, when we first sat down, I wasn't sure where to sit. I expected Ruby to go into the corner of the sofa, maybe because that's what I remember her doing back in the day. But she sat in the middle, grabbed the throw blanket and put it over her lap, then pulled the large footstool closer and made herself comfortable. I sat kinda beside her, but left a gap as I didn't want her feeling like I was pushing in on her personal space.

Her choice of *Speak no Evil,* after considering all the options, surprised me. I'd expected her to pick something light or a comedy, considering everything that has happened. But I'm glad she picked it, as the movie was damn good. When it finished, I thought she'd just go up to bed, especially as it was already getting late. But when she picked up the remote the second the credits rolled and put on another movie, my eyes widened in surprise. I think she took it as my response to her picking *The Barbie Movie* to watch next, opposed to the fact I just hadn't expected her to want to stay down here and watch more TV. I was more displeased by the prospect of watching a movie about a doll than excited by her wish to relax and stay downstairs. Even if Margot Robbie was playing said doll. Ruby must have sensed my apprehension of her choice as she simply turned her head towards me, gave me a sweet smile, and said, "Just trust me. It's gonna be better than you think." I nodded in response and schooled my facial expressions.

It didn't take long for me to realize that she's already watched this. I wondered why she'd want to watch it again. But as the movie went on and I clocked onto the themes and messages being conveyed, it became crystal clear why she picked it.

This was for her. Not to entertain or distract. She picked this because of what happened with that asshole.

I don't even want to refer to him by his name. Every time I think about him, think about the fucking bullshit he said, pure fiery rage courses through me. What I would give to have ten minutes alone with him. It's weird because I thought my anger would have dissipated, but as each day passes, tension and frustration wrack my body. And the only safe way I seem to be able to let it out is in the gym. I think I've trained harder and longer in the last few days than I have in months.

Usually, I go to the gym four days a week, but I run every day. Which is funny, as I hated running when I was younger. I loved sprinting, loved that burst of power. But after my accident and the subsequent breakdown, it was actually my therapist who recommended I run to help clear my head and work through shit. It helped and I've been doing it ever since. Yet in the last few days, running hasn't felt enough. I've not gotten the mental relief that I usually get. Tonight is a win. A step forward for her. And hopefully tomorrow she will take another small step forward. I look over at Ruby and see she is fast asleep.

I turn the TV off and softly nudge her awake, but it's no use. Another thing that hasn't changed about Ruby is once she's in a deep sleep, a herd of elephants couldn't wake her.

Moving the blanket, I detangled it from her, then I slide my arms beneath her, lifting her to my chest. Slowly and carefully, I carry her upstairs and lay her on her bed as I'm hit with the memory of the last time I had her like that in my arms.

As much as I appreciate Ruby throwing this little get-together for me, it really wasn't necessary. We already had a party on the day of the draft. I thought we were only back here in Franklin Park to grab the last few boxes of our stuff. We've already got everything set up in our condo in Wisconsin, and it's been wild. There are still times I've gotta pinch myself that this is all real. Everything feels like it's aligned itself for me. The Greenbay Packers' quarterback retired and they drafted me in the third round. Training camp has been intense, but I've been so fired up and it's only fueled my hunger.

We've had all our preseason games that went better than I could have hoped as I got to play in one of them. And when I found out I'd gotten a place in the final roster... Man, that's a day I'll never forget.

The season start is only a few days away, and we've done a twenty-four-hour stop back home to grab what I thought were a couple of suitcases of Ruby's things and a chance to see our family before the season starts. And low and behold, Ruby had arranged a surprise party at her parents' house. My dad, sisters, uncles, aunts, cousins, as well as a couple of our friends, all showed up to show their support and wish me luck. I think the hardest thing is not being able to enjoy the food and drink as I'm making sure my body stays at its peak.

Even though this party wasn't necessary, I still enjoyed it and appreciated that it was also for Ruby. She's practically given up everything to stay by my side, come with me, and be the rock I need. I know Ruby definitely needed this.

It's late and everyone has left. Her parents are clearing the last few things from the yard, and I make my way inside looking for Ruby. I can't help but laugh when I find her asleep on the sofa.

"Hey, babe. Let's get you up to bed," I say as I rub her arm.

"Mmmm. Too tired. Stairs. Too far away," she mumbles.

"Alright. I'll carry you up."

Lifting her into my arms, I carry her to bed.

"I know I cried. But I'm not sad. I'm so proud of you,

Roman. And I love you with all my heart. Forever and ever," she murmurs as she rubs her face against my chest.

"I know. And I love you too," I say as I get her dress off and tuck her in under the covers. As I stare down at her, I silently promise to do the best I can, be the best. Not just for myself, not just for my team, but also for Ruby. She's given me everything by not only helping me fulfill my dream, but doing it at the cost of her own.

Last night was probably the best night's sleep I've had since we got here. I don't know if it was just my body giving into exhaustion, or because it was the first night I wasn't worrying about Ruby.

Feeling refreshed, I jump in the shower, get dressed, then make my way downstairs. Just as I'm snatching a cup for my coffee, Ruby walks in, also looking rested and definitely a bit more like her usual self.

"Morning."

"Morning. What time did the movie finish last night? I don't even remember heading upstairs," she asks as she also makes herself a cup.

"I'm not sure. Around midnight. Yeah, you fell asleep before the end and there was no waking you. So I carried you up."

I don't miss how her cheeks turn red and she suddenly looks very interested in the kitchen flooring.

"Damn, I hope it didn't cause you to put your back out. It explains why I felt so hot during the night and had to strip all my clothes off as I never sleep in anything more than a t-shirt. If that." Her eyes widen, and her cheeks turn an even deeper shade of red. My whole body heats and my pulse begins to race as I picture her stripping off and sleeping with practically nothing on, remembering just how delectable her body was. How good it tasted. How soft her skin felt beneath my fingertips. Clearing my throat, I try to stop my wayward thoughts as quickly as I can.

"Don't be silly. You're still as light as you've always been. I bench press more in my warmups. And regarding your clothes, I didn't think you'd be too happy if I'd have stripped you down while you were asleep," I reassure her with a laugh, but I'm surprised to see her staring down at her cup, chewing on her bottom lip with what looks like disappointment on her face. But that can't be right. I must be seeing things I wish were there. There's no way in hell she's disappointed I didn't undress her. Damn, I must really be losing my mind.

"I think I'm gonna have to eat some lighter meals. With you constantly making these great home-cooked breakfasts, lunches, and dinners, plus my lack of working out, I'm gonna end up needing to be rolled out of here when it's time to leave," Ruby jokes as she finishes the last of her coffee.

"Oh, don't be silly," I reassure her before taking a bite out of my apple.

"I was looking up some things around here and saw that there's something on today that I think you'll like."

"Oh yeah? And what's that?" she asks.

"Well, how about this? You tell me if you wanna venture out of the house today. If you say yes, then I'll tell you. If you're not up for it, that's fine and we can just chill here."

I unplug my phone, which has been charging all morning, and await her answer. Turning my head, I see her leaning against the counter beside me. Her eyes narrow, but a curious grin spreads across her face. I'm not trying to push her into anything before she's ready, but I think it would do her good to get out. I'm really hoping that she's tempted enough to find out what I looked up and agree to go.

"Fine. I guess it would be good to get out for a little while. But I have one condition," she stipulates.

Now my curiosity is piqued. "Hit me."

"I don't know if your suggestion is gonna be something I would actually enjoy doing or not. And to be honest, I think if you tell me what it is before we leave but it ends up being something I don't like the sound of, I'll just chicken out with going. So yes, I'll go, but don't tell me what we're doing. Keep it a surprise until we get there. Oh, and you have to wear one of the baseball caps I brought with me." The devious smile that stretches across her face suddenly gives me cause for concern.

"Now, hold on. Will I be able to choose which one I wear? And what color is it?"

"Nope. I'll be picking it, and don't worry, I'll go with a color I know you can pull off."

Damn. Ruby knows how much I like my ball caps, and how picky I am with the ones I wear. But seeing how excited she seems about this silly little trade, I'm pretty sure I'd agree to walk around with one of my nieces' princess tiaras if it meant that smile stayed.

"Alright, fine. You've got yourself a deal." I roll my eyes and grin as she bounces on the balls of her feet and claps.

"Time to get ready. Make sure you're wearing something comfy to walk in. Oh, and seeing as we've not started doing trades, I've just thought of a great way to up what I had planned. Let's just say that a few bets may be involved. So let the games begin." The look of confused curiosity that's plastered over her face is just what I was hoping for her as I make my way upstairs.

"I don't know what I'm more impressed by. That you found a flea market open today or that you came up with some pretty impressive challenges for my tasks?" Ruby says in an excited tone. I'm honestly surprised at how much she's enjoyed herself. I didn't think she would be so enthusiastic. I thought it could be fun because she used to make me watch this program about auctions at *Sotheby's* and *Christie's*. To me, it was one of the dullest things in the world. Even my sister thought it was so boring she actually banned Ruby from watching it when they hung out. So, I felt this was the perfect thing to get her out of the house and keep her mind occupied. Plus, when we got here, I started putting together a list of tasks.

I gave her a hundred dollars in cash and told her to find and buy four specific items, without exceeding that amount. She had to find something with a forest animal on it, a piece of jewelry, something that predated 1880, and an item she felt represented someone in my family. I'll admit I really struggled to come up with that last one. I gave her a maximum of two hours to find and barter for her items. And I guess I shouldn't be surprised, but she completed the task.

"Will you finally show me the things you got? I still don't

understand why you wanted to keep that bit secret. I'm the one that came up with all the suggestions."

I take a sip of my Long Island Iced Tea while we sit at this cool little place I found after our trip to the market. I was getting hungry and I'm sure Ruby was too with how much she was running around.

"I didn't wanna show you because I couldn't risk you saying some things were wrong or didn't count. But don't worry, I can tell you're desperate to see them, so I'll put you out of your misery."

She reaches into her bag and pulls out this dark blue glass bottle. It fits perfectly into the palm of my hand and makes me think of the kind of thing they'd have kept poison in once upon a time.

"I don't know why, but I'm tempted to smell it. However, I'm not risking there being some sort of poisonous residue still in there."

Shaking her head, she laughs at my statement before pulling out a worn-looking piece of fabric with a deer embroidered on it. Next, she hands over probably the thinnest chain I've ever seen. I'm sure if I squeezed it, it would break between my fingers.

"I don't think this is like a long-lost *Tiffany* or *Cartier* or anything, but it is pretty cool," I tell her before handing it back. Pulling out the last thing from her bag, I see that it's wrapped in a cloth. Unwrapping it, I find a small Spartan warrior statue.

"You're gonna have to help me with this. I can't work out if this is representing Serena since she's like a fighter for her clients and stuff, or is it meant to be my dad? But I don't quite get the connection."

"It's not Serena or your dad. It's you. You're a fighter. You picked yourself back up. I know you do a lot for others, like helping Rhett when he proposed to your sister. That wasn't exactly a small thing. I bet if it wasn't for you, most of it wouldn't have been possible."

"You did more of the coordinating and assisting on that," I interject, but she just shakes off my comment and continues.

"Look at what you've done for me the last couple of days. I think this is a good representation of you."

I have to swallow several times as my mouth is dry. My skin prickles as an overwhelming emotion works its way through me. "Thank you. I'm for sure not a warrior. But that's very kind of you to say."

Looking into her eyes, I let her see how much that means to me. Those words, especially coming from her, given our past, mean more than she could ever know.

Chapter 17

Ruby

Amazement washes through me as I mentally go through the list of things that Roman does now. I can't believe the change in him. He's matured beyond ways I could have ever imagined. Whether it be small things, like cooking and cleaning up after himself, or the way he is now conscious of his words and actions. There is so much that I can see, that I've processed and am acknowledging now that he does. Which is the polar opposite of how I was and dealt with things before. Because after he broke it off with me, there was a period where I literally blocked him out of my mind. Tried to eradicate anything and everything that would remind me of him. Didn't want to think about any small thing he did, any of his habits or behaviors, none of it. Which was really difficult considering my best friend is also his sister. Whereas now, I can't stop from seeing it all. Noticing every minute detail. Not just noticing things but studying him. Entranced. Fascinated, even.

Roman seems to have completely reset himself. It's like he hit rock bottom after the accident and subsequent depression, then built himself back up. There are still essences of how and who he used to be, woven in with the stronger and better version of who he is now.

The ways that he's been looking after me. Whether that's in a big way like helping me out by driving me down here when there were no flights, and I felt like I wouldn't be able to get here. Or cooking, keeping me company, talking, gauging what it is I need which can be space and silence or just the presence of someone around. Or like carrying me to my bed after I'd fallen asleep somewhere else. He used to do that a lot. Though back then, it often ended with me randomly waking up horny and wanting him. Obviously, no such thing happened last night. Or better said this morning.

My cheeks heat as I remember my word vomit earlier about waking feeling heated as I still had my clothes on.

Why the fuck was the first thought that popped into my head disappointment that he didn't try to undress me? What the hell is wrong with me? I pictured the feel of his hands on me. The friction of his calloused fingers against my flushed skin. Something must seriously be wrong with me. I couldn't even look him in the eye after that. Thank God he didn't notice, I'm sure there's a reasonable explanation for all of it. It's probably that my mind and body are overloaded with all kinds of feelings and emotions that can't work out which way is up at the moment. Yet why, in the deepest and darkest recesses of my mind, is there the smallest voice telling me I am lying to myself?

. . .

I don't care what anyone else says, there is nothing hotter than watching your boyfriend at football practice. Especially in this summer heat. Cheer practice has been canceled this week since almost everyone on the team has exams, so we're meant to be focusing on those. I should study for my finals right now, but the library's air-conditioning is nonexistent and I couldn't stand it in there a minute longer.

Taking another sip from my bottle of water, I finish the last few dregs while using my notes that I should go over as a fan. Although I found the only shaded section of the bleachers, it's not even making a dent with the humidity. Closing my eyes, I try to pretend that instead of being by the football field, I'm actually relaxing on a beach somewhere. I lay myself on the bench and zone out into a paradisiacal fantasy in my mind.

I must have actually drifted off for a bit, when I'm awoken by the shrill sound of a whistle blowing. Turning my head and looking down, I can see their coach has brought practice to an end. I don't think Roman knows I'm here, but he must have spotted me at some point, because unlike the rest of his teammates who are walking to the locker room, he's making his way to me.

Pushing myself up so I'm seated, my eyes scan over his wet, glistening skin. Drenched in sweat, he looks like he's covered in baby oil and I know all the other girls are jealous he's mine.

"I thought I saw you making your way up here earlier," he says before pulling me up, grabbing my hips, and giving me a kiss. Pushing up on my tiptoes, I wrap my arms around his neck as our tongues explore and caress each other. My arms slip with how wet he is, reminding me he really needs a

shower, so I give him one last kiss before pulling back and looking him in the eyes.

"As much as I can appreciate just how hot you look with your shirt off and body glistening with sweat, you really have to shower, babe."

"I know. Just wanted to give my girl a quick kiss before I do. You gonna be alright here? Or do you wanna walk down with me and I can quickly grab my keys so you can sit in the car?"

I don't know what's cuter; that I have the best boyfriend in the world who's always looking out for me, or that he's giving me an Eskimo kiss while he asks where I'll be more comfortable.

"I'll wait here. I'm fine. But I do wanna stop and grab an ice cream on the way home."

"Deal. I'll be as quick as possible," he says, giving me one last quick kiss before he leaves.

I splash my face with water as I wash my hands. Where the fuck did that memory come from? I've had such a great day. I don't remember the last time I laughed this much. Roman did such an amazing job of distracting me at the market today. Even the damn baseball cap I gave him that he wore backward and was meant to be funny, he looked hot wearing. Back in high school, he used to always wear a baseball cap and I'd spent ages telling him he'd look even hotter if he wore it backward. To which he said it made him feel like he was in some cheesy boyband, so would never wear it like that. That's why when he swiveled it round and wore it like that and goofily raised his eyebrows, I'd expected him to look just how he'd described. But that wasn't the case at all. The man looked damn fine. That cap worn that way unlocked another level of sexy. Like seriously give a girl a break. But even with the sexy hat, he did such an amazing job today, and here I am, having these silly memories from over a decade ago. I'm sure there's a simple explanation behind it. It's probably also because I walked in on him working out yesterday and my subconscious probably just latched onto a similar image from the past. Yeah, I'm sure that's it.

Patting my face dry, I scrape all my hair up into a high ponytail. We'd decided to go out for dinner tonight but thought we'd check out and see what's about in the other direction, heading away from the beach instead.

I make my way out of the bathroom and grab a light sweater to take with me, in case we end up sitting outside to eat. When I get downstairs, I'm not surprised to find Roman ready and waiting.

"I'm ready. Let's go, I'm starving."

His eyes widen slightly as my voice is unnecessarily loud, but he simply gives me a nod, and the corner of his mouth quirks in a half smile. "Sounds good to me."

Damn, I'm really gonna need a drink tonight to shake myself out of whatever the hell is going on with me right now.

We walked instead of driving, and as I finish my third cocktail, I realize I should slow down a bit. At least until after we finish our meal. We found this cute little French place I dragged Roman into, saying we had to go here in honor of Serena currently being in France with Rhett. Luckily, I got a grip on myself and have not been awkward around him since we arrived, although I'm sure the alcohol has played a part in that.

"Alright, so part of your job is working with companies and helping them bring in customers, right?" he asks sincerely as his fingers trace the tablecloth near my hand. I don't know if it's the temperature around us or because I can't stop focusing on the soft strokes of his fingers so close to mine but my skin feels hot and flushed.

"Well, yeah. That's my entire job. I help to put together sales pitches, identify customer acquisition opportunities, and work closely with the sales and marketing teams to find how to bridge their product to their customer base, then find ways and strategies that can differentiate them from their competitors. Why do you ask?"

"Well, a couple of months ago, Dad and I were at a car expo—one of the many we go to every year—and I met a guy there who does these amazing custom paint jobs. Long story short, he wants to do a partnership with a garage that focuses on vintage or luxury cars, and turns out he only lives about thirty minutes away from us. I looked through his portfolio and I'm telling you his work is insane."

A genuine smile spreads across my face as I watch how enthusiastic Roman is talking about this.

"He gave me his card and we've been chatting a lot. I really think this could be a great idea, something that could bring in a whole new wave of clientele. But I don't just wanna go to my dad with just the idea. I wanna put together a proposal or whatever you call it. And I was hoping you could help. At least maybe tell me the kinda stuff I'd need to put in it."

He takes a long sip of beer, and I'm surprised when I see a hint of nervous apprehension in his eyes.

"Roman, you understand I work with beauty and wellness companies, right? I don't know a thing about cars."

"Yeah. I know, I get that. I was hoping you could like, maybe, just give me a breakdown of the kinda information I should be gathering. What kinda stuff to look up or if there's any particular research I should do?"

My heart warms as once again he looks like he's waiting for me to say no; turn him down and not help. I press my knees against his under the table, not only to reassure him but I also can't help but want the contact. The touch. The connection.

"Of course. Like I said, I don't know about the car industry, so I wouldn't be able to help with anything relating to product knowledge. But I can help with which things you need to look into and at least the things I think you'd want to put together so you can present it to your dad."

His shoulders visibly relax and when he gives me that megawatt smile of his, I feel my cheeks warm.

We spend the rest of the meal brainstorming and can't deny how great it feels. Like we're a team.

I can't believe that we stayed at the restaurant until closing. The wait staff had asked if we wanted them to call us a cab, and I'm still not sure if that was because they wanted us gone or because we had a couple more drinks after our food. I'm not complaining, though. Not for the drinks and the exciting and engaged discussion we continued having regarding Roman's business idea, or the fact that we're currently sat in a cab on a journey that would only take us about twenty minutes to walk. I'm not drunk, but I definitely have a good buzz going.

"Thanks. Here's great," Roman tells the driver before handing him some cash. My reactions are a little slow to realize that we've pulled up in front of the gate. The whole cab ride all I could think about was that familiar scent of Roman's aftershave that feels like it's imprinted itself within me. He still wears the same one he did all those years ago. The one I had bought him for Christmas one year. A scent that whenever I've smelled always reminded me of him. And right now it's making me wet with desire for him.

The next thing I know, Roman's opening my door and reaching out his hand to help me get out.

"Do you remember the code? I don't think I remember it," I tell him.

"Yeah. But even if I didn't, I've still got it saved on my phone," he says, punching in the digits and the gate opens up before us.

"I know we chatted about a lot tonight. And I wasn't expecting you to remember everything. So maybe, like tomorrow or something, we can sit down and write all the points down." My words aren't slurred, but even I can hear the slightly tipsy breathlessness in my tone.

Opening the front door, Roman steps aside and lets me in first. "Yeah, that sounds good. But there's no rush. I don't want to put you out or anything."

Standing at the bottom of the stairs, I turn towards him and roll my eyes. I don't know if it's the alcohol or just my imagination, but I swear I can see the beat of his pulse in the vein along his neck. My tongue runs along my bottom lip, desperate to instead be running it along his throat, tracing that beating pulse.

"Don't be silly. It's not putting me out. I enjoyed it. Besides, there might even be something in it for me."

"Really? And what's that?" The deep timbre of his voice feels like it's vibrating through my chest. He's taken a step towards me and my eyes bounce between the stunning green of his and his full mouth. Desire tingles across my skin as I watch his tongue glide across his pillowy lower lip.

"I... I... I might finally have a better understanding of cars. And why you enjoy playing with them so much."

I swear I can hear a rumble vibrating through his chest as I bite my lip. The surrounding air is thick and palpable.

"Mmmm. How I like to 'play with them?' That's what you think I do?"

This time it's me that takes another step closer, feeling like a magnet pulled to him by some unseen force.

"Yes. I think you enjoy playing with them. You like using your hands."

We're now millimeters apart. And looking deep into his eyes, I can see he knows I'm no longer talking about cars. I want him. I want his mouth. I want to feel his lips on mine. His pupils are blown and his jaw clenches as it's causing him physical pain from not touching me, not having me. From the look he's giving me, I can see he wants the same.

Pushing onto the balls of my feet, I close the remaining distance between us and kiss him.

The second my lips touch his, I'm awash with sensation. A mix of nostalgia, that feeling of coming home, and knowing that right now I want more than just this kiss. As his tongue caresses mine, Roman swallows down my moan.

Wrapping his arms around me, pulling my body flush against his. Despite the layers of our clothes still between us, I can feel the heat emanating from the thick, hard muscles of his chest.

The vibrations of his groan travel through every molecule of my body. What had started as soft and sensual has now turned into a frenzy. Without breaking the connection of our lips, he presses me against the wall, the feel of his solid bulge against my hip. Knowing he's as turned on as I am only spurs me on further. My body feels like it's going to explode.

Hands wrapping around the back of his neck, I graze his skin with my nails. That seems to set something off within him, and he lifts me up, wrapping my legs around his waist, and begins walking us up the stairs.

I don't know if it's leading to my room or his. Either way, I don't care. I just want him. Roman slows our kiss and rests his forehead against mine.

"Ruby... I want you so much right now. God, what I want to do to you right now."

I brush my lips against his. Showing he can have it all.

"I can't believe I'm doing this and saying this right now, but I think we should stop. I want you so damn bad. But I don't want us to just have fun tonight. Then tomorrow morning you wake up filled with regret, blaming it on us having been drinking tonight. I know I want you just as much now as I would if I were sober, but I care and respect you too much for us to do something you'd regret."

I pout as my body is burning with desire and my initial thought is why does he have to be so goddamn noble. But then, clarity makes its way through me.

I'm horny and tipsy and still have my legs wrapped around the man I thought thirty seconds ago I was about to fuck. As his words settle in, I know he's right, but that doesn't change the fact that I want him right now. Looking into his eyes, I can see just how torn he is. And I know deep down, no other man would be this respectful to me in this situation. That realization takes the sting out of my frustration.

"I understand. And I appreciate it."

Slowly unwrapping myself from him, I reach behind me to feel the cold metal of the door handle. As the door opens, I can see it's my room. Looking back at Roman, the rapid rise and fall of his chest from his labored breathing mirrors my own. I give him one last chaste kiss before walking into my room. Just before I close the door, I look him square in the eyes, so he can see the honesty in mine.

"Everything you said is understandable and valid. But just so you know, I'd want this just as much in the light of day as I do right now. Goodnight."

Closing the door, I lean against it and wait for the racing beat of my heart to subside. I meant what I said. This isn't just alcohol-fueled hormones, but I can't begrudge his apprehension. I don't know what this is between us, nor do I understand what it means. What I do know is that tomorrow I will do everything in my power to get him to give in. To understand, I don't need a drop of alcohol in my system to still want him.

Chapter 18

Roman

I 've never struggled so much to fall asleep as I did last night. I was tossing and turning nonstop until I basically passed out. Beating myself up, fighting what my body was desperate to have. Also, there was a part of me that was surprised, I guess. When I woke up yesterday morning, if anyone would have told me that several hours later, my lips would be locked with Ruby's and we'd be one step away from fucking, I'd have laughed in their face.

I have never denied my attraction to Ruby and have always known how hot she is. That's never been in question. What was in question was the unexpectedness of her desire. I honestly hadn't expected her to be interested. Both because of our past and everything that happened, but also given everything that she has just gone through with that asshole. And even though the second her lips touched mine, that feeling of familiarity and comfort, and those banked embers of desire reignited, the moment I started thinking about how much she'd drank, I knew despite how much my body craved her, I needed to stop.

Lying here, I start to wonder if maybe she was just eager for some form of comfort and attention, and I was just the most convenient option. That thought leaves a bitter taste in my mouth. I drag myself out of bed and head to the bathroom. I really can't stand the idea that if I weren't here, she could have had a similar evening with a random stranger. Another man would have been lucky enough to have her mouth, the touch of her fingers, the feel of her body. Frustration and annoyance bubble through me. Then I remember the last thing she said before closing the door. *That she would want this just as much in the light of day as she does right now.* Did she really mean that? Was that true or simply something she said in the throes of desire and under the cloak of alcohol-fueled passion? Suddenly I'm desperate to know. That gets my ass into gear as I chuck some clothes on and make my way downstairs.

As I walk into the kitchen, three of my senses are hit at once. First, the sound of music playing in the background, followed by the delicious smells of food. Then my eyes find Ruby by the fridge, and she is wearing the tiniest bikini I have ever seen her in. The small sapphire blue slivers of material are a bold contrast to the soft creamy tones of her skin as her hips sway to the beat of the music.

Fuck.

That body. The way she moves. Damn, I want her so badly. Desire instantly shoots down my body as my cock begins to thicken. It's not like she's doing a striptease or lap dance, watching the way her body moves so seamlessly. The soft hourglass shape of her curves makes me think of one of those old paintings of goddesses. Hypnotizing, entrancing, otherworldly. She's sexy and subtle, tempting but also composed. She must sense my presence because when she turns towards me, she doesn't seem surprised by me standing here. Instead, there's a cute little smile that plays on her face that stretches up to her eyes.

"Good morning," she says cheerfully.

"Morning. Have you been up long?" I ask.

"Yeah, been up a while. I've already eaten, but left you a breakfast burrito in the oven. It's probably still warm as I wrapped it in foil, but you can heat it up if you want it hot."

I'm trying really hard to concentrate on the words she's saying, but I'm finding it harder with each passing second as my eyes continuously feast on her mouth-watering curves that my fingers are twitching to touch. She must know exactly what she's doing as she walks over to the other end of the kitchen and begins wiping down the counters. The way her breasts bounce as they are barely constrained in that triangle bikini has me biting my lip and swallowing down a groan. It takes me a second to realize that she's continued talking.

"I think I'm gonna take a dip in the pool. After you've eaten, you should think about trying the water out yourself," she says with a purr.

Her hip grazes my hand as she passes me, and I have to clench my fist because even just that slight touch sets my skin ablaze. I watch her like a hawk as she makes her way to the pool. Not even daring to blink as I follow her every step until she gracefully dives into the water. Only once she swims her first lap, do I shake my head to get myself out of the trance-like state I'm in.

Snagging the breakfast burrito she left me, I take a seat at the kitchen island and position myself to have the best view of her in the pool. Warmth and a slight sense of eagerness work their way through me as I think back on her words. Not wanting to preemptively jump the gun but also realizing her attire and coy smile before she went to swim are possibly her way of showing that she wants the same thing today as she did last night.

What does this mean? Is she wanting one-time thing? Or just some fun while we're here? Either way, I know for sure I won't question if this is something she wants.

After finishing my food, I clear away my plate, then get changed to go for a swim. I had to give my cock a quick tug while I was getting undressed because of how much it aches. Finding a pair of swimming trunks, I put them on, then quickly make my way back downstairs, remembering to bring a towel with me.

The second I step outside, I realize she's no longer in the water. Scanning around frantically, I panic that I've missed my moment with her. I'm just about to kick myself when I finally spot her lying on her back on one of the sun loungers.

At the sound of my approach, she reaches down, clutches a bottle, and sprays sun oil on her legs, stomach, and chest. I'm stopped in my tracks, mesmerized at the way her fingers glide across her glistening skin. There is no hiding the tenting of my trunks, and I don't care. She knows I'm here. Watching her. She's putting on a show for me, and it's one I'll gladly watch until my dying day. I don't know how long I stand there just entranced by her, could be minutes or seconds. Then she finally locks eyes with me.

"Could you give me a hand? I really need to do my back."

The fact that she runs her tongue along her full bottom lip after that statement has to be one of the goddamn sexiest things I have ever seen or heard. And she doesn't need to ask me twice. I would give her anything she asks for.

The strong thread of desire pulls me closer as I take the last few remaining steps towards her. Her skin glows, not just from the sheen of oil, but also the raw sexual energy that just oozes out of each one of her pores.

Dropping my towel beside her lounger, I lick my lips as she rolls over onto her stomach. Reaching back, she pulls on the strings of her bikini top. The only item of clothing still on her is the thong-style bikini bottoms that make her already great ass look like the ripest and juiciest peach. My mouth is watering to lick, bite, and suck on it. Grabbing the oil, I cover her body, not wanting to leave out a single inch of skin. Bending over, I start rubbing in the oil first down one leg, then the other. Her soft, muffled moans as I increase the pressure has me biting my cheek.

Slowly, I make my way up the backs of her thighs as I move into a comfier position, straddling her. When I reach the apex of her thighs, I look down as my thumbs are just millimeters away from her pussy that's only partially covered by her thong. My cock strains painfully against my shorts and I can feel the tip begin to leak with precum. There is a glistening on her lips, and I know it's not from the oil. My teeth clench and my nostrils flare with the desperate desire to sink into her tight, wet heat. I'm so hard that it's almost agonizing.

I bypass her ass for now because the second I have my

hands on it, I'll want to eat it. Starting on her lower back, I work my way up, massaging the oil into her skin. She continues moaning as I work in slow circles. When I reach her shoulders, I have to lean forward even more, and there's no way she can miss the feel of my hard cock against the cheeks of her ass.

I know for sure that she can feel it when she slightly lifts her hips and rubs her ass along my shaft. This time it's me that lets out a deep groan and precum leaks from the tip. As she continues grinding, I struggle to maintain my rhythm and concentration. Then Ruby unexpectedly twists onto her back. The soft expression on her face is a total contradiction to the burning fire in her eyes. She looks like the most angelic temptress.

With my knees still on either side of hers, I brace my hands above her head, caging her in. I can feel the heat of her gaze and her eyes leave a burning path as they move down my chest, then my abs, until finally landing on my cock. Her eyes widen slightly before she licks her lips and I know she's noticed the damp spot from my leaking precum on my trunks. My chest rises rapidly as my yearning for her reaches fever pitch.

"I want this Roman. I want you. I've not had a drop of alcohol. I've been recently tested, I'm clean and I have the implant in. I want you to fuck me. Right here. Right now. Fuck me, please, Roman."

Chapter 19

Ruby

I'm so breathless, I struggle to get my words out. From the moment he walked downstairs, my body felt like a live wire. Attuned to his every move. Even while I was in the water earlier, I could feel his gaze on me. I knew my bikini was going to be the first step in getting his attention. Just as I made sure he could watch as I oiled myself up when he was only a few feet away. Then, once he started massaging my skin, it took everything in me to stay focused and not just melt away to the sensations as his strong fingers relaxed the tension in my back.

My breathing is still as erratic now as it was when I turned around and saw the wet stain of his arousal and the enormous bulge in his trunks. My pussy clenches as I remember his thick girth and length. There hasn't been one single guy I've been with since Roman who has filled and stretched me the same way he does.

I meant what I said. I want this; him. I need to feel him

buried deep inside me right now. Hating that the reason I recently got tested was because I hadn't trusted Julian and had suspicions that he'd maybe cheated on me. So, after I went to the clinic to get tested, I was happy to receive a clean bill of health. None of that is important right now. What is, however, is the desperate need I have to be filled and taken by the man above me.

"Roman, please. I want you. I want this. I'll even get on my knees to show you how much I want this."

He dips his head, taking my bottom lip between his teeth, and bites gently. Then his mouth crashes onto mine as he kisses me.

Roman swallows down my moans as he bears his weight down onto me. The barely there material of my bikini bottoms does nothing to shield the delicious friction as he rocks his hard cock against my public bone.

Wrapping my arms around him, I match his rhythm as desperation for more seeps out of me. And from what I can tell he wants this as much as I do, Roman is taking his time. Exploring my mouth, his tongue massaging mine. fingers trailing along my rib cage until they reach the swell of my now-bare breasts. The calloused tips of his fingers send a delicious shiver from the top of my head to the tips of my toes, making my back lift and arch, only adding an extra layer of stimulating sensation that's already vibrating through my body. Lifting himself slightly, his fingers circle and pinch my peaked nipples. But once again, his touch isn't hard. Almost frustratingly soft. Like he's teasing my body with featherlike strokes. Strong enough for me to feel, but not enough to satiate the burning fire.

My pleading moans grow louder as he works my other breast in the same way.

I lift my hips to get more friction, but he pulls away. Never allowing me more. Sweat beads at my temples as my desperation grows and just when I think I can't take any more of his soft teasing, he kisses his way down my jaw and along my collarbone. Working his mouth along the swell of my breasts, I finally cry out as his tongue flicks over my nipple. He goes from licking to biting to sucking over and over again, building a relentless rhythm that has my eyes rolling back. "Oh, god. Yes, oh, Roman, that feels so good," I say in a breathless garble.

I've never had an orgasm from nipple play alone, yet I'm edging closer and closer to that euphoric feeling. As though he can read my mind, he stops working my nipples, which has me moaning in protest. He pulls on the strings of my bikini bottoms before tugging it off and throwing it to the ground beside us. He groans and I know from the way he's looking at my pussy, he can see how wet I am.

"Mmmm, I won't tell you how many times I've thought about your pussy. Not just in the last twelve hours. And I'm going to feast."

He doesn't even give me a second to respond as he grabs my legs, pushes them wide open, and licks me with a wide, flat tongue. I scream out in pleasure the second his tongue hits my clit, as though every nerve is currently centered on that one point of my body. Roman eats me out like he's on death row and I'm his last meal.

His tongue pierces my pussy, like he's fucking it, working it in and out. My hands frantically reach out and my fingers wrap around his hair holding him in place, desperately needing him to keep using his tongue like that before he works his way back up to my clit.

"Oh my goodness!" I moan in an orgasmic state of bliss.

His tongue laps before he sucks on my bundle of nerves into his mouth, sending me over the edge as my body detonates into a thousand pieces. My thighs tremble, squeezing his head, holding him in place as my orgasm surges through me. It feels like a million fireworks explode throughout my body. The brightest and most vibrant colors swirl in my vision, yet he doesn't slow his pace, prolonging my pleasure as I struggle to catch my breath. My body tingles as I languidly return to reality. I can't recall the last time I experienced such an intense orgasm.

My lungs feel like they're on fire due to my heavy breathing and the struggle to catch my breath while the gentle breeze around me feels incredibly strong and intense against my oversensitive skin.

I open my eyes as he releases his hold on my legs, his mouth glistening with my juices. Even though he's just eaten me out, he looks hungrier than ever. He rises to his feet and pulls down his trunks. My mouth waters at the memory of the taste of him as his thick, long cock springs forward and juts proudly before him. My eyes follow the vein that runs along his shaft, and drops of precum leaking from the mushroom tip. Before I muster up the energy to sit up and taste him, he lifts me like I weigh nothing and places me in his lap, so I'm straddling him.

In one swift motion, he spears me with his cock. Stretching and filling my pussy to the brim. I scream as my walls stretch to accommodate his thick girth. Pulling my face down to him, he swallows my cries, capturing my mouth with his. I can taste the sweet tang of my juices on his tongue, which floods me with further desire. Roman continues kissing me as he gives me a moment to adjust and accommodate his size. He must be able to feel me relax because as soon as I do, he thrusts, his hands gripping my hips, rocking me forward and back. Energy finally returns to my limbs after my orgasm, and I ride him, increasing the tempo as I grind my clit onto his pubic bone.

"Your... pussy... feels so good. Fuck... the way you're squeezing down on my cock is going... going to make me come."

Good. I want him to explode just like he made me. The muscles in my thighs begin to burn as I bounce and grind down on him. Both of us gripping, touching, stroking, caressing one another with reckless abandon. Each of us acting with feral desperation to get and feel as close to one another as possible. We're both fucking each other senseless, like wild animals unlocked to our basal instincts. His mouth finds my nipple and he sucks, sending my body into the abyss. Stars cloud my vision as he once again sends me over the orgasmic precipice. My head rolls back as I let out a soundless cry, my body quivers and trembles, sending pins and needles running from the top of my head to the tips of my toes. Goosebumps prick my skin and I can feel the burning blush that rushes across my chest.

His cock swells and he clamps down on my hips, letting out a deep, growling moan, finding his own release. Fucking up in to me, his arms wrap around me like steel bands holding onto me as he unloads every drop.

Sweat glistens across his deep caramel skin, and there is a slight shake in his arms as he wraps them around me to pulls me to his chest. My body feels so relaxed right now. For the first time in a long time, both my mind and body are content.

My fingers absentmindedly trace circles along the almost faded scar by Roman's shoulder from his accident. The last time I saw it, it was still raw and raised as the stitches had not long been taken out. He shifts beneath me and I sit up. Anxious apprehension fills his eyes. Something I can't quite place. At first, I think it's because I touched his scar and maybe set off the memory of the collision. But when I see the way he's searching my face, checking in and trying to gauge how I am and where I'm at. That's when I realize he's worrying. It's nothing to do with the scar or the accident. Roman's worried that I'm regretting what we just did. If he thinks I'm having second thoughts, he couldn't be further from the truth.

Leaning forward, I give him a gentle kiss, letting him know there is nothing to worry about. As his cock softens and slips from me, our combined release trickles down my thigh. He must also feel it and I can't help but giggle.

"I'm glad I did nothing to have you giggling like a schoolgirl before now."

The deep timbre of his voice sends a shiver down my spine. Looking up at him, I have to suppress another giggle by biting my lip. And when I see the soft smile on his face, I'm glad that there's no trace of the worry that seemed to plague him. "Well, do you know what will have me laughing even more?" I ask playfully.

"What is that?" he asks as I lean further back until his arms drop to his sides.

"When I see you wearing one of my dresses, as that's what the loser will have to wear."

"The loser of what?" he asks, his brows crunching in confusion.

"The last one in the pool," I say before quickly climbing off him. I'm already laughing before my head goes under the water, and as I push back up, he's diving in, in all his naked glory.

Chapter 20

Roman

My head still hasn't caught up with my body in fully digesting the events of the last twelve hours. There's a deep-rooted part of me that thinks this has all just been a dream. That I'm still asleep after telling her we should stop and wait 'til we're sober.

I swear to god, if I wake up soon, and instead of being in the afterglow of one of the hottest sexual encounters I've ever had, I'm waking up with a sore head and likely wet sheets, I'm going to lose my fucking mind. But as I dive into the pool, I know this feeling is too real to be a dream.

I break through the water right in front of Ruby and just as I'm about to grasp onto her, she laughs and swims off. Alright, if that's how she wants to play, game on.

Swimming behind her, I splash about as much as possible so she looks behind, then squeals when she sees I'm following her. The second she faces forward again, I dive under. My eyes burn with the chlorine, but I keep them open so I can see her naked body. This also allows me to pick the exact moment to grab hold of her waist and throw her up in the air. She lets out a cackling laugh-like shriek before she crashes back into the water.

She wastes no time, swirling her arms, splashing me back. Seeing her this relaxed hits something deep inside of me. It's like she's back to the Ruby I used to know. Just like she was when we were younger. And right now I just wanna keep her like this.

I'm filled with a lightness, a level of contentedness I haven't felt for so long. I can't help myself. I need to feel her. Touch her. Hold her. It takes no time for me to get hard again. The feel of her soft, supple breasts as I cup them and the way she grinds herself back against me sets my pulse on fire. Wrapping my arm around her waist, I pull her back to me so her back is to my chest. My hand moves up to hold her jaw, allowing me to capture her mouth with mine and kiss her. Once again, showing I want her. Need her.

My fingers go back to explore and gently pinch her nipples. Ruby moans into my mouth and the little slither of restraint I have snaps. Walking us through the water, I continue kissing her until we reach the corner of the pool. I bend her over the edge, pressing her breasts to the sun-warmed tiles. Her ass glistens as droplets of water trickle down her creamy skin. My tongue follows the line of each and every drop. Getting myself into the perfect position behind her, I grip her ass, easing her cheeks apart, then dive in. My tongue explodes with the taste of both of our combined release, even with the added tang from the chlorine, and she still tastes like the sweetest delicacy in the world.

The only sounds around us are the moans coming from

her lips as they echo and bounce across the surrounding water. I'm not pinning her down and the more my tongue works and explores around her lips and holes, the more she wriggles and writhes, finding it harder to stay still as I continue eating her out.

"Yes... uh... oh, fuck, yes."

Hearing her struggle to talk through her pleasure only turns me on more. I can tell she is getting closer as her legs shake and none of her words make sense. Pushing two fingers into her hot wet walls grip me tightly, pressing downwards, the tips of my fingers brushing against the soft spongy tissue deep inside her. My thumb circles her swollen clit and I watch the delicious sweet essence of her drips out of her, and it's such a sexy sight. One I didn't think I'd get the chance to see again and now I want nothing more than to have it every day. It only takes her a few seconds before she explodes and I greedily bend down and lick her up, drawing out her pleasure as her juices full in my mouth. As she continues riding out the waves of her orgasm, I stand back up, line myself up behind her, and bury myself deep inside. I know I should be savoring it and taking my time, but my skin is bursting. I'm ravenously desperate for her. Her walls clench down on me so tight it makes my eyes roll to the back of my head.

Fuck. She feels so good.

I wait until she finally seems to be back in the moment with me, then thrust deep inside her. Despite being in the pool, sweat drips down my back and, even though I already came not that long ago, I know I won't last very long as her pussy just feels too good.

Her ass ripples with every bounce and her hands claw

along the edge of the pool. She turns her head and seeing the way her pupils are blown has me increasing my tempo.

"Jesus. You feel so good. So. Damn. Good." Each word in time with my thrusts. "I don't think... I... I will last much longer."

Her moans sound as good and sexy as they always have and just like she used to, her hot tight walls clamp down on me more. My grip on her hips must now be bruising as I fuck her with everything I've got. Reaching round, my fingers find her clit. Knowing that it won't take much to send her over again. And after only a few strokes, she tumbles over the edge, setting off my release. I let out a deep growl, her body knowing mine just as well as I know hers, and she milks every last drop out of me until I'm finally spent.

Leaning over her, I kiss along the back of her neck as I struggle to catch my breath. Pushing up onto my forearms so I don't crush her, I push her wet hair out of her face. The sexy, lazy, satisfied smile that spreads across her face makes me feel so warm and happy. Like a soldier that's finally come back home. There is no better feeling. It's one that has haunted my dreams for years with the belief that I'd never get the chance to see or feel it ever again. No one has ever felt as good as Ruby. And I will do everything to make sure I can hold on to this for as long as possible.

"You okay?" I ask.

"Yeah. Great," she says breathlessly. "I don't think I can move. I think you've turned my legs to Jell-O."

I laugh at her dazed tone. Giving myself another few minutes to get my strength back, I kiss her neck and gently massage her shoulders. When I see goosebumps break out along her arms, I know it's time for us to get out.

"Well, as you can't use your legs, it looks like you'll need a helping hand."

Before she has a chance to protest, I throw her over my shoulder in a fireman's lift. Using the handrail, I walk us up the pool steps, tightening my grip on the backs of her thighs, and soundlessly laugh at Ruby's shrieks and giggles.

I guide us back into the house and straight for the shower in her en suite.

Turning on the water for the shower first, I then place her back on her feet.

"How on earth did you manage that? I know I'm in shape, but I'm by no means light." I roll my eyes and grin at her silly comment, watching as she backs up and dips her head so the water can rinse her hair.

"For one, let's not make out as if you're heavy. Two, I might not have played for years, but I sure a shit can still lift."

Snatching the body wash she has on the shelf, I squeeze some in the palm of my hands. Now that she's standing in front of me, I can see the indentation lines from when I pressed her up against the edge of the pool. I'm torn as a part of me feels bad at seeing those marks on her otherwise flaw-less skin, but at the same time, it turns me on knowing just how desperate I felt to touch her, taste her, have her. I rub the lather into her skin, gently cleaning every inch of her body. To my surprise, Ruby reaches over and squirts some shower gel into her hands.

"Considering the orgasms you just gave me and that you carried me up here, I think it's only fair that I return the favor."

"I won't say no to that." Having her hands washing me

like this, I'm not surprised I'm getting hard again. Though neither one of us pays my cock any attention.

My head rolls back as she continues to touch me everywhere. This is something I could get used to. I catch myself just in time as I almost say those words out loud. I can't allow myself to get into the enjoyable comfort of the feeling of her hands on me. As much as I love her touching me, I can't get carried away. I have no idea what exactly it is that's going on between us. I hate not knowing where I—where we—stand, but I don't want to come across as pushy, especially given everything she's already gone through. Still though, it doesn't take away from how good it feels to have her again, to feel her touch and be this close to her after all these years.

We finish up in the shower and both dry off before climbing into her bed. "Do you wanna address the elephant in the room or should I?" she asks as we lay facing each other.

My pulse picks up.

"I'll take your silence as letting me go first. Alright."

My fingers rub circles along her arms, and I do everything to keep my breathing even and controlled.

"As much as it turned me on and was a massive boost to my self-confidence." She pauses and mirrors my actions, slowly tracing her fingers along my chest. "And as tempting as it was when you got hard in the shower and still have a semi, from what I can see." We both look down at the slight tenting under my towel. "But as much as I know you're more than capable of giving me another round of pleasure, I'm sorry to say I think my pussy needs a bit of a break," she says then bursts out laughing. I managed to hide my relief behind a chuckle. I really thought she was going to talk about what we're doing. Fuck. Not going there. Nope. Not right now.

"I'm sorry. I think... I guess," I say, unsure of the right response.

Her cheeks have a rosy tinge to them, and it takes everything within me not to lean over and kiss them.

"You don't need to apologize. It's just... well, I guess with how intense we've now fucked, twice, and given your... um... size, a girl needs a bit of a cooler to recover. Not every guy is as fortunately well endowed as you are. At least I haven't met anyone else that is."

It takes everything in me not to smile, laugh, and celebrate at the way she's blushing. There is also no better ego boost for a man than when a woman tells you she needs a time-out because of how much you're packing. Especially now knowing that anyone else she's been with since me has been lacking.

"I have an idea."

"Yeah, what kinda idea?" Ruby asks with a purr as she wraps her leg around mine.

"Well, we can't have you feeling sore or uncomfortable. No. You need to be more relaxed."

"Oh, is that so? And how will you help me relax more?"

Leaning forward, her lips find mine. Our kiss is much softer, more tender than our last few. The moment her mouth is fused with mine, my hands need to feel her. Touch her. Caress her. It's like she turns me into an addict. Desperate; needing another fix. But she's just told me she's sore and the last thing I'd ever want to do is hurt her. Even if my cock is already straining and dripping to feel her again. I keep my touch light. Not in the teasing way I'd been doing down on the lounger by the pool. But letting my fingers softly trail along her skin that I remember as clearly as I did all those years ago. I'm not playing a game or trying to edge her. Every touch has a purpose. Words aren't necessary as I pour everything into each and every kiss. Cupping her face, I pull her in closer, wanting to fuse her body with mine, and wishing I'd never have to let her go. Because if it was down to me, she'd never leave my side again.

Rolling over so I'm lying beside her, I pull her onto my chest as we both continue to kiss and hold one another. The last thing I remember before drifting off to sleep is how heavenly it feels to have her arms and legs wrapped around me, the sound of her soft and steady breathing, and emotionally feeling the most relaxed and content that I have in years.

Chapter 21

Ruby

Warmth and comfort are the first sensations that seep in as my mind clears through the hazy fog of sleep. Letting out a soft sigh of happiness, I stretch my arms and legs out. It takes me a second to realize what's blocking me, or better, who's caged around me.

Gently opening my eyes, I see the man who I thought was a long lost chapter from my past but has somehow found his way back into my life.

His thick, long lashes fan across his cheeks and his chest slowly rises and falls as he sleeps. This was honestly the last thing I ever imagined happening. And now...? Well, I don't quite know how to categorize what's happening between us. Clearly we both still have a sexual and physical attraction to one another, there's no doubt about that. Even just thinking about how amazing he made me feel, how he played my body like an instrument with such knowledge and understanding, sends a wave of warm satisfaction through me. I understand that I've been in somewhat of a sex haze since last night, but as fun and delicious as all of this has been, I know we can't continue to put off having a conversation about where we stand.

My bladder screams in protest, and I untangle myself from his embrace to make my way to the bathroom without waking him up. After finishing up, I climb back into bed and continue to watch Roman, trying to work through the emotions circling through my head. I don't know how long I lie there, but his eyes eventually flutter open.

"Good morning," I whisper.

"Hey. What time is it?" he asks with a slightly raspy voice, stretching his arms up above his head. My eyes instantly stare at his chest and I'm once again amazed at just how good he looks. He's still in phenomenal shape. Part of me wonders if he's even hotter now than he was back then. Maybe it's his mental maturity that has made him even more insatiable to me.

I find my phone on the nightstand. "It's almost four o'clock."

"Damn, so we slept for like three hours. I don't remember the last time I had a nap that good or that long," he says, the deep baritone of his voice vibrates through the mattress, sending tingles through me. I shuffle myself further down the bed so I can lay my head on his chest. My fingers make aimless patterns across his six-pack and pecs as I hum in agreement.

Even just the way he plays with my hair, his fingers wrapping around the strands almost hypnotically, has me luxuriating in relaxation. Neither of us speaks for several minutes, but I know I can't put this off any longer. Leaning my head back so I can see him better, I glide the tips of my fingers along his jaw, feeling the rough stubble that's begun to grow out.

"As much as I would like to just stay on this comfy cloud of sexual bliss, I know we need to talk."

I try to gauge his reaction. I guess a part of me is expecting to see annoyance, frustration, or maybe even anger that I've brought this up. Maybe that's just my own insecure reaction because that's how Julian would usually respond when I tried to bring up a serious conversation. But all I see is a softening in his eyes as the corners of his mouth lift slightly with a warmth that's so kind, and nods. It only again proves just how different he is from Julian.

"The first, and I guess the most important thing I want, no need you to understand is that I regret nothing that's happened between us. Not a single thing. I know you said before you didn't want me waking up the next day thinking I'd maybe made a mistake." I push myself up so I'm sitting facing him before continuing, "But when I woke up this morning, I felt just as much pull and desire as I had last night. Maybe even more." His loud sigh of relief sounds so weighted, like the biggest weight has been lifted off his shoulders, and I'm surprised how emotional it makes me feel.

"Good. I'm glad. I think for me, my biggest worry was that I didn't want you to think I'd take advantage of you. That's the last thing I'd do to you." I can see the sincerity in his eyes as he speaks, and I know he means every word.

"I know, Roman. I really do. I also understand that this, us, what's going on isn't just complicated and entangled by just one thing. There are layers to it. I'd initially come here to take some time, have some space to work out if there was any way for me to repair things with Julian. Obviously, that's now never going to happen. It's done. Over. But even beyond that, we have a past. Our history isn't one that's filled with only happiness. At the end, the way we ended, fuck, that was so hard on me."

Roman takes my hand in his and I really appreciate the gesture. He's giving me his undivided attention and is really ready to listen to what I'm about to say. It's something I'm not used to from the men in my life.

"If it's okay with you, I'll start with everything regarding Julian and all that? I just feel that if I explain all of that to you, maybe you'll have a better understanding of why I feel the way I do. Why I've reacted and dealt with things in a way that perhaps you wouldn't expect me to."

Shifting himself, he pulls my leg to rest across him. I don't know if it's because he wants to just keep close contact or maybe a way of covering himself more. I can understand being naked and me saying I want to talk about my ex can't be what any man would want to do in bed.

Giving me a reassuring smile, he nods and starts gently rubbing along my calf, not in an erotic way. I get the feeling it's more to keep his hands busy and maybe help me relax at the same time.

"So, I already told you I met him on my birthday night out but can't fully remember exactly how much of what I'm about to say I've already mentioned. So, sorry if I end up repeating myself."

"That's okay."

"Anyway, as I'd said, everything progressed from there pretty quickly. To be honest, everything went faster than I've ever had with anyone. I'm not sure if that was my doing or his, or a combination of both of us. I wouldn't even be surprised if someone on the outside looking in said I was just so desperate to settle down, that I clung onto the relationship, jumping in head first. A therapist would probably have a field day with me."

Laughing nervously, I continue, "Anyway, everything developed quickly, which I can now see made me blind to the red flags he started displaying. I wouldn't say he was always bad. No, not at all. But he definitely has two sides to him. There was his fun-loving, carefree, enjoy-life mentality that felt contagious. And he had a soft, tender side. I know that something happened in his past, either when he was in his late teens or young adult, I'm not sure. But there were several times when he'd be drunk that he'd start rambling on that it shouldn't have happened to him. I've no idea if it was a trauma, something that only affected him, or a particular incident that he never got over or something. He never opened up about it, but I know it's something that really affected him. In my gut, I know it was an enormous source, or I guess the seed of why he does things or reacts in certain ways."

"Surely it's gotta be something that only happened to him or involved only him, otherwise wouldn't Serena have brought it up if it was something that affected the whole family? Her and Rhett are really open and share everything with one another," Roman suggests.

"Yeah, you're right. That's why despite me trying to get him to open up, it felt so frustrating that he didn't. I just wanted to be able to understand. I'm sure Serena has told you her opinion of him, and I would never take away the fact that they, well... don't have a great relationship. But despite all of that, I still was holding on to some kind of hope because he made me laugh more and got me to let my hair down. I started throwing some caution to the wind, but it got so tiring after a while." I start picking at my cuticles, something my mom always used to tell me off about when I was a kid as I did it whenever I felt uncomfortable.

"And all those little things I pushed down or tried to ignore, I just couldn't unsee them. Couldn't keep burying my head in the sand. There would always be excuses and reasons. Whether it be family, the stress of his dad being ill, the death of his dad, or Rhett firing him. I felt terrible as I could see he was on this downward spiral, but there was nothing I could do. His friends are all bachelors who love to party, so they were only encouraging his destructive behavior even more. My gut was telling me I needed to end things weeks ago, but I felt that if I did, I'd only have been kicking the man when he was already down, and I just couldn't bring myself to do it. So I started to slowly pull away. Create some space. Give myself some time to see if there would be any way to salvage everything. But with how everything imploded, it's clear that it was already at the point of no return, even before me coming here. I should have listened to my gut. I guess this is the part that connects the past to the present. The part where you come into the picture."

"How do you mean?" he asks. There is no animosity to his tone, just genuine curiosity, and his facial expression is soft and empathetic.

"When you had your accident, it was honestly the scariest moment of my life. I hated the feeling of helplessness, wishing that I could endure the pain that you were going through instead. I felt like I was on the sidelines, watching the man I loved, the person I thought I was going to spend the rest of my life with, not only dealing with the physical injuries, multiple surgeries, and physical therapy, but also the emotional trauma. This isn't me having a go at you and I'm not blaming you, but it was so hard. Are you sure you want to listen to this?" I ask, watching as the muscle in his thigh twitches incessantly. No idea if that's an involuntary reaction or a nervous tick. He follows my line of sight and it stops shaking, his hand holding onto his legs as if he can't stop his fidgeting without restraining himself.

"Yes. I know we spoke again after everything, but let's be honest, that was very one-sided. I never really asked for you to explain everything you went through. And that was wrong of me. So please tell me. Don't hold back. Please," Roman says empathetically. It almost sounds like he's pleading.

Emotion bubbles to the surface as memories I thought I'd long laid to rest come back.

Seeing the raw sincerity in his eyes makes my own water. Taking a deep breath, I muster up all my strength, since I know this will be difficult.

"When you drove me down here, I'd already told you how I felt a part of me was hanging on, trying to work out if there was any way I could not only fix things but maybe also fix him. Try to do and repair with him all the things I couldn't with you."

Jerking his head back he winces. His brows crease slightly and I watch as he closes his eyes and lets out a deep breath. I'm sure this can't be easy for him to hear.

"You see, after your accident, you shut down and shut me out. I'd try talking and you wouldn't open up. I tried comforting you, but I always felt like you thought I was nagging. Like I was always hovering in your space." My knee bounces as I fidget with my fingers.

"We were still so young and very naïve, I couldn't really understand where your mind was or how you were mentally coping. And where you weren't talking or sharing anything, I had nothing to go on. Essentially, I was guessing how you felt. It continued to get harder and harder as each day passed, and it felt like we were trapped in this dark place." I vividly remember that cold, distant atmosphere in the apartment. Like we were at a wake or something.

"But even as difficult and physically and emotionally draining as it was, I never, and I mean never, thought we wouldn't get through it," I say plaintively, though the more I talk, the easier it feels to finally get this out in the open.

"It's kinda ironic, really. With you, with us, it was hard. Everyone around us could see the struggle, the difficulty both of us were having with trying to navigate handling your injury and all that came with it. We never spoke about how hard it was. Never opened up. We both could feel it, but never addressed it. Yet I was just so convinced we would get through it. Every night I'd reassure myself that there was a light at the end of the tunnel. Whereas with Julian, everyone around us would think that everything was okay, when in reality we were a boat out at sea with holes continuously appearing and me trying to patch them up. Deep down, I knew we were a sinking ship. Yet, as much as both scenarios were different, the results have ended the same."

Leaning further onto him, I shuffle up the bed not only to get closer but also needing the support to stay upright, not just physically but also emotionally. I'm sure he can feel the slight tremble in my fingers. Each time I pause while talking,

I expect him to interrupt, or state his opinion, but he doesn't. It's like he fully understands that his silence, him just listening and absorbing it all is exactly what I need.

"I couldn't understand how you could break us up. I felt that you saw me as something disposable. I... I... in the days after you ended it, I was catatonic. Questioning everything. Doubting if you'd ever loved me. Convincing myself that you thought I was worthless, inconsequential. To me, it felt like those were the only plausible reasons why you did what you did. You were just done. There was no fight. No desire to see if we'd work through it. *Nothing*."

Roman threads his fingers between my own before lifting my hand and kissing each knuckle while looking deep into my eyes. Those beautiful green eyes of his are holding so much emotion. I can see the sorrow, the grief, the torment of thinking back and reliving that time. A time that was so difficult for both of us in such different ways. I take a moment to get myself together. These thoughts, these feelings aren't ones I've openly talked about in such a long time. If ever. And I want to be both honest, yet respectful to Roman. I don't want to just sit here and admonish him. That would be entirely unfair.

"Obviously, I eventually found out what a dark place you were in. And despite still feeling hurt, it broke my heart that you'd gotten into such a state and I didn't even realize. That you felt you had no other options but to..." My voice breaks and I can't finish. Even to this day, I can't say those specific words out loud despite everything that happened.

Roman will forever be my first. My first love. The first man I gave my body to. The first man I ever pictured spending the rest of my life with. I could never—absolutely never—imagine a world without him in it. Without him being around.

Roman pulls me close so I'm now sitting on his lap. "I've got you," he whispers as he kisses the side of my head. My chest and shoulders shake as I think about how close things got to Roman no longer being here.

He strokes my hair, and I can feel the slight tremble in his fingers. Turning my head I see the unshed tears in his eyes and can only imagine it must be horrible having that memory, mentally going back to that scary time. Leaning forward, I gently kiss each of his eyelids, wanting him to know I see him. I appreciate him. I'm grateful for him to walk through this with me. Kissing his forehead, I try to pull myself back together and not think about that horrible, dark time.

"I hated how you had gone through that. Hated that I wasn't able to be there, wasn't able to support you."

"Ruby. Ruby, please look at me." I slowly lift my head, and his face becomes blurry as my eyes fill with unshed tears, just like his. The way he lifts his hands, holding my face close to his feels like he's creating a protective bubble for the both of us. The rest of the world disappearing around us. As if right now, naked and in bed, we are cocooned in the safe security of one another. Each drawing strength from the other.

"What I did was wrong. Pushing you away like that was awful. Unforgivable. But I need you to understand that it had nothing to do with you. Everything was on me. I didn't push you away because I didn't care or because I didn't love you. It was because I hated what happened so much. I was so consumed, so convinced that my life was over. I had tunnel vision on my career from as early as I could remember. Then, in a split second, it was all over. It took me a really long time in therapy to work through everything. I was taught to grieve the life, the idea of the future I thought I was going to have. I had to learn that it was okay to be devastated by what had happened, but appreciate the fact that yes, I'd been injured, yet those injuries weren't life-threatening. Yes, they'd ended my football career, but I could still make a life for myself. Of course, it would be a different life, but I could still do something. Set a fresh path, an alternative course for myself. I also spent a long time working through all the shit that had happened with my mom. I realized how important it is to talk to someone. To open up. I'd had such a distorted perception that, as a man, I needed to get over it. As if talking through everything that was going through my head was a weakness, when actually, it was a strength. To this day, I still see a therapist. I don't go every week, but I book in sessions when I find myself struggling."

My eyes widen in surprise as I hadn't expected that. My hands hold onto his thick muscled shoulders, wrapping around him in both awe and so much respect.

"I feel so awful, especially as I now understand how detrimental it was that I didn't open up to you. But I didn't know how to."

Tears silently roll down my cheeks, and Roman gently wipes them away with the pads of his thumbs. I let out a sad laugh-like huff.

"You shouldn't be comforting me right now Roman," I sniffle, the tears continuing to fall down my cheeks. "What you went through, the strength it took to reach out and seek help. How you've managed to rebuild your life, knowing that it's not just a one-time fix, that you're still seeing a therapist. Roman, you are stronger than I ever could have imagined." My lips quiver as I struggle to get the words out.

"Ruby, I am so, so sorry that my actions affected you so much. I hate that you got to a point where your instant reaction when a man isn't treating you how you deserve is to trying to find the good and fighting for things to get better. When instead, you should kick them to the curb because you deserve the best. You deserve the absolute world. You deserve to be worshipped like a goddess." His tone builds with strength, determination, and confidence with each word spoken. Tucking my hair behind my ear, before cupping my face, I see how much he believes what he says. Even if I don't have the same belief.

Laughing through my tears, I shake my head at his words. "I don't agree with that."

"The biggest mistake I've ever made was how I treated you after my accident. And if there was any way that I could go back and change things, I would. I don't know what direction our relationship would have taken, but I'd have opened up. You'd have understood where I was really at, and the biggest thing is you'd have known that you'd done nothing wrong. Not a single thing."

My chest feels like it's been cracked wide open, and the pressure has been released. It literally takes my breath away. I truly feel that things have been laid to rest.

As much as I know we should now talk about what's going on with us, I resolve that we can do that this evening. Roman looks just as tired and emotionally empty as I do. I feel drained and I really need to eat. After that, we can talk about the rest.

"Why don't we have some dinner, then watch a movie? That sound good to you?" I ask.

"Yes. That sounds perfect. Let me quickly go and grab a pair of shorts," he says before kissing my forehead and dashing out of the room. I watch the sculpted cheeks of his ass until they disappear out the door.

I give him a silly and teasing pout when he returns wearing a pair of loose gray basketball shorts. My pout turns into a smile when I see he's brought one of his hoodies for me to put on. The soft worn material glides over my skin and I push the sleeves up before we make our way downstairs.

All through dinner, I had a smile on my face. It's been so relaxing, so enjoyable. I can't remember the last time I felt this at ease.

"I have to say, I think this has been my favorite meal so far. And look, we finished everything." I laugh. Even though I agree, I find it funny because I'd initially hoped to keep some leftovers for tomorrow.

"Yup. I guess we both had a real appetite," I say with a grin.

Looking at Roman as he sits on the couch, legs spread, with one hand holding the remote on his stomach as he looks for a movie for us to watch, while the fingers of the other run along his jaw and mouth. With the orange, red and coral hues of the sun setting behind him through the wrap around windows, he doesn't just look sexy. He looks fucking beautiful.

"Stay right there. Don't move a muscle. I need to get a

picture of that," I say, getting up to quickly grab my cell. "I mean it. Don't move."

He murmurs "yes" as I dash upstairs and grab my phone from the bedside table. As I run back downstairs, I notice I have eight missed calls and a voicemail from Julian's sister, Kara. Confusion and unease slither through me as I call my voicemail and listen to the message.

"Hi Ruby, it's Kara. I've tried to call you a couple of times, but there was no answer. I know you're away at the moment, but I felt it was really important that someone reach out to you. Julian apparently went out, got drunk, then ended up in a bar fight. Police were called, and he got arrested. When he was searched, they also found drugs in his possession. Our lawyer got the charges dropped, and as there were only trace amounts of drugs found on him, he was able to get an agreement. He's been taken to a rehabilitation facility and needs to complete the three-month program. Those are the terms of the agreement. I don't know what else to do or say. But please call me back as soon as you can. I'm so sorry."

Chapter 22

Roman

Goosebumps spread across my arms and down my back the second I see Ruby through the windows standing dead still, holding her cell to her ear. She looks the polar opposite of how she had minutes ago when she'd dashed upstairs. Her face looks ashen, and with wide eyes, her facial expression is one of shock. Unease hits my gut that something bad has happened, and I get up and make my way over to her as she ends the call.

"Hey. What's happened? Is everything okay?" I ask as softly as I can, even though right now every worst-case scenario is running through my head.

"Uh... I... Umm, that was Kara, Julian's sister. She'd tried calling me, but my phone was on silent. Just listened to her voice message."

My pulse spikes as I'm really worried she's about to say something terrible.

"She told me Julian got drunk, got into a fight at a bar,

and got arrested. They found drugs on him. Or like trace amounts or something."

Her eyes squint and she motions with her hands like she's still grappling with remembering what was said.

"I don't know how, but his lawyer got the charges dropped, but only on the condition that he goes to rehab. It sounds like one of those three-month facilities."

Taking her hands in mine, they are icy cold. Guiding her to the couch, I snap up the throw and cover her when she sits.

"I know this is probably a stupid question, but are you okay? How are you feeling?"

I take a seat beside her, close enough to reassure her I'm here and listening, but not overcrowding her.

"I just can't believe it. I'm not surprised about the drinking. I am surprised that he got into a physical fight. I never thought he'd ever go beyond verbal. But what I can't wrap my brain around are the drugs. *Drugs*. Like, is he for real?" she asks, her voice cracking and filled with sorrow.

Closing her eyes, she hangs her head. I hate seeing her like this. Seriously, what the fuck is wrong with this dude? It's good that he's not seriously injured or dead. Not because I give a shit about that asshole, but I know that despite everything, it would still devastate Ruby. I can't stand guys like him. Born into privilege, has more money than sense, been handed everything he could ever want, and still messes everything up. People like him don't know how difficult life can truly be. The more I hear about the guy, the more I struggle to understand how he and Rhett are actually related. Focusing back on the matter at hand, I give her arm a reassuring squeeze.

"Hey. I know this is shit, but this has nothing to do with you. You know that, right?"

"I... I... "

The vulnerability in her voice is like a punch to the gut.

"I just can't. I don't understand. Now all I keep thinking is, was he using drugs all along? If he was, then how stupid was I not to notice it? How could I have not suspected it? And if it's new, then is it because of everything that happened with me? Did that push him over the edge?"

It boils my blood that her mind has gone there, but I'm not super surprised she did. As much as I wanna tell her that it's not her fault, I know I have to be careful right now. She's already been through the wringer because of this asshole.

"I've never met the guy, and I have no way of knowing for sure what he's done or why. However, my gut is telling me if he was using during your relationship, you'd have known. And if, let's say, he was using drugs, then it's likely he's been doing so for years, where even those closest to him wouldn't even notice the direct effects from whatever it is he takes. He'd be a habitual user, his mood swings would have been a regular part of his overall behavior. But if that were the case, then I honestly don't see how Rhett wouldn't have known. And if he did or even suspected, he'd have definitely done something about it. Especially after him and Serena got together I can't imagine that he wouldn't have told you. Even just to cautiously warn you. Also, as much as it kills me to say this, you don't know for sure what drugs they were. For all we know, it could have been his friend's drugs that he was holding onto or something. And he might not even have touched or used the stuff, but it was just found in his possession."

I'm not even trying to make excuses for him. I just hate seeing the way she's pulling herself into a ball, as if she's trying to make herself as small as possible. Her shoulders hunch and she can't even look at me. Just seeing the way Ruby is retreating within herself, I know I will do anything to stop her spiraling.

"Listen, you've just been dumped with all this. Right now, you have no more information. Nothing is going to change this evening, but I understand that you're in shock. So how about you head upstairs and have a nice hot bath? While you soak, I'm gonna clean up down here, then make you a chamomile tea. I'll bring it up, then you put one of your favorite movies on, and I'll sit with you until you fall asleep. Then tomorrow, after a good night's sleep, you can work out what you wanna do. How does that sound?"

The lost look in her eyes breaks my heart. To my surprise, she leans forward, wraps her arms around me, giving me a hug. Pulling her close, I hug her back, stroking her back and giving her a kiss on the top of her head.

"Thank you. You've really been just so... I don't know how I'd have managed all this without you. Thank you."

"No worries." And I mean it. There's nowhere else I'd rather be.

Helping her up off the couch, I watch as she makes her way up the stairs. When I hear the door to her room close, I head back downstairs and try to keep myself busy but find myself pacing in the kitchen instead. All I can think is that I honestly don't know what to do. These past couple of days, and especially today, showed me how much I've missed her. What I would give to have a second chance. Would she even consider giving me one? Giving us one? And as much as I want her, there's no denying the timing couldn't be any worse. She's got so much going on right now that this surely would be the worst time to even talk about it.

The sound of my cell ringing interrupts my thoughts and when I pick it up from the counter I see Serena calling.

"Hey, what time is it over there? It must be in like the middle of the night or something?" I ask when I answer.

"It's just after 1 a.m." Her voice sounds as tired and drained as Ruby's did earlier. "So I'm guessing Ruby knows what happened?" she asks.

"Yeah. Rhett sister called and left Ruby a voicemail." I quietly make my way out onto the decking area, not wanting Ruby to overhear.

"Yeah, I'm so sorry. She sent me a text saying she'd tried getting hold of her. She doesn't know everything that's happened between Ruby and Julian, so she was desperate to let her know."

"Is that how you guys found out?"

"No. Their family lawyer is super close with Rhett. He's actually his godfather. He called him when he was on the way to the precinct. I didn't wanna tell Ruby anything until we had all the facts."

"So, do you know what exactly happened?"

The sound of her sigh is audible through the phone.

"Apparently he'd gone out last night with a few of his buddies and some of them decided it would be better to carry on drinking instead of going home and getting some sleep. They'd gone to their usual places, then found somewhere serving breakfast, so they were eating and drinking until they got asked to leave. Stumbled from one place to another—bear in mind it was only lunchtime—and they, or at least Julian, hadn't slept in over twenty-four hours. God knows what his alcohol level must have been. Anyway, they ended up in a bar and apparently, one thing led to another.

"One of his friends got into an argument with someone, then Julian escalated it by throwing the first punch. Police were called and when they searched him at the station, they found two broken pills in his pocket. I know it got sent off for testing, but Rhett hasn't told me yet what they were. Or he's still waiting to find out. Anyway, given the connections that Rhett and his brother's family have, their lawyer sorted a deal that Julian goes into a rehabilitation facility immediately. The judge was only going to make him do twenty-one days. But Rhett said Julian needs to get help and sort his life out. So between Rhett and their lawyer, they actually got it to three months."

"Wow. That's surprising, but probably the kindest thing Rhett could have done for his brother."

"Yeah, I know. There's still a shitstorm of stuff to sort out, though. And we knew we needed to head back as soon as possible. So we're packing up our stuff now and Rhett arranged a private jet. I thought it would be best to pick Ruby up along the way. So we're gonna fly into Virginia Beach first, then fly back to New York. If you could drop her at the airport, that would be amazing. Between the time difference and the flight time, I think we should arrive just before lunchtime your time. But I'll text you the exact time once we board."

The tiredness and frustration are clear in the tone of her voice. And as much as I know she will never say it to anyone, I can imagine she's annoyed they're coming back from their trip early because of her fiancé's dickhead brother. Which only gives me another reason to hate the man.

"How's Ruby holding up? I've been really worried about her and this all now happening has me even more concerned."

"I wouldn't say she's great. And the timing of this has also been pretty shitty."

"How do you mean?"

"So she was really upset after what happened a couple of days ago. That had hit her really hard. But she'd slowly started coming round. Or I guess you'd say she started coming back. Back to her old self. She wasn't sad anymore. Started to relax and seemed to see that she was gonna be alright and get through everything. Things were turning good. Then *BAM*, she's hit with this news, and it's sent her reeling. Questioning and doubting whether she missed signs of drug use. Wondering if their blow up pushed him to use. Obviously, I told her she wasn't to blame for any of it, but I don't think she understands that yet. What's your take? Do you think he's been using the whole time?" I ask with genuine curiosity. If anyone would have had any suspicions, it would be my sister.

"Definitely not. Don't get me wrong, the guy is a complete and utter asshole, and I hate him for what he's done to Ruby. And yeah, his behavior seems to reach another level when under the influence of alcohol. But I never got the vibe that he was also on anything. Besides, since their dad's death, Rhett's apparently had someone monitoring him, so they'd have spotted, or at least suspected something."

"Do you mean he's had someone following him?" I ask in a rush, genuinely shocked if that's the case.

"I didn't exactly push Rhett on specifics, but from the sounds of it, there was someone who would discreetly check in on Julian, then report back to Rhett."

"Ah, I see. I was gonna say, if someone had been following, then they hadn't done a good job of preventing shit kicking off."

"I know. I know. Rhett is fuming."

"I'm sure he's pissed that his brother's behavior means he has to end your trip early."

"Well, yeah, there's that, but I already told you how bad things were between the two of them. Their relationship was already so strained, I feel like this was the final straw for Rhett. I think where he feels he's had to take the mantle as head of the family, he's taken on the responsibility of a grown-ass man. He shouldn't have to do that."

Serena and I continue chatting for a few more minutes. I don't tell her anything that's happened between Ruby and me. Not because I'm ashamed or embarrassed but it would feel wrong to talk through things with my sister when Ruby and I haven't even addressed where we stand. I've not even had the time to really think things through and work out what I'm gonna say.

Chapter 23

Roman

After finishing up my call with my sister, I take a moment as I look out at the darkening sky and just take a breath. When I first agreed to my sister's request to do Ruby a favor, I honestly would never've guessed the whirlwind of events that have occurred.

I don't even realize that I'm box breathing—something my therapist taught me years ago to help with anxiety and the feeling of being overwhelmed. Right now, it helps calm the storm of emotions in me. Whatever happens next, I'll need to book another session, maybe two, when I'm home. So much has happened in the past week. Locking up the doors behind me as I head back inside, I make her some tea to hopefully help her relax. Right now, I feel like it's the only thing I know I can do to help.

Once it's ready, I head upstairs, careful not to spill it. But when I go to knock on her door, I find it ajar. Walking in, my eyes are first drawn to the bed that's still unmade and wrinkled from our nap earlier. It's wild that just a couple of hours ago she was asleep in my arms, relaxed and content, and now she's lost in troubled and worried thoughts. All because of the actions of an idiotic man.

The bathroom door is open, so I lightly knock before entering. She might not have believed me when I said it before but she really is a goddess. She looks like one, as she sits there in the bath. Her skin glows from the water and steam surrounding her. She's piled her hair on the top of her head and the way the column of her neck is exposed has me wishing I could run my lips along it.

She gives me a brief, sad smile I wish I could replace with the orgasmic bliss she had earlier.

"Here's your tea. But be careful as it's really hot," I tell her, placing it on the ledge next to the tub. She lets out a sigh, pulling her knees up to her chest, and resting her head on her forearms to look over at me. I don't get the impression that she's trying to cover up because she's naked. She used to always sit like that when something bothered her, and she didn't know how to voice it.

I take a seat on the floor next to the tub and mirror her actions by resting my head on my arm propped on the lip of the bath.

"Do you wanna talk about it?" I ask gently. If she says no, that's fine. If she wants space, I'll leave her in peace.

"I just don't know what to do or what to think anymore." Her voice is barely above a whisper.

Not knowing quite the right words to respond, I stay quiet, looking at her encouragingly to carry on.

"There's a part of me that's just so angry. I'm angry that, once again, I feel like I'm being pulled into the crazy circus that seems to be Julian's life. Angry that every time I start to feel one thing, I'm then dragged in another direction."

She lets out a sad laugh before carrying on, "Do you know what's so ridiculous? When I came here, I was trying to convince myself that I was doing this for me. To have the time, space, and distance to work out what my next step was going to be. Try to weigh the pros and cons of what to do with Julian. But even before I arrived, I knew in my gut that we were already way beyond saving. Yet there was a part of me that needed to have this actual physical trip. It's like if I'd just stayed at home and made this decision, I'd have somehow berated myself down the line. Convinced myself that I hadn't really taken the time to fight. To push through. I don't know."

I can see the conflicting emotions as they cross her face. It's almost as if I'm intruding as she wades through the wavering thoughts in her mind.

"Don't take this as gospel. This is just my opinion. What I think is that you're someone who is and always has been, a warrior. A champion. Whether that is for yourself, the people close to you, or even just strangers that pop into your life. You've always been a woman that, when you think or feel something, you don't do it halfheartedly. You give it everything you've got. You're one hundred percent in. It's one of the many amazing parts that makes up who you are. It means that when you say you're going to do something, there's literally nothing that can get in your way. But that same passion applies when you decide you don't want to do something. When you're done, you're done. Once you've shut that door, there's no turning back."

Saying those words out loud makes me realize that I

likely have zero chance of something ever happening with Ruby again and it leaves a bitter taste in my mouth. Right now, though, I need to think about her, not me.

"Like you said, your gut was telling you something, but knowing your nature, it's understandable that you'd be cautious and apprehensive, letting your mind and heart catch up. Especially considering what I now know; your worries and fears regarding relationships. It's perfectly understandable that you want to make sure you feel settled enough within yourself to know that you made the right choice."

I don't think she's noticed that she's stretched back out and relaxed again in the water. Droplets run down the slopes of her breasts above the water, with her nipples sitting teasingly along the waterline. The sight is both erotic and beautiful at the same time. She's a temptress and angel all at once, luring me in with both heat and innocence. A picture could never capture the beauty she's exuding right now, so I do my best to take mental snapshots to look back on and cherish for as long as my memories will allow it.

"Can I ask you a question?" I ask.

"Sure."

"If you could, if you had the power to pick how things could be right now, what would you want?"

She takes a little while to think it through. I watch, almost hypnotized, as her fingers skim along the surface of the water.

"Well... I... Do you mean life in general or just right now with everything that's going on?"

"Either. Whichever you prefer."

"I guess regarding everything right now, I'd say I'd hope

that Julian gets the right help he needs to fight whatever demons he's dealing with. That maybe one day, he can live a life that's not dependent on drink or drugs or filled with animosity towards certain members of his family. So that if I ever bump into him because of our mutual connection of Rhett and Serena, we'd be able to at least be cordial to one another."

"Okay, but what about you? What do you want for yourself? Not anything that would be beneficial to anyone else. Just you."

The way she looks deep into my eyes, I can tell how difficult that question is for her. She's one of the most giving people I know. Is always the first to help and support others in any way she can; too often putting everyone else's needs before her own. But that's exactly why I'm asking. Even if she doesn't know the answer right now. I want her to dig down and think about it.

Despite the uncomfortable position I'm sitting in, I stay as still as a statue, not moving a muscle, as I don't want to interrupt her train of thought. Eventually, she closes her eyes, takes a deep breath, then rests her head back against the bathtub.

"I just want to be happy. I don't need any flashy gifts. I don't want things to be like a rollercoaster, nor am I expecting my life to be happy rainbows and unicorns or silly stuff like that. I just want something simple. Something solid like my parents. They've been married for almost forty years. Worked in jobs that made them happy. They have a love for one another that's only gotten stronger with each passing year. I want my other half. Someone to make memories with, have a family, live each day as best as I can. Falling asleep in the arms of the person who'll always be there for me, no matter the ups and downs. That. That's what I want."

I swallow deeply as tears slowly roll down her cheeks. Scooting forward, I reach out and gently wipe them away. It warms and breaks me with the way she pushes her face in the palm of my hand. Appreciating the fact she is letting me be here at this very moment. Witnessing the raw vulnerability as she lays herself bare. I know how careful I need to be with what I'm about to say.

"Ruby. I promise you that one day you'll have that. *All* of it. I know that for a fact."

I push myself up onto my knees and kiss the top of her head.

"Not just because you deserve it but because, like I said earlier, when you put your mind to something, you give it your absolute all. Now, you're going to soak as long as you want in the bath. Then, like we planned, you're gonna get into bed and find something to watch. I can stay with you if you want. I can stay with you until you fall asleep or sleep beside you. I know we haven't spoken about what's happened between us today. And I'm not saying we shouldn't, but right now, the only important thing is you. I think it's pretty clear all I want is the best for you. I want to be in your life. Really, in your life. However and wherever you'll let me. Obviously, I know now isn't the time to think or even discuss all that, but I want you to know I am, and will continue to be, here for you."

It feels good, kind of freeing really, to truly tell her this. I've suppressed it for so long and remember all the times I'd wished I'd felt the strength or courage to just pick up the phone and call her. Telling her all of this. But I couldn't.

Either the timing wasn't right, she was in a relationship, or I just chickened out. So now that I have, it feels like I've unlocked something. Finally setting something I'd been harboring within myself free.

Looking into her stunning hazel eyes that are filled with so much, I can't even begin to decipher it.

"Serena called me earlier. With everything that's happened, they have decided to come back early. Rhett's arranged for a jet to fly them over. Obviously, I didn't tell her anything that's happened between us."

I think I see the briefest flicker of dejection across her face, so I carry on talking to make sure she understands what I mean.

"It's not because I'm wanting to hide anything. God, no. But we haven't talked about it, and now, with the timing and everything, I just want to play things by ear. The ball is in your court. My sister's arranged it so they fly into Virginia Beach, pick you up before the three of you fly back to New York."

I realize that not only have I given her even more to digest now, I've also possibly cemented the opening for her to end this—whatever reignited between us—before it's even properly started again. I just have to keep reminding myself and her that I will be there, even if we are miles apart. And hope and pray that maybe we can blossom at the right time.

"Then once you are back at home, and you've processed everything, then we will chat. Perhaps I could come visit, and we can work out where we stand and how we can navigate our next steps. And see how we do this together. How does that sound?"

Letting out a contented sigh, I love seeing her shoulders

relax as she smiles at me. Her eyes pierce mine as if she's trying to see deep into my soul. I'm taken aback when she leans over and kisses my bicep. It should feel like a silly gesture but it feels so sweet, so caring.

"Yeah. I would really like that. I think you coming over and maybe we just have a whole weekend together where we can work it all out. Just us together. No distractions."

Giving her a nod, I sit and stay with her until she's ready to get out.

"Roman, would it be okay if you sleep here tonight?"

"Of course."

"Also, could I wear one of your sweatshirts to bed, please?"

Hearing her ask this feels even better than it used to when we were younger. Back then it just made me feel like a man. I was stoked, and it was hot. Now it warms me. I love that she finds comfort in wearing my clothes.

"Not a problem. Let me go brush my teeth and I'll grab one for you."

Jogging over to my room, I quickly brush my teeth, grab a hoody, then make my way back to her room and see that she's already climbed out of the bath and has a towel wrapped around her. I have to close my eyes as she removes her towel and puts my top on, as now is really not the time for me to think inappropriate thoughts. Finally, once she's gotten herself comfy in the bed, I quickly change out of my clothes, leaving my boxers on, before climbing in beside her.

Once we put a movie on, it doesn't take long for her to fall asleep. Ruby rolls towards me, and by default, I put my arm around her, bringing her in close. And just like old times, I fall asleep with her in my arms.

Chapter 24

Ruby

This is just so ridiculous and so unfair. I really don't see how Roman has flipped my suggestion of getting a dog into an argument. Like, how the fuck did he go from us having dinner, to me showing him the photos of the pups I'd seen at the dog shelter earlier, to somehow believing that it was me showing that I'm unhappy here?

I get that he's tired from pre-season training, and even though he hasn't admitted it, I can imagine he's nervous for the season to start, but still. Now I wish I'd never said a goddamn thing. If I'd kept my mouth shut, he wouldn't have stormed off in the car and we'd probably be sitting on the couch, watching a movie. Fine. He can go and be a child, have his little tantrum as he drives around. I know what he's like. By the time he comes back, he'll have realized how much of an ass he's been. Which usually results in him being very apologetic to make it up to me.

That thought puts a big smile on my face as I clear away

our plates. Once everything is tidied and put away, I head to our bedroom and change into one of his hoodies. I don't know why but they always feel so much more comfortable and comforting than my own. I can give him a taste of his own medicine. Knowing how much it turns him on when I wear it, let's see how frustrated he feels when I'm stretched out, only wearing this and I don't give into any of his attempts to smooth talk his way to an apology.

I'm so engrossed in the movie I've put on, I don't hear my cell phone ringing. When I do hear it, I reach over and snatch it off the coffee table.

I expect it to be Roman already willing to apologize, but it's a number I don't recognize. "Hello?" I answer.

"Is this Ruby Tanner?"

"Yes, speaking."

"This is Deputy Craig Wilson. I'm calling because you're listed as the emergency contact for Mr. Parker."

Fuck, I really hope he hasn't gotten himself into any kind of trouble. That would be the last thing he needs—bad press and the team's management breathing down his neck—just before the season starts. I really hope it's not something bad. Shit. What on earth has happened?

"Is everything alright?"

"I'm afraid he's been in a severe accident. From what we can tell, Mr. Parker's vehicle was involved in a T-Bone collision which caused the car to flip and crash into the central reservation. The fire department was able to cut him out and the ambulance is currently transporting him to St. Vincent Hospital. His injuries appear to be severe but not life threatening."

It feels like all the blood has left my body. Falling forward

I struggle to catch myself from tumbling to the floor. Tremors run through my legs. My arms shake as I attempt to wrap them around myself. I can't hear anything except the blood pounding loudly in my eyes. My chest feels like a steel band wrapped around it, suffocating me, making it impossible for me to breathe.

"Ms. Tanner, are you there?"

I wake, gasping for air. My hands shake as I wipe the sweat off my brow, feeling trapped as I try to untangle my legs from the bedsheets. The sound of a toilet flushing makes me look over towards the bathroom. Roman must be in there. He stayed, just like I'd asked.

Laying my head back down on the pillow, I attempt to get my breathing back under control. Fuck. I don't remember the last time I dreamed about the day I got the phone call from the police officer telling me Roman had been in a car wreck. I haven't thought about it in years. A shiver wracks through me as I remember the complete and utter fear I felt at that moment, not knowing how bad his injuries were. The panic and terror I felt as I made my way to the hospital and waited for what felt like years for him to be brought out of surgery.

I honestly think that was one of, if not the worst, days of my life. It's not like you see in the movies where it's all high intensity, fast, loud, and chaotic. It was the opposite. Like I'd fallen into some sort of catatonic state. My limbs felt immovable. Sounds around me weren't clear to decipher. As if my head was underwater and all the voices and sounds from the hospital were muffled. It's something I wouldn't wish on my worst enemy.

I wrap myself up more in my duvet, trying to warm up, but it's fruitless since the cold is coming from within. The only reason I can think that I had that dream was because of that phone call I got about Julian yesterday. I understand those situations are completely different, but they both were phone calls I know are going to be pivotal moments that'll take my life in a different trajectory.

Everything feels like the worst scrambled mess. The blow up with Julian, the then downfall of him and the world around him, and while all of that was going on, Roman and I have somehow reconnected. Like entangled paths, we've woven back into one another.

I can't really work out what's going on between us. What it means. None of it. I know for sure we can't just ignore what's happened. I will address it. I'm not ashamed of it, nor do I feel like it's just a distraction or rebound, especially because he isn't just a random guy. We have a past. So I know we will talk about it. It's just on the long list of things I need to work through. But I also feel worried that time is running out and where I'm leaving it feels too unresolved and that scares me.

I feel terrible about what's happened to Julian. There is no shadow of a doubt that he is in a much darker place than I ever could have imagined, but I can't help noticing the differences between him and Roman. Not the Roman from after his accident. The person he is now.

I was surprised when he mentioned that he still sees a therapist. Even just how he communicates with me, the patience and understanding and selfless approach in which he now does things only goes to prove, to show, just how much he has grown and developed as a man. He still has that twinkle, that spark, just like he did when we were younger. But now there's an added depth of maturity that I can't help but to be drawn towards. Yet as much as I'm attracted to that, there's no way to deny that right now would be the worst time to start something new. Things have only just ended with Julian, plus the ongoing issues and drama that follow in the wake of that man.

I know I will need to really work and process through all of that. Then, on top of it all, Roman and I don't even live in the same state. How would it work? Would we start off long distance for a while and see how things go? It's something we really need to discuss and work out.

Letting out a groan, I cover my face with my hands. I could analyze all of this to death and still not be any closer to working out what I want, where I stand, or what my emotions are right now. Just then, the door to the bathroom opens and Roman walks out wearing a tight white t-shirt that looks like it's been molded onto his body and those gray sweatpants that I swear the devil created just to tease and torment women. My eyes scan over his muscular chest and abs, causing tingles to spread all over my body at the memory of the pleasure he gave me less than twenty-four hours ago.

Noticing that I'm awake, he gives me a soft smile before taking a seat at the end of the bed. "Good morning. How did you sleep?"

"Surprisingly good, considering everything. How about you?" I ask, pushing myself up.

"Was out for the count," he says before leaning over and stroking my leg through the duvet before continuing, "It's just past ten and Serena messaged saying their flight is scheduled to land at 12:15. So I was thinking I could make us some breakfast, then pack everything up. Once we're done, I'll drive you to the airport, then you guys fly back to New York, and I'll drive Rhett's car back home. That sound okay with you?"

Once again, I am so touched at how supportive and understanding he is.

"Yeah, that sounds good to me."

Our eyes lock, and it's as if there's an imaginary thread tethering us together. Despite the silence, there is so much being said. Giving me a nod and a quick squeeze of my leg before he stands, I know he felt it too.

"I have to say I've really been surprised at how good your cooking has gotten. I'm not saying you were bad before, but you've definitely reached another level," I say as I finish the last mouthful of eggs, pancakes, and bacon.

He huffs a small laugh. "Well, there are two reasons for that. One, I'd basically gone from living at home where Dad or my sister would cook, so I never really needed to, to then us moving into the apartment where you cooked most of the time. And back then, I was so strict on staying on the plan the nutritionists gave us. Let's be honest, I was mainly eating either steamed fish or chicken with veggies. That shit was bland as hell."

Nodding along, I remember how serious he was about eating as clean as possible. There were times I'd sneakily eat a Taco Bell in the car before picking him up from training because I felt bad for wanting it. Though I always suspected that he knew. Especially if he checked in the secret hatch under the armrest where I stashed the empty wrappers.

"You said there were two reasons. What was the other?"

"So after my breakdown, a teammate heard about what happened and reached out. He was like this life coach. At first, I thought it was all a load of bullshit, but what he really helped me do was get organized. Get a kind of structure and routine in place for me. Instead of me just trying to do everything all at once to fix myself, he helped give me the tools I needed to build myself back up. He called it establishing the foundations. So the first two foundations were physical and psychological. I attended all my regular appointments with my therapist, adding extra sessions on days I was struggling. That was working on my mental health. Then physically, we worked on a new fitness plan that I could follow that would incorporate everything that my physical therapy required, but I also started making all my meals from scratch. It would give me that additional routine of planning and prepping. It helped me get into an order. And even though I'd started it to just try to get into a better daily routine, it just stuck."

I love that. It's crazy because I knew everything about Roman before. We practically grew up together. Then obviously, after our breakup, I'd hear bits and pieces from Serena and see him on occasion. But now, hearing all these little things, it feels like I'm getting a new insight into his life.

"So how long will it take you to finish the work to Rhett's car?" I ask as we make our way to the airport.

I don't think Roman realizes the hidden meaning to my question. There's a part of me that really wants to know if there's any chance he'll be coming to the city soon. I know it's stupid, but I feel like if I had some sort of timeline, it would help me. I'd know how long I have to weigh up everything.

"I'd say a couple of days, a week tops. As long as I don't hit any bumps and there are no issues along the way, plus depending on how many hours I do a day, yeah, I reckon a couple of days."

I have to bite my lip as he clearly didn't understand what I was getting at. Bless him.

Annoyance works its way through me when I realize we're pulling into the drop-off zone at the airport. I don't want to go. Don't wanna deal with reality. I wish we could just stay in the little bubble of the beach house. Taking a deep, steadying breath, I push down that annoyance, muster up my strength, and open my door. Roman lifts my bags from the trunk before joining me.

"Listen, everything will be okay, I promise. I know it might not feel like it right now, but things will work themselves out." His hands clasp my face and his thumbs gently caress my cheeks. The confidence in his eyes reassures me and makes my heart ache at the same time. As much as I know I need to, I don't want to go. I don't want to leave our bubble. But most importantly I don't want to leave him.

He wraps his arms around me and pulls me in for a hug. I feel safe, like I'm protected in the cocoon of his chest. Breathing in the warm, comforting scent of him that feels nostalgic and new at the same time.

"You've just gotta focus on things day by day. Don't let yourself be clouded by worries that are out of your control. You can reach out to me whenever you want. We've both been through so much, but we've managed. You'll get through this. And once you have, once all those other obstacles have been overcome, I will still be there. I need you to be the happiest and strongest version of yourself. Both of us deserve the best while giving our absolute all to one another. So when you're ready, let me know. It doesn't matter what time of day, I will pick up and get my ass right over to you. I will do anything it takes. And I need you to do the same. I will fight for you. Fight for us. And I really believe you do too. You just need some time. Okay? That sound good to you?"

Craning my neck, I look up into his warm green eyes. There isn't a doubt in my mind that he means every single word, not telling me what he thinks I want to hear. He's being mature, rational, and understanding. Gratitude and appreciation spread through me.

"Yes. That sounds perfect. Thank you. For everything. I honestly don't know what I'd have done this past week without you. It truly means so much."

My lips brush across his, tentatively exploring as my subconscious affirms the need to cement our promise. Threading his fingers into my hair, I gasp when he grips the strands tighter. Fusing me closer to him like he's desperate for there not to be even be a millimeter between us. Not to know where he stops and I begin. Roman's mouth consumes mine with a bruising kiss. When we finally come back up for air, I give him one last squeezing hug before taking my bags and make my way inside the terminal to where I need to meet the private jet.

I ended up asking for some help, as I couldn't work out where I needed to go. Which I guess worked out well, as I was then given a ride in the buggy to the private jet hangar. I don't even have the chance to pick up my bags before my ears are filled with the sounds of my best friend making her way down the steps of the aircraft and running towards me.

"Ruby. Ruby," she says breathlessly before squeezing the life out of me in a snakelike hug. My heart warms with how much I've missed her. Not just because she's been away. Even before then, I really didn't get to see her as much as we used to. And I know a large part and the reason for that is my doing. First, I was wrapped up in the excitement of when Julian and I first met, then the fact that she and Julian didn't get along that put a strain between us. As everything descended, I just couldn't face her. I felt embarrassed and shamed. Plus, I knew if I was open and really honest with her, there'd have been no way I could have kept my head buried in the sand.

"I've missed you. I've really missed you," I say, burying my face in her hair and swallow down the emotions that bubble up in my throat.

"Oh, babe, I've missed you too. I've missed you so much. I am so sorry. I am so sorry for everything that's happened. Man, I just... I just..." Hearing her voice break sets off the tears I've been holding back. Pulling back, I hold her hands in mine and give her a smile.

"It's been a fucking rollercoaster. That's for sure."

"Come on, let's get you on board and we can have a proper chat."

She doesn't even have time to reach for my suitcase and handbag that are at my side when Rhett's hand reaches around her, picking them up. I hadn't even realized he'd also gotten off the plane.

"Ruby, it's great to see you. I obviously wish it were under better circumstances," he says before giving me a kiss on the cheek.

Rhett and Serena look like they've stepped straight out of a vogue photoshoot as opposed to having just been on a ten-hour flight. As always, there isn't a single blonde hair out of place on his head. Plus he's the only person I know who would wear slacks and a crisp white shirt on a flight. And even though my best friend is dressed more relaxed in a soft lilac linen shift dress that only seems to heighten the glowy tan of her smooth dark caramel skin, with her curly hair blowing wildly in the breeze around us, she still looks stunning. They really look so good together.

"Yeah, but I don't know how we can top the last time we saw each other."

My heart warms the look Rhett and Serena give one another, as we all know the last time the three of us were together was at the big surprise engagement.

"That was really the most magical day," Serena says brimming with glee.

Her entire face lights up, her cheeks spreading with a rosy hue, and her eyes soften as she continues looking lovingly at her fiancé. Seeing that joy spread across my best friend's face is one I wish and hope she has every single day for the rest of her life. However, it doesn't take long for a somberness to blanket us.

"We should get going, our flight is scheduled to take off in thirty minutes, and I don't think the pilot will be too keen if we keep him waiting," Rhett says keeping his tone empathetic.

Serena grabs my hand and leads the way onto the huge,

stunning private jet. It's only once I step foot onto the aircraft do I realize, or I guess remember, the crazy level of wealth my best friend's fiancé has. Giving a nod to the flight attendant who stands by the aisle offering a glass of champagne that I gladly take, I almost feel bad stepping on the plush cream carpet that lines the floor. There is no way if I had the means to be able to fly private would I ever set foot on a commercial flight ever again. Damn, I feel a pang of jealousy at the life Serena now has. The only thing that takes the sting out is how much I love her and know she deserves it.

Chapter 25

Roman

It's been three days. *Three days* since I dropped Ruby off at the airport, and it's taken everything in me to give her the space and time she needs. And even though I've kept myself busy working on the custom job for Rhett when I do finally get home, I spend a couple of hours on the laptop putting down ideas for the expansion project. There's no escaping the one woman consuming my mind.

When I go to sleep, my mind replays every single minute of our time at the beach house, like a high definition montage of every single glance, word spoken, touch, and every kiss. The whole thing was like a pendulum going from one extreme to another. From being an outsider looking in, standing on the sidelines as I watched Ruby break. Getting mentally torn apart by the fucking bullshit that asshole Julian spewed. Seeing her withdraw, retreating within herself, was horrible to witness. And what made it even worse was that there was a time several years ago when she'd have reacted and behaved in the same way, all because of *my* actions. *My* choices. *My* decisions.

When you hurt someone, intentionally or not, you should bear witness to their pain. It wasn't right that I hurt her, even if it wasn't what I had wanted, even if I was in a really dark place and felt there was no other option. It still isn't fair that I caused suffering, and she was made to deal with it.

Well, I've witnessed it now. Seen the aftermath, and one thing I can bet my life on is that I will never do or say anything that could hurt her like that again. After seeing that pain, that suffering, all I wanted to do was take it away from her and make her feel better. And even though it wasn't perfect, I felt that in those last couple of days, I was able to help, even if it was just with small things. Making her relax, getting her to smile, keeping her distracted, and obviously the biggest surprise of all was giving her body the pleasure she deserved. I'd never expected things to reach that point. Never. Especially considering how we ended things. But there was no way I was going to deny her. I'd happily have continued giving her everything she wanted, but then that jackass and his stupid, pathetic actions made everything come crashing down on her once again.

Shaking my head, I stop myself from going down that road. I swear to god I would love nothing more than to knock his motherfucking lights out.

Glancing up at the clock on the wall, I realize I need to hurry up and close up the garage to drive back home in time for kick-off.

. . .

The loud, distinctive voice of my cousin, Anthony, echoes around the house.

"Yo, Uncle E, Ro, I come baring food."

By the time I get downstairs, my dad's taken the beers out of the fridge and Anthony is making himself at home on the couch. My stomach rumbles at the delicious smells coming from the bags of food that are still unopened on the coffee table.

"You realize there's nothing stopping you from grabbing some plates and serving out the food, right?. I'm the one who put in the order and paid in advance. The only reason I got you to pick it up was because you were passing it on your way here," Dad says matter-of-factly.

It always makes me chuckle when my dad berates my cousin. It doesn't matter how old we are, he will always call him out. And seeing just how fast Anthony jumps up from the sofa and grabs some plates from the kitchen, I would bet anything that if anyone asked, my cousin would admit he's more terrified of my dad than his own.

"So what we are eating?" I ask as I take a seat on the couch.

"I went with the rib platter, brisket ends, cornbread, and creamed corn. I wasn't in the mood to play waiter and take everyone's order."

"What the hell is going on with their offensive line today? Even our center back in high school made better snaps than he has this evening. Sheesh, pay me his salary and I'll do a damn better job," Anthony brags.

"Dude, you bring a whole new meaning to the term fumble. I swear you get reality and your dreams mixed up sometimes. I've seen you play. Well, try to, at least."

Dad bursts out in a loud belly laugh. Mainly because he knows I'm speaking the truth.

I needed this evening. Just sitting back, having a nice cold beer, enjoying some good food, watching a... well, a shit game, but still. And despite all his flaws and ridiculous behavior, Anthony's wild running commentary is the perfect addition to a pretty chill evening.

I got most of the bodywork finished on Rhett's job by lunchtime, so I started getting to work on some of the other bookings we've got in the shop. I'd planned to work through lunch in order to get out early, but I'm gonna need another coffee, to boost my energy levels back up.

"Dad, do you want a coffee?" I shout.

"No, I'm good."

Making myself a cup, I reach into my coveralls for my phone and scroll through my messages. I look at the last exchange I had with my sister, letting me know they had dropped Ruby off at her apartment. Taking a seat on the couch in the office, I decide to call Serena and see if there is any update on how she's doing.

"Heya, can you talk?" I ask.

"Sure, hold on, let me quickly get the door." There is a soft click of her closing it. "How are you? How's Dad?"

"We're good. We're good. How's it being back at work after your vacation?"

"Obviously, I loved being away. We had the most amazing time. But I won't lie, there's a huge part of me that's glad to be back in the office. Just don't tell Rhett."

I gotta laugh as she's always loved her job, and I swear she's one of those weird people who is genuinely happiest when she's at work.

"Don't worry, your secret's safe with me."

"Good. Also, it was the longest I've been away, so that felt like I was itching to get back. And as much as I know he'd never admit it, I know Rhett was struggling to only be updated with the daily reports he was getting emailed. That's another thing I love about him and us. We both love to work."

It's crazy, she's now been engaged for over a month, but I swear this is the first time I've heard her talk about being in love with him.

"Anyway, I guess the only bad thing or, let's say, difficult, wasn't that we had to come back early. It was the reason we had to."

That's what I was planning on talking to her about.

"Yeah. How's Ruby been holding up?"

"Well, on the flight back, she told me everything."

My fingers twitch on my coffee cup as I wonder just how much Ruby told her. I wonder if she told my sister about anything that happened between us. Not that I'd have an issue with that. I'm just intrigued.

"Ro, I knew roughly what had happened, as you've given me a rough summary, but it broke my fucking heart when she explained everything. I knew they'd been having issues. You knew how much I couldn't stand the guy and prior to the trip, she'd only given the smallest indications of what was going on. But after hearing everything, knowing she'd been dealing with all this shit alone? Ro, I wanna fucking kill him. I don't care that he's Rhett's brother. That son of a bitch had no right to treat her that way. He shouldn't treat anyone like that, but especially not Rubes."

My anger grows and matches that of my sister's. "Trust me, I get it."

"Anyway, so as I'm sure you can imagine, the flight was emotional, and she was super drained by the time we dropped her back to her apartment. I've been messaging her multiple times a day and we've chatted on the phone several times. Plus, I'm cooking dinner for her tomorrow night."

"Has she been eating regularly? Been going to any of her gym classes or anything?" I ask casually, still not sure if Ruby told her what happened between us.

"Yeah, I've been making her send me pictures of her meals. I don't think she's eating enough, which I keep telling her, but I can tell she's getting annoyed, like I'm mothering her."

"Well, it's good she's eating. Maybe suggest something like a multi-country food challenge."

"What do you mean?"

"Something like making a list of countries and she picks a dish from each place. It'll be something fun, exciting. Keep her busy and I reckon it'll help keep her mind pre-occupied."

"Ooh, that's a good idea. I like that."

"Yeah, I think if she gets herself into a good routine, I'm not sure how she'd do things regarding her work schedule, but if she can get into a good balance with that, eating, getting her body moving and most importantly talking, then that would really help. Opening up in some shape or form. That can be with you, any of her other friends, a therapist, or even just a journal. She just can't get lost in her head. If she does those things, then I know she'll get through it. She's a lot tougher than she knows."

"I know. I know. I just wish there was more that I could do."

"But you are doing everything you can by being there, supporting her, and just giving her what she needs, whenever and whichever way she needs it. I know you, sis; you're probably itching to just dive in and make everything better. But trust me, not only will she 100% get through it, but knowing she put in all the work and built herself back up will make it so much better."

I hate that she's going through this. My chest aches with sadness that I can't be there to do more.

"Yeah, I know. You're right. Who'd have thought the same boy who used to find it funny putting tomatoes in my sneakers and telling me if I eat a handful of M&M's and shove them in my mouth in one go was the equivalent of eating just one as you only swallow once—which would either get me in trouble with Dad or make me puke—would grow into the same man giving such great advice?"

I laugh at that. I used to have so much fun pranking my sisters when we were younger.

"Listen, I've always given brilliant advice. You just haven't always been quick or smart enough to take it."

"Well, I'll give you this one." She laughs.

"Practice makes perfect. Well, I hope you and Ruby have a wonderful dinner tomorrow, and keep me posted on how she's doing." I would never admit this to my sister, but I'm jealous. Jealous that she gets to spend time with Ruby when I'd love nothing more than to do the same.

"Will do. Love you, bro."

"Love you too, sis."

Finishing my coffee, I'm just about to head back to work when my dad walks in and takes a seat on the couch next to me. I can feel his eyes on me without even needing to look at him. "So, how's Ruby holding up?"

I turn to look at him. "I see your hearing is as sharp as ever."

He grunts with a grin, then raises a brow, waiting for me to continue.

"Well, I'm sure you can guess that was Serena on the phone. She said that she's been in regular contact with her, and she seems to be alright. Or I guess as okay as she can be. And Serena's gonna be cooking dinner for her tomorrow."

"That's good to hear. Now, how about you tell me what happened at the house?"

"What do you mean?" I ask, even though I know exactly what he means.

"Don't play dumb. I raised you better than that."

Stretching my arms above my head, I realize I do wanna open up to him.

"So you probably knew more about what was going on when I originally left than I did, considering how much you chat with Serena?"

"Kinda. I got the impression that things were bad. And you obviously explained that you were doing Serena and Ruby a favor by driving her to the vacation house. Then you sent a message saying she'd had a big argument with him, that everything blew up and they broke up. Then you asked if it was okay for you to have a couple of days off because you wanted to stay since you were worried about her."

"Yeah. I didn't go into details about what that asshole

said. Even now I don't think I can repeat them, it still makes me so damn angry. Dad, you don't know how much I wanna smash his face in."

"I'm not surprised. If the things were so bad that you can't even speak of them, then I know they are awful. Ruby's always been like another daughter to me, so even I wanna deck this prick."

A smile breaks out across my face as I appreciate just how much he has always cared about her.

"Yeah, there's definitely a queue forming."

"So, now can you tell me what happened in the days after everything blew up and since your return?"

"I'm not gonna get into too many details, but yeah. We reconnected, we're just taking things easy, enjoying each other's company. Then that ass-wipe got arrested. And when I dropped her at the airport, I told her just to take care of herself. That when the time is right and she feels ready, then we can talk."

Dad nods his head, and I guess a part of me was expecting him to be a bit more surprised. Which must be evident on my face.

"Okay, that's kinda what I thought had happened."

"You did?" The genuine surprise clear in my voice.

"Yeah. Listen, son, I know you think you're subtle and give nothing away, but it's been clear as day that you never stopped loving that girl. Any time your sister would so much as mentioned her name, your neck would be on the brink of snapping with how much you were straining to listen. Child, give me a little credit."

Shaking my head, I roll my eyes but can't help but smile. He's right. He's always goddamn right.

"But what I want to know is how *you're* feeling? That's what's important to me. How are you handling all of this?" I can hear the genuine concern and worry in his voice, and I know it's because of what happened in the past.

"It's weird, like I feel clear about what I want. Or what I'd like. But I'm not stupid. I get that this is all a bit of a shit-show, and there are so many layers to everything. Ruby opened up about things she went through after I broke up with her and... well, it made me feel like shit. I guess there was a part of me that didn't want to acknowledge the extent of her suffering. Probably because that was never my intention."

"Anyone that knows you, knows that you weren't in the right headspace."

"I know, I know, but still. It made me really open my eyes and realize that I want to make her happy. I dunno. I guess it just took me a really long time to realize what I had and see clearly what I wish I could have again."

Rolling my neck, I try to ease some of the tension building.

"I think with everything that has happened, I'm gonna book an appointment with Dr. Stainer to make sure I don't get caught up in my head."

Dad squeezes my shoulder. "That's good. I'm proud of you, son. And always here if you need me."

"Thanks."

It's been a couple of weeks since I've had an appointment,

but just as always, I feel comfortable sitting in the soft bucket armchair in my therapist's office.

"So, Roman, considering everything you've told me, it sounds like you are dealing with the trauma that Ruby went through and then the subsequent entanglement between the two of you really well. You were respectful, understanding, and have kept your lines of communication open. That's all great. But I still get the sense that you're holding something back. Do you think you can dig deeper and let go of what else is bothering you?"

Resting my elbows on my knees, I hold my head in my hands. Unprompted, I do my box breathing as I feel panic work its way through me.

Something that people never talk about when you've reached your deepest and darkest depths before is the underlying fear that seeps into your bones and stays there forever. The fear of you hitting that rock bottom once again.

"I'm scared. I'm scared that I'm not as strong as I need to be. Or wish I was. I don't know if it's because I had to look back on the time I've buried for so long now."

My knuckles dig into my eye sockets. I know I need to get this out. It's just so hard.

"When I was younger, I thought nothing could ever push me to the point where I'd want to end it all. Never. Yet after the accident, the way everything felt like it was drowning me. I... I was so convinced that my life felt like it wasn't worth living. Couldn't see any other way out. There was no solution. Convinced things would never be better."

Sometimes it still scares me at just how close I'd gotten to ending it all. I kept everything in, stupidly believing that if I opened up and talked about my struggles, it would have somehow made me less of a man.

"There's a part of me telling me I'm too damaged, that there's something wrong with me because I'd reached such a low point before."

"Do you feel worried that you'll start getting those dark thoughts again?"

I think about his question carefully. "No... I... no, not exactly. But it's like the fact that I have done that, considered ending my life, that just feels like this black stain I carry with me every day that I can't get rid of."

Looking up, I see Dr. Stainer nodding as he writes on his pad.

"Roman, we've had many sessions together where you've expressed stress, things that have given you anxiety, and problems that have troubled you. You've spoken about fears and regrets and have worked through them successfully. What do you think it is about this situation, this dynamic, that seems to trigger a direct correlation to the breakdown you had in the past? Do you think it's because Ruby is involved with both?"

"Yeah. But not in any kind of blame way. It's more like before, I let her down. I let myself down. I just couldn't live with myself if I did it again."

"But from what you've told me and the way you've left the ball in Ruby's court for her to decide what she wants, whenever she is ready to do so, could some of your fear also be with the possibility that she may not want the same thing as you? Could it be that maybe the fear of rejection, of being on the receiving end of it is something you're not wanting, something you're not used to? Maybe not wanting to acknowledge or think about it? And instead, you're clinging to the one fear you're comfortable with?"

I know he's right. But I just don't feel like it's as simple as that.

"In some ways, maybe. I dunno. Couldn't it be both?" I query.

"There is no right or wrong answer. I just want you to be open and see that it's also possible to have other fears. It doesn't always need to be the worst or most extreme case scenario."

As usual, after finishing a session with Dr. Stainer, I find myself in a quiet, contemplative mood. Sitting in my car in the driveway, I cut the engine and snatch my cell from the console. He was right. There is a part of me that's worried that when the time comes, Ruby won't give me a second chance. But the choice is up to her. As much I want us to give things another go, I can't just plow into it. I just need to be there, ready, and make sure my actions speak louder than just my words. Pulling up my text thread with Ruby, I begin typing a message.

> Heya, just wanted to say I've been thinking of you and wondering how you're doing. And like I said, I'm here if you need anything X

Chapter 26

Ruby

These past couple of weeks have been such a mix of emotions. The first week after getting back from Virginia Beach, I was a crying mess, probably heightened because I got my period. It was weird, as it wasn't just that I'd been crying over Julian and how insane everything had ended. It was as if the floodgates had opened and all the emotions that had been building up, that I suppressed for the past couple of months, finally came to the surface. Once I finally accepted the clear toxicity of the relationship, I realized I was better off without him. It wasn't my fault and there was nothing I could have done. It felt like an emotional breakthrough. Almost as if I'd finally forgiven myself for the way I treated myself, the way I would always find flaws within my own emotions and handling.

There is no denying the appreciation that I have for Roman. We left things completely unresolved, not even addressing us hooking up at the vacation house. We hadn't had a chance to, and given all the drama that had already occurred, and how I was so fresh out of a relationship, there were so many layers to it all.

Time, healing, and understanding were all things I needed. And I've been so grateful for the way he understood that. For the past three weeks, we've messaged each other throughout the day and talked on the phone almost every day. It's never anything heavy or directly related to him and me.

I've been helping him with the proposal for the garage, and it's been something I've enjoyed. The only thing I have struggled with has been the growing pull I feel towards Roman. The girlish excitement every time my cell pings with a message from him. Or the sexual tension that runs through my body on multiple occasions while we've talked on the phone. His velvety deep voice has always affected me, but now it just hits harder. I'd never admit to him that there have been a couple of occasions after we've talked on the phone, where I've then gotten my vibrator out of the nightstand and desperately chased my release while replaying what we did at the pool. I could never bring myself to actually do it while on the phone. No. But I do enjoy the thrill as I save it for after.

The sound of the door buzzer interrupts my thoughts and considering I know that it's my best friend coming over for dinner, now is a really inappropriate time to be thinking about how I've gotten off to the memories of what Roman and I had done. I am however, planning on telling her that something happened. She's been so amazingly supportive these past couple of weeks, and where I had kept quiet when I was going through all that shit with Julian, I don't want to do the same again now.

Opening the door, I'm greeted by two of my favorite sights. My best friend smiling and she's holding a bottle of Sancerre Rosé.

"Now I would happily open the door to this every night," I say, giving her a kiss on the cheek before she makes her way inside.

"I'm gonna allow myself to believe you're mainly talking about me, not the bottle."

"Well, obviously," I reply, putting as much skepticism in my voice as possible. "Ow," I shriek. I'm guessing by the hard way she just slapped my ass she doesn't appreciate my joke. "Damn girl, is the palm of your hand made of steel?" I ask, rubbing my poor backside.

Serena chuckles. "Maybe you better be careful. Now what's on the menu tonight? It smells fantastic and I'm absolutely starving."

"I've made a Greek chicken tray bake."

While I plate us each up, she pours the wine.

"That was damn delicious. And no, I have no shame in the fact I went for seconds, then thirds. To be honest, if there was any left, I'd take it home so I could have it for lunch tomorrow. It was that good," Serena tells while refilling our glasses.

"Next time, I'll double the recipe."

"Atta girl," she says with a wink before clinking my glass.

I've really enjoyed tonight. Since coming back, we've both attempted to make time for each other. Either nights of cooking dinner, or getting our nails done, or even just a quick coffee. Even when I protested that she's newly engaged and

I'm sure her fiancé would eventually get annoyed, she shut me down so quickly. Plus, I've gotta give it to her. She's going to be marrying one of the few good eggs out there. My girl did good. It's reminded me again just how important our friendship is. Which is why I know I need to tell her about her brother.

"So, there's something I need to tell you."

"Okay. Is everything alright?" I can hear the worry in her voice and I nod with a reassuring smile.

"Yeah. It's nothing bad. Basically, I did something I never thought I'd do again."

Her eyes narrow as I'm sure she's trying to guess where I'm going with this.

"When I was at the beach house and all that madness happened, I was a wreck. Just like I explained to you. My self-confidence was shot and I honestly just felt so hurt."

She gives my leg a comforting squeeze and I remember how difficult it had been for her on the plane when I'd recited that phone conversation word for word.

"Well, the first couple of days I... I don't even know what I was. I couldn't get out of bed, and if it hadn't been for your brother, I probably wouldn't even have eaten."

Resting my arm on the back of the couch, my fingers trace along the pattern of the throw blanket.

"He was so sweet. So caring and understanding. He didn't push or pry, he just was there. Looking after me. To be honest, I was pretty surprised by it. I couldn't believe how much he had grown and matured. Anyway, one night we went out for dinner and had a couple of drinks. When we got back we kissed, but nothing happened. Then the next day, well, everything happened. Several times. And before we had time to talk about what we were doing or what it meant, I got the call about Julian getting arrested," I say in a rush, as even though we are best friends, Roman is still her brother. And one thing we never did was talk about my sex life with him. No. That'd just be wrong. When I finally turn my head to face her, I'm a little confused why she has a grin on her face.

"What?"

"I knew it."

"Knew what?"

"I knew something had happened between the two of you."

"How on earth could you have known that?"

"Ruby, I love you. Always have. You're my bestie and we've known each other since kindergarten. And well, considering the fact that you stayed in a house together for a week and since you've been back, haven't mentioned his name. Not once. So I wondered if there was a particular reason you hadn't."

My eyes narrow at her and her stupidly good observational skills.

"You said two reasons. What's the other?"

Her grin only gets bigger, which just winds me up more.

"I know my brother. Not only has it been crystal clear to me that he's wanted and missed you all these years, but it was also the way he been continuously calling, wanting updates on how you were doing. Plus, the way he thinks he knows you better than I do just pisses me off, making suggestions on the things you need or might want as if I wouldn't already know the answer," she says then takes a sip of wine before continuing. "Oh, but I will give him credit for one thing. It was his idea to suggest you do that world cooking challenge. Which I definitely benefitted from tonight."

My mind is reeling as my best friend just sits back and takes another sip of wine. I can't believe she knew and never mentioned or showed anything.

"So I know this is probably a silly question, but do you think there's a part of you that's going to give this thing between you guys a second chance? Like, how would you guys do it?"

"You're not asking a small question there now, are you?" I say before taking a large gulp of wine. "I honestly don't know. Part of me is really drawn in, eager to see if we would or could ever work again. But I'm like, surely this is the worst timing. I've just come out of a clusterfuck of a relationship. I'm not finding the same joy I once did with my work. Plus, we don't even live in the same city. Not even in the same damn state. Is this not just the universe's way of showing how I really don't have my life together?"

"Okay, how about we break this down? About your relationship with Julian. Yes, you guys ended not that long ago. What is it now like five weeks ago?"

I do a rough calculation in my head, then nod that she's correct.

"And from what you said, your head and your heart weren't truly in it for some time before that. You'd already emotionally detached long before it ended. You just let yourself believe you needed to fight for it. There's no timeframe or rulebook of when you're allowed to start thinking about a new relationship. It just happens. If you're wanting it and ready, then who's anyone to say otherwise?" she says, giving my knee a squeeze before continuing. "Now about your job. If you could pick anything you wanted to do, what would it be?" Serena asks curiously.

"I'm not exactly sure. I thought I wanted a career, this career. The pay is great, the hours aren't crazy demanding. I should count myself as lucky. I guess I just feel like another cog in the machine. There's nothing defining to me. If I were in a movie or like a fairytale, then my dream would be to find someone to settle down with, start a family, and maybe on the side work for myself in some shape or form."

"You know that's perfectly achievable."

"I get that logically. It just feels beyond my grasp."

"I get that. And that's normal. Alright, let's say we put the man and the kids on hold just for now. What kinda business would you want to be in that could be your own?"

Excitement bubbles through me as I grab my laptop off the coffee table and show her some ideas I've already started putting together.

"There are so many groups and forums of people asking for help and advice. I'd still be in the same sector, but I'd be working with start-ups or businesses that are small and don't have the right marketing experience that could help elevate their business," I say in a rush. My legs bounce with excitement at even just talking about this.

"Well, why not start putting together a plan and maybe start by going freelance? Then build from that? Start it small, keeping it manageable, maybe beginning with a niche market. Then, as that grows, you build from there, setting up your own place, and hiring your own staff when the time comes to expand. Just like your mom did."

I never really thought of it like that. For the first time in god knows how long, I feel small sparks of hope ignite within me.

The next morning, I wake up with a banging headache, and only just make it to the toilet to puke my guts up. It feels like I'm running a marathon as I walk the few steps from my bathroom back to my bed.

I don't get it. We only had a couple of glasses of wine last night. That shouldn't be making me this ill. Maybe there was something off with the chicken? But surely that should have made me sick last night, not this morning. Or maybe I've come down with something. Urrgh, I can't think. It hurts my brain to concentrate. Whatever it is, I feel like I'm knocking on death's door.

New business planning will have to wait until after I sleep this bug off.

Chapter 27

Roman

T his week has been absolutely nonstop. It's as if every customer within a fifty-mile radius booked in for either a service, oil change, repair, or upgrade, all within the same four days.

My muscles relax as I soak in the steaming hot bath, glad to have the next couple of days off. Snagging my phone off the side, I realize I haven't messaged Ruby since my sister went over to hers for dinner, so I send her a message.

It's been great hearing the way she's slowly been getting back to normal these past few weeks. Like the dark, heavy cloud that's been hanging over her has shifted, and the lightness that had been missing is slowly emerged again. I've heard it in the tone of her voice as we've chatted. The way she's joked more, spoken more animatedly. Even the silly videos and memes we send back and forth have just been more positive. It's been kinda crazy, the way the dynamic has changed between us. Especially when you compare it to how things were ten-plus years ago. From her looking after me, supporting me, being there for me when I was at my lowest—albeit, I was an idiot and hadn't appreciated it at the time—to now, where I've just been trying to be there for her and wishing I could do more.

"Dinner should be ready in about twenty minutes," I shout to my dad as he walks through the front door.

"Looks like I timed that well. Let me go jump in the shower as I still can feel the Castrol GTX on me from working on that oil leak on that Rolls Royce earlier."

Grabbing a beer from the fridge, I take the twist cap off and realize I still haven't heard from Ruby. That's super unlike her. She usually messages back within minutes. Sliding my phone out of my pocket, I check to see if she's read my message. Nope, still unread. Huh, I hope she's alright. Giving her a quick call to check and see, the phone rings and rings, worrying me until she finally answers.

"Hello," she says groggily.

"Hey, are you okay? What's wrong?"

"I feel like shit. Think I'm coming down with something. I'm still in bed, been sick, and feel hot and sweaty one minute, then freezing cold the next."

She sounds ill. Even just speaking those few words, she sounds out of breath.

"Damn, I'm sorry. Do you have anything you can take?"

"Mmmm, um... I dunno. I'm not sure."

I don't enjoy hearing her like this. I really don't like that she's going through this alone. I don't even need to think twice about driving up to see her.

"Okay, Ruby, I've got the next couple of days off. I'm gonna jump in the car and drive up to you. I reckon I'll take around two and a half hours. I'll also stop at the pharmacy to pick up a couple of things. So why don't you try to get a little sleep, and I'll call you again when I'm outside?"

"You don't have to do that." She coughs. "That's too much. I can't ask that of you." Her voice sounds hoarse as she sniffs down the phone.

"You're not asking. I'm offering. I want to. Let me do this for you, I'll worry too much otherwise."

"Okay. I'll keep my phone on loud."

"Good. Alright now try to get some rest and I'll see you in a couple of hours."

"Mmmm hmmm. Okay, see you soon," she says with a croak.

Plan in mind, I eat quickly before putting Dad's plate on the counter. I'm just about to walk up the stairs as he makes his way down.

"Hey, just spoke to Ruby, and she's not doing great. I think she's come down with something. So, since I've got the next couple of days off, I'm gonna drive up and help her out."

His eyes widen slightly before a wide grin spreads across his face.

"Dad, I really don't get how anything I just said could make you smile right now," I snap, slightly confused.

"It's not what you said. Obviously, I hate to hear that Ruby isn't feeling well. I guess I shouldn't be surprised that you're biting to go and help her."

"Dad," I exclaim, rubbing the back of my head to ease the tension I can already feel beginning to build.

"No, no, I don't mean it as a bad thing. Calm down," he says, holding both hands in front of him as if I'm being hysterical. "Look, you told me what happened between the two of you and I've known for ages that you've had feelings for her. I don't think you ever stopped caring about her. I just didn't realize how strong your feelings were. Seeing you so eager to rush to her side, like you can't bare to not be near her, I guess shows I was just slow to realize just how intense and current your feelings for her are."

"Dad, I don't have time for this."

"I know, I know. It just feels like lost puzzle pieces are falling into place. Anyway, thanks for dinner. I'll leave you to get ready in peace. Please drive safe, and send Ruby my love and a speedy recovery."

Patting my back as he passes, I shake my head at the old man and quickly pack a bag of clothes for the next couple of days.

The traffic really wasn't too bad. And ignoring the implied point Dad was making in his parting words, I stopped at the pharmacy and filled an entire basket of things. As I'm not sure exactly what's wrong, I thought it would be best to cover all bases.

Parking the car, I throw my rucksack over my shoulder, the shopping bag in my other hand, and make my way to Ruby's apartment block.

I'm too impatient to wait for the elevator and instead take the stairs two at a time up to her on the fifth floor. When I reach her door, I can feel a bead of sweat run down my back and my cheeks puff out as I'm slightly out of breath. Damn, I thought I was in decent shape, but I took those stairs hard. I knock first, then when that goes unanswered, I ring the buzzer, wondering if she's still asleep. For a second, I wish I'd gotten her to leave it unlocked so I don't have to wake her, but the second that thought pops into my head, I realize how stupid it would be. I'm just about to grab my phone out of my back pocket and call her when I hear the bolt of the lock slide before the door slowly opens, showing Ruby is hunched over, holding onto the frame. Her skin is pale. The dark rings around her eyes give her a pained and hollowed look. My heart fills with both longing and heartbreak, wanting nothing more than to wrap her in my arms and not let her go until she begs me to. At the same time, it physically pains me to see her look so ill. So frail.

"Hey, were you asleep?" I ask, walking through the door. Even despite her being ill, I still take in every single inch of her. She could be spewing her guts up and she would still be the one person I long for the most. There was a time when it had been years where I wasn't close to her, away from her presence, yet these past few weeks have felt so much longer. My skin has been itching to touch her, hold her again.

"Yeah, I think so," she says as she shivers.

I place my rucksack down on the floor and the bag of meds on the counter.

"Can I?" I ask, raising the back of my hand towards her forehead, wanting to see if she's warm. She nods and I can see from the glassiness of her eyes that she's really not doing great.

"Yeah, you're really warm. Have you been able to eat anything?"

"No. I was sick this morning. Haven't been again since, but don't wanna eat anything. Not yet."

"Why don't you get yourself back into bed? I'll make you a tea. And I brought some medicine. Hopefully, once you take them, it'll ease things, and you'll get a decent chunk of sleep. Then tomorrow we see how you're feeling, and I'll make a soup or something. Sound good?"

Reaching out, she takes my hand, squeezing it lightly, giving me a watery smile and a nod before making her way to her bedroom. Unpacking the bag of meds, I turn her kettle on and am glad I also picked up the cold and flu tea bags. I use the bedtime one, hoping that'll get her to sleep nice and quickly. By the time I've got it all ready, I find her wrapped up in her duvet, looking like a cute little bird in a nest, watching the TV in her room.

"Alright, here's water for your meds," I say as I place it on her nightstand. "This tea will help you sleep too."

I then grab the meds out of my pocket and hand them to her as she pulls herself up into a seated position. The only color on her face is the dark smudges under her eyes, which are glassy and unfocused and her hair has escaped the bun she had put it up in, but she's still beautiful to me. I don't think I'd ever not be drawn to her. The thought makes me smile.

"What's funny?" she asks, tentatively blowing on the cup of tea, making the steam swirls disappear.

"Nothing funny. Just that even being sick, I still think you're beautiful."

She coughs at that and for the first time since she's opened the door, I see the faintest hint of color on her cheeks.

She huffs a pitiful laugh. "Now I know that's a big fat lie. I look awful. But it's sweet that you're trying to cheer me up."

"Ruby, one thing you know about me is I don't bullshit. Nor do I lie."

Raising a brow, I wait to see if she tries to argue, but she doesn't.

I scan a look around her room, this being only the second time I've been to her apartment.

Two years ago, she threw Serena a surprise birthday party here. I remember how weird I felt coming as it was the first time I was around her in her home. I only found out afterwards that she had a boyfriend but didn't invite him since she hadn't wanted to make me uncomfortable. I had such mixed feelings about that. There was a part of me that couldn't stand her being with another man. But then there was another side that appreciated that she'd been considerate of *me* over her boyfriend. Especially when she really had no reason to be kind.

I take a seat on the edge of the bed, careful not to disturb the cocoon she's made of her bedding, and watch the home design show she's got on. I don't know how long I sit there, weirdly drawn to the program, when I hear the deep breathing coming from behind me. Turning, I find she's fast asleep. This is what I wish my life could be like. Obviously, I don't want her to be sick, but I want to be close with her at all times. For her to be the first thing I hold in my arms when I wake, and the last thing I kiss before I fall asleep. Ruby, us, it just feels right. She's always been the one and I hate that life, the shit that happened, broke us apart. But that has never changed what I have always known deep down. There has only ever been one Ruby Tanner and she will always be the only woman who not only captured my heart but possessed it too.

I fell asleep on Ruby's couch and forgot to draw the curtains, so the bright sunrise wakes me early. I didn't sleep as uncomfortably as I thought I would, which surprises me.

Silently, I check on her and find she's still fast asleep.

After the bathroom, I lay back down on the couch and turn the TV on. I must have fallen back asleep because the next thing I know, I wake to the sun higher in the sky, and the sound of the toilet flushing. Rubbing the sleep from my face, I turn just as Ruby emerges from the bathroom barefoot, wearing a fluffy oversized white robe that seems to drown her. Her face is still pale, but she seems a little steadier on her feet.

"Morning. How are you feeling today?"

"Better I think but still not great," she says, pulling the tie of her bathrobe tighter.

I make my way over and feel her forehead again.

"You're still warm but not as hot as last night. Why don't I run you a bath, hopefully sweat some of this out of you, then I'll make something light while you soak. Take some more meds and maybe you chill out here for a bit. I'll open up the windows to get some fresh air in here too."

"Yeah, I'd really like that. Thank you." Wrapping her arms around me, she gives me the sweetest hug. Her hand stroking along my back and she kisses my chest just where my heart is before heading to the bathroom.

While she's in the bath, I find a recipe for soup. As it simmers on the stove, I strip her bed, put on clean bedding, start a load of laundry in the machine, then do a quick tidy of her apartment. By the time she's done in the bath, the place is clean.

We're sitting on the sofa and I pull her feet onto my lap, gently massaging them. She's got a bit more color to her face since the bath, taking the meds, and eating. We've just been chilling here watching some TV. She's snagged her laptop off the coffee table, bouncing her attention between the TV and the screen in her lap.

"I know I mentioned yesterday that I'm off for the next couple of days, and since you're still feeling awful, I was thinking I could stay here just while I'm off. I can help with any bits you need, and when you're better, maybe we can also go over the proposal. I can show you all the updates I've got."

"I feel like all you're doing is looking after me at the moment. You've really gotten the short straw recently. But yeah, I'd like the company."

"What the...? When on earth did I do this?" Ruby exclaims in shocked surprise.

"What are you talking about?" I ask, scooting closer to her. She turns her laptop to face me.

"Umm, I'm not exactly sure what I'm looking at."

"This," she says, pointing to an email at the top of the screen.

"Okay, so what is it? What's it about?" I ask, still not exactly sure about what I'm looking at.

"I wasn't sure at first. But then I remember that last night, no, the night before when Serena came round. I was showing her this Facebook group that's dedicated to small start-up businesses. Reading the various posts, I saw how many of them were having the same or similar issues. There's such an enormous gap between them and those really making it. But it's such a fixable thing. Some of these have so much potential but, like with so many start-ups, don't have the funds or the experience to really use their marketing. Especially with the use of social media."

Her voice is still ropey, but even through that, it's easy to hear her enthusiasm.

"Okay, so what does the email say about this?"

"Well, Serena encouraged me to make a post on that group, making some suggestions and just pointing out a few areas they should invest in to help, and so on. Because of my job, I didn't want to post under my name so I did it anonymously as there was no way I was going to risk getting into trouble with work if they found out. Anyway, the admin from the group emailed saying several people saw the post then reached out to them asking if there'd be any way they could contact me because they'd want to hire me."

"Wow, that's amazing. But would you have the time to take any of those on, around your work?"

Stretching her head back, she lets out a deep sigh. "That's the thing. For a while, I've felt like something is missing. I don't enjoy my work anymore. Well, not exactly the work, more the company." Placing the laptop back onto the coffee table, she shifts to face me.

"I know I've been really lucky with my job. The money is great and the actual daily tasks aren't things that give me stress. But I do feel like I'm boxed in. Like it's all gotten so monotonous. The brands and companies we work with all feel the same. They all have crazy large budgets so money can be thrown at everything to easily make it all possible." Her fingers trace along the tassels of a cushion that's wedged beside her.

"It's just... I want more of a challenge. I want to make a change. I've thought about switching things up more and more; going freelance and working with small companies, challenging myself with a much smaller budget, seeing just how creative I can be with limited resources. On my own, I feel like there is just so much room for me to grow. New ways to improve. Yeah, staying where I am gives me stability, but I feel like I'm just another cog in the machine. Nothing special. Just show up, work, day done. That's it."

It's mad. When she talks about going freelance and working for herself, she completely lights up. Even with the little energy she has, her passion shines through. Yet when she speaks about her company, her face is completely different. It's like it drains all the joy and energy out of her. Her eyes begin to get heavy and I can tell all this talk has completely taken it out of her.

"You're getting tired. I don't want you overdoing it. Do you wanna take some more medicine before having a nap?"

"Yeah. That would probably be for the best." She looks so tired, so vulnerable. And as much as I hate seeing her like this, I'm just really glad I'm here because I love nothing more than taking care of her.

Pouring her a fresh glass of water, I follow her into her room. She's standing at the foot of the bed, completely still. "Am I hallucinating or am I just super tired? I swear those aren't the same sheets that were on there when I got into the bath."

"You're not hallucinating. I put fresh ones on. Thought it

would be more comfortable," I say, chuckling when she grasps my arm in genuine shock.

"If I had more energy, I'd make some kinda joke about you just wanting an excuse to go through my drawers, but my brain can't do it."

That has me bursting with laughter.

"Man, you're really being too good to me. I wanna give you a hug, but don't want you to catch what I have."

I gently wrap my arms around her waist and give her a hug. "Don't be silly. My immune system is like Teflon." My lips brush the column of her neck and I can feel her steady pulse beating. *Home.* That's what she feels like. Right now, in my arms, this is what home feels like.

"Now get some rest and I'll be just out there if you need anything."

"Thanks again, Roman. Really, it means a lot."

Giving her a smile, I leave her in peace to get some sleep. When I open her laptop, which luckily isn't password protected, I get a start on my little pet project. She was so passionate as she spoke about going freelance, and I know if she wasn't so sick, she'd be researching the hell out of this. I want to help her, but this is in no way my area of expertise. But I do know who I think will be able to help me. Grabbing my phone, I send a message to my sister.

> Sis, I need your help. And maybe also a favor. Gimme a call when you get a chance.

Chapter 28

Ruby

It takes three days for me to start feeling human again. Once the fever broke, I was awake longer. Thankfully I was only sick the one time because I absolutely hate throwing up. Roman has been amazing. Before I even asked for something, he'd already had it ready and waiting for me. And having someone here, that continual sense of company and companionship, has really been something I hadn't realized I craved so much. I think that's the one thing that has been bittersweet. I've loved having him here. But I've been aware of the countdown to his departure. As much as I've tried to ignore it, especially while I was still feeling like shit, there's no avoiding it now. He needs to head back home this afternoon as he's gotta open up the shop tomorrow morning.

"Do you think you feel well enough to head out? Get out of the apartment and get some fresh air?" Roman asks as we lounge on the couch. His t-shirt has risen up from where he was rubbing his stomach and a shiver runs through me as my eyes follow the lines of his cut muscles. Even when he's not even trying, just sitting there relaxing, this man oozes sex appeal. I know for sure I'm feeling a lot better than I was since my mind races with ideas of running my tongue along that bare section of skin.

"Yeah, I'd be up for that. Maybe not like a super long walk or anything, I think that'll drain me."

"Of course not. I was thinking maybe we walk a block or two and find somewhere to eat?"

"Sold. I think my appetite has come back with a vengeance. Especially now that I can taste again."

"Now, that's what I like to hear. Is there anything in particular you're in the mood for?"

I catch myself just in time before I make a really inappropriate joke, like I'd gladly give him something to taste.

"Let's just see which place either sounds or smells best."

The sound of his laugh wraps around me like a warm hug.

"Sounds good. Alright, shall we make a move?"

"Yeah, let me go grab a sweater."

Putting my sweater on, I get my handbag and lock up as we make our way out. The gentle breeze hits my face as we walk down the sidewalk and I'm glad I put my sweatshirt on. Roman stays close by my side as we make our way down the street, avoiding the people passing us by. I swear I can feel the warmth emanating from his body. It takes everything within me not to reach out and hold his hand. I desperately want to but where we still haven't talked about us, I can't quite bring myself to do it. Now that I'm feeling better, I wonder of we will. I just hate that once again time is against us, he has to head back home when I'd love nothing more than to spend the whole evening with him in bed.

I've noticed several women greedily take in the fine specimen that he is. It sets off a shiver of jealousy in me. Yet he seems complexly oblivious to what's going on, chatting away.

His body still has the build and definition of an in-season athlete. He's never been one for labels or designer clothes—always opting for comfort and practicality over what's on trend. But, my god, the man doesn't realize the damage he does when he rocks a pair of gray sweats. "So, what do you think? You've probably already been here loads of times," Roman asks, interrupting my thoughts.

"What? I missed that. What was the question?"

My face warms in embarrassment that I completely zoned out.

"I was saying how about we check this place out? It's not too busy and smells good too. Whatcha think?" he repeats with a smile.

Looking up, I see we're outside a cute little Italian deli I've been to a few times.

"Yeah, here's good."

"Shall we grab a table inside or out?"

"Inside please."

Roman opens the door and holds it for me to enter first.

"Hi, do you have a table for two?" I ask the waiter.

He leads us to the table in the back. My tummy rumbles at the delicious smells coming from the kitchen. After sitting and placing our orders, I turn towards Roman, needing to finally address everything that has been going on between us. Nervous excitement works its way through me.

"So, I know we never had time to talk about everything that happened when we were at the beach house. And I know you said that I just needed to focus on myself to properly process and heal and all that."

He nods along slowly as I speak.

"I wouldn't say I'm healed. I feel like that's too big and extreme a word. But I have processed everything."

"That's good."

I hum in agreement. "Well, I don't want you to think that I haven't thought about what went on. And there's no denying how great you've been ever since. Like, come on, look, you're here. Now. And have been taking care of me while I've been ill."

"I know. And like I said to you before, it's because I want to." He places both his hands on to the table, just in front of my own. Placing my hands in his palms, he covers my hand with his own and soothingly rubs his thumb along my knuckles.

"Now, we've talked about how things ended between us and the impact it had on me, I think we can now truly move on. You've been through enough and so have I."

The corners of his eyes soften and his shoulders slump slightly. As much as the movement was only small, I can see just how much of a weight has lifted for him.

"I want you to know that when we slept together, I didn't do it because I was in some weak and vulnerable space. It wasn't the kinda thing where I simply needed attention and would have just gone with anyone. I honestly wouldn't have given anyone else the time of day. But with you, it just felt so right."

I need him to know I'm being utterly sincere. He wasn't just a rebound screw. There was definitely more to it.

"I believe you. Yeah, that first night when we kissed, I

was unsure. Especially as we'd been drinking. I didn't want to take advantage. Nor did I want you to regret anything the following day. That's why I stopped. But I was more than happy that you were still keen on it the day after."

My whole body tingles as memories of what we did resurface. Closing my eyes, I bite down on my lip as the flashbacks play before me. His hand squeezes mine, making me open my eyes. I can tell from the flare of his nostrils and the hoodedness of his eyes that he's probably doing the same thing right now.

"Ruby," he growls in a deep, warning tone. There is something deeply empowering about the thought of him struggling to hold himself together right now, simply from a memory.

"I know." Taking a deep breath, I pull myself together. "Where was I?"

"You were saying you didn't want me to think that what happened was just by default."

"Yeah," I say, clearing my throat and getting back on topic. "Look, we have history. There's a thread that will always keep us connected to one another. We still have a strong mutual physical attraction to one another. And along with all that, you've grown and matured in such an amazing way, it's unbelievably impressive." Puffing out his chest slightly, his eyes light up and his excited energy is palpable.

Taking a sip of my coffee, I give myself a second to breathe.

"We have something. Something very special between us. Even now thinking about you heading back home and not being nearby, me not seeing you every day, I... I don't like it. I really don't like it. But I'm not sure how we could even entertain the thought of giving things another go. Or if you'd even be interested. Or how it would work. Or how—"

"Ruby," he says, interrupting me. "I've known, and I'm sure you have too, that I've regretted ever letting you go. I've never stopped wanting you. Yes, I always believed that I would never get the chance to fix things. Or never believing that you would ever give me, give *us*, another shot. But my feelings for you have never changed."

The waiter chooses that precise moment to interrupt us with our food. I'm not even sure I can eat right now as my heart is beating so hard I'm surprised it hasn't burst out of my chest. We wait for him to leave before Roman reaches over, taking both my hands and holds them tightly, sending a bolt of electricity up my arm.

"I know I'm far from perfect, and I'll never claim to be. When we were together before, so much of our lives and relationship was built around me. My training, my football, getting drafted and moving. All of it. And now I can see just how unfair that was. How much you sacrificed."

I shake my head. "But I didn't see it as a sacrifice. I was happy to go with you. I wanted to be wherever you were."

"I know. And even though I appreciated it, I don't think I showed enough gratitude. I really want you. I want us. And I will be happy to do whatever it takes to make things work. So, how about, for now, we give long distance a go? Yes, I know it's not ideal, but we aren't super far away from one another, and if that means me coming up here every week on my days off, then so be it. I don't mind the drive. And if you're working on those days, then that's still fine. We'd have the whole evening together."

Excitement and hope bubble through me. Yes. I want this.

"Roman, yes. *Yes*. I want this so much. We deserve it. I know it won't be easy. I promise I will make the effort. I... You don't know how much I want this to work." Emotion bubbles up inside of me. I never would have thought we would ever get back to this. Never in my wildest dreams.

"There'll be a lot visiting back and forth, but it'll be fun. I know my parents will be happy to see me more often too. The times between visits will feel long and hard but I know, I just know it's going to be so worth it when we do get to spend time together."

He lifts me up and onto his lap. I don't even care that there are people around us probably looking and wondering what on earth we're doing.

"If you're in town and have come down to visit, there isn't a single thing that could keep me busy enough to keep me away from you."

Taking hold of my chin, he tugs me closer before brushing his lips across mine. Starting slowly, he kisses me, pouring every ounce of what he's just told me into the kiss. Every promise, every hope, every potential glimpse into the future.

Finally, he pulls back slightly, giving me a warm loving smile.

"So, is this you agreeing to us giving this a real shot again?"

"Yes. Yes, it is." I don't remember the last time I felt this light. This free or as happy as I do right this second. Like Christmas and birthdays all rolled into one. My whole body is trembling with excitement and I give him another quick kiss before going back to sit in my seat.

"Good. Like I said, we can do long distance at first. Then when the time comes, we can see where we are and what we wanna do, seeing where we are with our jobs and can work out what our next step will be. I will do whatever it takes. And I just want you to go with your heart. Whether that is with us or with your work and career. Can you do that for me?"

"Yes. I will."

"Now let's eat before our food gets cold."

Chapter 29

Roman

4 *months later*

"You know it would have been quicker if I'd have just gotten a cab? There was really no need for you to come and pick me up, I'm sure there are enough things you need to do," I whisper in Ruby's ear as we sit in the back of a luxury town car.

"Don't be silly. Plus, I know your sister will be relieved that everyone arrived. Especially with everything that's happened."

Yeah, that was some unexpected drama. My sister and Rhett are getting married this evening here in St. Barts. The initial plan was for the twenty-four of us attending the wedding to fly out together. Rhett even chartered a large private jet. However, last week, there was a tremendous storm that swept across the island, and part of the runway was damaged, so they were told none of the larger jets were able to land. Only the smaller ones. So, instead of everyone flying together, he had to arrange for us to go into smaller groups.

"Well, there's no need for anyone to worry. I'm here. Everyone else already got here safe and sound. The weather is looking great. I know everything is gonna run smoothly," I tell Ruby reassuringly.

I pull her closer into my chest, caressing her arm and tenderly kissing her on the head. These past few months have been better than I ever could have imagined. It's not been easy, as once we decided to really give things another go, all I wanted to do was spend every waking moment with her. But I couldn't. With me in Philly and her in New York, we have done it so that we see each other a day or two every week. After the third month, things really progressed and she finally decided to leave her company to set up on her own. Though it's been tiring and non-stop for her, one big bonus is that she now spends half her week with me in Franklin Park.

"So what time does the bridal party have to get ready?"

She looks at the time on her phone before turning to me. "In about two hours. The ceremony starts at six. So we're getting ready from two o'clock to allow time for hair and makeup plus the photos. I think they will nab your dad at around five-thirty."

"You know he's gonna get all choked up when he sees her in her dress. His little princess," I tease.

Ruby gives me a shy smile, but there's an anxiousness to her eyes.

"Hey, baby, what's up?"

I think I know what's bothering her.

"I just... I just feel a little nervous. Or, I guess a little uncomfortable. I haven't seen Rhett's sisters yet. And even though I know Julian isn't coming, I still feel weird. I don't want it to be awkward around them."

Just as I thought. I knew this was likely going to be coming up at some point.

"From what you've told me, besides Rhett, his sisters seem to be the only other decent ones from that family."

"They are. Both of them are really sweet. So is his nephew. I guess I just feel like it's going to be uncomfortable, and that's the last thing I want on this day of all days."

Pulling her legs onto my lap, my hands massage along her soft creamy calves and along her thighs, glad that she's wearing a short sundress because I've got something in mind.

"Don't forget, they reached out to you after they found out what had gone down. I wouldn't be surprised if you made them more nervous than they make you. And Rhett was so adamant about keeping the day relaxed and comfortable he didn't invite his mother or brother."

I was so damn happy when I found out neither of them were coming.

Leaning forward, I run my mouth along her throat, kissing her just below her ear. "Let me help you relax a little. But you're going to have to stay as quiet as possible," I whisper.

Her mouth opens in a silent gasp.

Glancing up, I see the driver is completely unaware of what is about to happen, but still, there is no way I'm going to allow him to see my woman in any kind of sexual state so I press the privacy button on the door and wait until the privacy screen is fully up. Capturing her mouth with mine, my tongue leisurely explores and strokes hers, while my fingers slide beneath her dress, pushing her panties to the side. The heat emanating from her gets me rock hard so fast, I'm almost lightheaded. Applying just the lightest of pressure, I run the tip of my finger along her slit, finding her clit already wet and swollen.

"Mmmm," I hum as I brush my lips against her cheek.

Continuing to gently circle her clit, my fingers get wetter and wetter with her essence. Her arms twitch as she struggles to contain her movements and staying quiet. I kiss her deeply the moment I push my fingers into her hot, wet heat, swallowing her cries as my fingers pump in and out.

Her walls clamp down on my fingers so tightly, it's almost too tight to move them. Pushing her hips up, she rocks against my hand, allowing me to reach a deeper angle. I know the second she can feel me pressing against the spongy ridge as her eyes burst open. As much as I would love nothing more than to have her soak me as she reaches ecstasy, I can't risk it. Changing up the angle, I continue fucking her with my fingers.

Ruby pants and I can tell she is close. With pleasure-filled, hooded eyes, she kisses me deeply the moment she comes. Swallowing her moan, I wait as she rides out her orgasm, only pulling back once she quietens down so I can watch the ongoing waves of pleasure wash across her face.

It takes several minutes until she gets herself back together. Once she does, I make a show of rubbing my fingers which had been deep inside her, across my lips before sucking them clean of her juices. A smirk creeps out of the corner of my mouth when I hear her moan.

"Well done for staying quiet. You did very good," I purr quietly.

"Thank you," she says breathlessly, blushing before resting her head on my chest.

"I'm always happy to do whatever it takes for my girl."

"Now don't we all look mighty fine?" Dad says as he pours a drink for the male guests, including a little juice for Rhett's nephew, Kai.

"I would like to make a toast. Rhett, you have continued to show me just how much you love and care for my daughter. Even when there have been hurdles, you both have overcome them. Which has only strengthened your relationship. And boy, was it darn impressive the way you managed to reorganize everything after the fiasco with this place."

Everyone chuckles and nods along in agreement.

"As you know, family is sacred to me and I'm glad it's being extended. Wishing you both a lifetime of love, joy, good health, and happiness. To Rhett and Serena."

"Rhett and Serena," everyone repeats as we all toast.

As the string quartet plays, we all stand as my two nieces walk down the sandy aisle, scattering rose petals. The guests say a collective "aww" before the two of them take their seat beside my sister, Olivia. The maid of honor, my gorgeous girlfriend, walks down the aisle next, in a turquoise silk dress and her hair lightly blowing in the breeze, looking like a goddess that's been painted by one of the masters. And walking beside her is Rhett's best man, his nephew Kai, looking very dapper with his bowtie as he holds her hand. He's probably the only guy, besides my dad, that I wouldn't get jealous of watching her with. I give her a wink and a smile as she takes her place. She really looks breathtaking, especially with the sun-setting backdrop behind her.

Turning, I watch my sister, looking beautiful as she walks down the aisle arm in arm with our dad. Honestly, I just feel true happiness for her. The second she takes her place beside him, I swear you can feel the happiness between her and Rhett. It's palpable. Seeing the emotions from both Serena and Rhett as they say their vows only cements my feelings for Ruby even further. I want to spend the rest of my life with her.

Her eyes then find mine as if she had heard my thoughts. I want this. I want to marry this woman. Spend the rest of my life showing her just how much she means to me. How I will never make the same mistake again by not realizing or appreciating just how lucky I am to have her. And I will spend every waking moment showing and proving to her she deserves the absolute world. I've always loved Ruby. That's been a constant. But with each passing day and especially at moments like this, the love I have for her is so deep, it's imbedded within my soul. Part of my DNA. And I never want that to change.

"It is my greatest honor to now pronounce you husband and wife. You may now kiss the bride," the officiant declares before everyone gets to their feet and applauds the happy couple.

Following a sit down dinner, there are the toasts. My

dad's and Rhett's make everyone emotional, Kai's is very short and sweet and showed great confidence for a five year old, and Ruby's has everyone in stitches. I also didn't miss the looks my sister shot her when the stories were getting very close to embarrassing.

Wrapping my arms around Ruby, we watch as the newlyweds take to the mini makeshift dance floor.

"Hasn't today just been perfect? It's been simply magical," she gushes as she leans back into my arms.

"Yeah. I don't think it could have gone any better. Well, with how Rhett seems to pull off the craziest things, I am a little surprised he didn't do something like hiring someone to train dolphins and fish to be jumping out of the ocean and start singing like in *The Little Mermaid*. That would have been some crazy shit."

Twisting to look at me, she rolls her eyes and laughs. But I catch her mouth with a kiss before she can turn back. She doesn't need to tell me twice when she pulls my arm, leading me onto the dance floor. With Luther Vandross's "Never Too Much" playing, my family happy around me, and the love of my life, my soulmate, in my arms, I've never been happier.

"I love you. I love you so damn much," I murmur to Ruby.

"Aww baby, I love you too."

"Today, seeing the love they have for each other, everyone just being happy and supportive, wanting to share and celebrate the two of them, I want that to be us one day," I tell her.

Her eyes mist up with unshed tears, and she gives me the most beautiful smile I have ever seen.

"Yeah, I think one day this could be us too." Her voice cracks and I can feel my throat tighten with emotion.

We dance away in our own little bubble before Kai interrupts us.

"Ruby, my mummy said I'm meant to dance with you," Kai says with his back straight and a look of determination on his face.

Bless this little kid. Ruby glances up and looks over at Rhett's sister, Kara, who gives her a kind nod back. I knew Ruby was worried about how they would be towards her, but both sisters have been so kind and supportive. Reassuring her that they only want the best for her. Crouching down, I smile at Kai. "Can you look after my girl while you take her for a dance?" I ask him.

"Yeah. I won't let anything happen. I promise," he says, jutting his chin and we seal the deal with a high-five.

"Now did you two girls know that it's tradition for the groom to dance with the flower girls?" I tell my nieces who are standing at his side.

"Really? With both of us?" they ask, their faces lit up with excitement.

"Yup. Now, why don't the two of you grab Rhett, and show him that our family are the best dancers?"

Chapter 30

Ruby

3 *months later*

"Mom, I swear you are the only person I know who thinks eggnog is better than mulled wine. Like seriously? I sometimes really question both your judgment and taste in things."

I love teasing her, especially when it comes to anything Christmas-related. It's like she has this little battle within herself. Torn between wanting to continue the Croatian traditions she grew up with, while also being fully aware that she's been living in the States for over thirty-five years, so our American traditions are pretty deeply ingrained by now.

"Oh, stop it, you. And we both know if I had to pick something to toast with at Christmas, it would always be a glass of Rakija." Shaking her head, she links her arm through mine as we continue making our way through the little Christmas market. Despite the clear blue sky with the sun shining down on us, it's absolutely freezing. It feels like forever ago that we were under the glorious sun in St. Barts, celebrating Serena and Rhett's wedding. Damn, I can't believe that was three months ago.

"Alright, so what else is left on our list to get as I'm really getting cold, Mom?"

"We need to pick up the wreath for the table and get some vanilla powder for the crescent cookies. You already picked up those limited-edition books for your dad, right?"

"Yeah. They're already wrapped, and I'll keep them at Roman's until Christmas Eve. Dad's too nosy, plus I just know if he finds them, he'll work out what they are too easily. He's been wanting those books for too long to not suss it out."

My dad is like the biggest little kid. I swear that man goes on a mission every year to find his presents. Even when I was a kid, I was the one who ended up telling him to behave himself and stop looking, otherwise, I'd tell Mom.

"Is it just me, or does it feel like it's getting colder here every year?" Mom asks, pulling her scarf tighter.

"Yeah, I think it is. However, at least it's that dry cold. So as long as you wrap up and keep moving, it isn't too bad," I tell her.

"Now speaking of moving, come on, let's get going," Mom orders, before rushing inside the store.

I would never have the patience to be doing this with her back in Manhattan. The mad rush from all the tourists and everyone trying to get all their shopping done in time for the holidays? Yeah, give me Franklin Park's two blocks of shops, and one mall any day.

There was a time when I never could have imagined myself considering moving back here. I was convinced that after I spread my wings at eighteen, the only thing that would bring me back was visiting my folks. But with the lease ending at my apartment and given how I'm spending several days down here a week with Roman, it just makes more sense to move. But even bigger than the logical part of it, I just don't want the distance between us anymore. I want to be with him as much as I can. For our relationship to keep growing flourish, which I know will only be possible once we're fully together.

Roman and my relationship has only continued to grow stronger. And every time that I've had to go back, I've hated leaving more and more.

"I think I'm gonna move back here," I blurt as we look through the racks of the boutique store.

My mom turns to me, grinning from ear to ear with her hands holding onto her face, looking cute and comical at the same time.

"Are you being serious right now? You're not teasing me, are you?"

I've gotta laugh at how the pitch in her voice rises.

"I'm not kidding you, Mom. Come on, I doubt you're really that surprised. I've told you my lease was up. I already spend more time down here than I do in New York. Besides, with how well everything is going with Roman and my work, it just makes sense. I can work from anywhere. As much as he's said he'd have no problem moving and finding a new garage, there's no way I'd want to let that happen."

She crashes into me and gives me the biggest squeeze. "Oh, sweetie, you don't know just how happy I am to hear that. It's been so hard the last couple of years only seeing you every few months. Those visits always felt too short and too irregular. That's why I've loved that since you and Roman got back together, I've gotten you back. My sweet girl, this is the best gift I could have asked for."

"Mom, you're acting like I was living on the other side of the world. Besides, we either messaged or spoke on the phone every single day. I think you're getting more emotional in your old age," I tease.

"What do you mean in my old age? You cheeky girl."

"I know. I'm just kidding. Come on, half the time people think you're my older sister. Not my mom."

She preens, loving the compliment. It's true though. My mom looks great for her age.

"Anyway, back to the important point. My baby is moving back. So do you know where you'll pick? You know, you're always more than welcome to stay at home. Or will you go to Roman's? Or will the two of you get your own place?"

"Woah, woah, calm down. I literally only decided less than five minutes ago. I've not even thought that far ahead yet."

"But surely you two have talked about the possibility?"

"Well, yeah, but it's been more in that hypothetical sense. Roman has been so accommodating that any time it's come up in conversation, he just presumed he'd move up to me."

"The two of you will obviously need to discuss it all, but in the meantime, I know just the thing."

Grabbing my arm, she drags me out of the store so fast,

I'm surprised the shop assistant didn't suspect we were shoplifting.

"Slow down, slow down. Where are we going?"

Despite the chill, I'm panting as I try to keep up with her. "You'll see."

Two minutes later, we walk into a realtor's office. I can't help but glance upward in frustration. It's like she's worried I'm going to change my mind, so she's desperate to get me locked in somewhere as soon as possible. I entertain her for a little, and let the relator pull some brochures of places she thinks would be a good fit.

The two of them are chatting away, discussing the various listings when my eyes catch on a poster in the corner. It's not been put on display yet, so I'm guessing it's already been sold. Before I know it, my legs are taking me over to it.

Crouching down, my eyes are transfixed on the picture taking center stage. There sits the most beautiful house I've ever seen. The two-story beauty looks like something you'd find in the deep south, with acres of golden fields surrounding it and it sits before a stunning lake. One I vaguely recognize from when I was younger.

Looking closer, I notice there's a little dock and a wrap-around porch. The whole thing takes my breath away.

"Ruby, you okay over there?" Mom asks, walking toward me. "Oh, wow. Now that's stunning," she says before I even have the chance to answer.

The realtor joins us and jumps right in, telling us all the details. The more she describes, the more I fall in love.

"It's going on the market next week. I think the seller was hoping there'd already be an offer before we list it. However, when you compare it to the other properties around town, it's almost double the price. But I'm hopeful we will get an investor, or someone, say, out of town who is looking for the perfect weekend getaway. If we get the asking price, it'll be our record sale," she says with glee.

"It really is beautiful. I'm sure someone will snap it up. There's no way a place like that will stay empty for long."

A sense of sadness washes over me and I already envy the lucky buyers.

"I would like to make a toast," Dad says, holding up his glass of wine and rises out of his seat at the head of the table surrounded by people they invited to their pre-holiday dinner, including Roman's dad Elijah.

"As you all know, history has always been something that has both fascinated and intrigued me. Hell, I've been lucky enough to make a career out of it." His cheesy chuckle makes everyone laugh.

"But right now, I don't want to talk about the history out of my favorite books. Instead, I'd like to note all of ours. It has been many years since the five of us have been together like this. And despite life and all its hurdles and difficulties, I am beyond happy that we are all back together. So as we kick off this holiday season, I would like to make a toast to Roman and Ruby. To family, friends, reunions, and most of all, to love."

"To love," myself, Mom, Roman, and his dad repeat, all raising our glasses.

"If I may?" Elijah asks. "Thank you for having me over.

It feels like all the puzzle pieces are finally back in place. Ruby, you've always felt like one of the family and you always will. It's great to have your back. Especially as I've seen how much happier my son has been in these past few months, and I know that is all because of you. Thank you for putting the smile back on his face. Now let's dig in, this spread looks amazing."

My heart feels so full right now. Emotion washes over me, and I have to take a second to breathe and compose myself. Damn, why am I so emotional right now? Just like always, without even a look or any prompting, Roman knows. Taking my hand from my lap, he threads his fingers between mine and gives me a light squeeze. Always the caring and reassuring presence whenever I need it.

Roman and I clear the table as Mom brings out the desserts. And I'm not the least bit surprised when she steers the conversation back to my move.

"Do you know, I didn't realize how many places are currently available for rent. Now there was one on Banks Street that I thought looked really nice. They must have done a lot of work for that one. Though the outside doesn't look as good and now doesn't really match the interior. Oh, but that one was nothing compared to that dream one you found, Ruby." Shaking my head, I laugh. I can tell she is going to be like this; non-stop until I've found somewhere.

"What's this about a dream place?" Roman asks, his cheeks raising as he grins curiously.

"I'm telling you, this place is absolutely gorgeous. It goes up next week, but Ruby spotted the poster. I think they were meant to keep it hidden. It sits right on a lake, has five bedrooms, four and a half bathrooms, and looks like something out of the movies."

"Maybe you should look into getting a broker's license, Mom. You've conquered your salon, now maybe it's time you move on over to real estate," I say as she goes into more detail about the place than I can remember.

"I think you might be on to something there. She's made that place sound pretty special," Roman says.

"I think your mom is a little excited about you moving back," Roman says as he takes his shirt and pants off, throwing them onto the chair in the corner.

"I think it's safe to say she's going to be turning this move into her own little pet project and doing everything in her power to make it all happen as fast as possible out of fear of me changing my mind."

Even as we finished our desserts earlier, most of the conversation was geared towards my decision to move back. And although I kept teasing her eagerness, it still was sweet that she was that excited about it.

"But who can blame her? When you called and told me, it felt like my birthday and Christmas all rolled into one." That makes me smile, as those exact words went through my mind when we'd decided to really give us, our relationship another shot.

Climbing onto the bed, he covers my body with his, holding himself up on his elbows on either side of my head.

"Is that so? Does that mean you don't need any

presents?" My voice comes out in a breathy tone as he pushes his hips to mine. I push up against him, desperately chasing the friction against his solid muscular body.

"You moving back here is the ultimate present I could ever ask for. So since you being here is my gift, I think it's only right that I get to unwrap you."

He doesn't even give me a chance to respond before his mouth takes mine in an all-encompassing kiss. Taking my breath away as his lips fuse with mine, the weight of his body pushing me deep into the bed.

Opening my legs, he slowly begins rocking against me. His long, hard length edging along my slit, making me moan. His fingertips leisurely trail along my side, over the soft material of my nightdress, the featherlight touch bordering on ticklish. By the time he reaches the hem of my silk slip, I'm squirming for more. Achingly slow, he pulls me up as he sits on his haunches, sliding my dress over my head before discarding it on the floor. His pupils are blown, eyelids hooded, and his tongue trails across his full lips as he takes me in. The look of complete and utter lust, love, and devotion sets my skin on fire.

Wrapping his arms around me, he pulls me onto his lap. Kissing, stroking, and grinding me along his hard cock. I'm so wet I can feel myself dripping against him. Lifting me slightly, he positions me above the thick head of his cock and slowly pierces me.

His lips brush against mine as I let out a soft moan. Ripples of euphoria cascade through me while he continues rocking into me. My body is on the precipice of pleasure and pain. I love the fullness of being filled by him while breathing through the slight sting as he stretches me. This angle allows him to get even deeper. Hitting just the right spots and I have to turn my head, biting into his arm to stop the loud cry that's worked its way up as my back arches off his lap and into him. My nipples harden as they brush against his hard pecks. Linking my arms around his neck, I roll my hips, adding to his slow and gentle thrusts. The tender and consuming way he's fueling my desire only makes me more desperate for him. Chasing that surge of passion, I rub my clit against him with every thrust. Tingles ricochet down my spine as he buries himself in and out of my wet heat. Every single atom of my being is absorbed by the feel of him.

"Oh, god... yes... oh fuck, yes," I moan.

The second I utter those words out loud, it seems to ignite something within him because he tightens his hold around me and increases his tempo. Laying me back down on the bed, his thrusts never falter.

"Fuck, Ruby. Your pussy is gripping me so tight."

Leaning down, he licks and bites one nipple, then the other flooding me with mind-numbing pleasure. My skin feels so sensitive, it's practically feverish, making me gasp. His thumb finds my clit, and presses down and circles it, making me cover my mouth with my hand to muffle my screams. My knees clamp down on his hips, locking his hand in place as his fingers strum and pinch my clit. My damp quivering thighs struggle to stay locked around him as he pushes me further and further until finally, my body shatters into a million pieces. Fireworks explode in my vision as my lungs struggle with my ragged breathing. Waves of burning pleasure wash over me from head to toe as I come. My arms and legs shake as the aftershocks of my orgasm reverberate through my body, yet Roman's pace and rhythm never break, only prolonging my orgasm as I continue to shudder and tremble. I struggle to get my eyes to focus and my chest to stop heaving from the relentless potency of pleasure that consumes my body.

"Mmmm... yes... fuck... mmm," he cries.

He lets out a deep moan as he comes, which vibrates right through him, sounding like a lion out in the wild. Seconds turn into minutes, as we both make our way back into orbit. Roman's arms tremble slightly as he still holds himself up, brushing his lips down my temple, along my jaw, and peppers kisses softly along my lips. Once we both finally get our breath back, he grazes his mouth on my forehead, kissing me gently before detangling himself from my arms and legs to make his way to the ensuite.

Stretching my arms and legs, I let out a contented sigh as my skin brushes against the cooler sheets around me. Roman then returns with a damp washcloth and softly cleans me up. Treating me like I'm the most delicate flower and making my heart swell even more than it already does for this man. He presses a kiss to my forehead. "You are the best present ever. Now get a little rest as I'm going to be unraveling you all night long."

Chapter 31

Roman

These past couple of days have felt like an exciting dreamlike blur. Once I finished working on the final booking I had before we shut up shop for the holidays, I could put all my time and energy into arranging Ruby's surprise. I ended up taking a leaf out of my brothers-in-law book, enlisting some help to get it all done in time.

The only thing she knows is that she needs to be ready at one o'clock.

Checking my watch, I see I need to get a move on. Most nights she's been staying at mine, but last night she stayed with her folks since she and her mom were having a girly night in watching a Christmas movie and wrapping presents. Like the perfect woman she is, she's ready and waiting on her parents' porch as I pull up. Watching Ruby running over, I can see her excitement as her fingers twitch and she bites her lip as she opens the door and climbs into the car.

"Hey, baby," she says sweetly before leaning over and kissing me as she puts her seatbelt on.

"You ready for your surprise?" I ask, putting the car into drive.

"Yeah, I've been trying to work out what it is, but I can't guess.

Despite the feigned and exaggerated pout she's pulling, I can tell by the look in her eyes that she's excited.

"You know," huffing a laugh, "you're a really hard person to do surprises for. "

"Are you trying to distract me and stop me from asking more questions about where we are going?" she asks with mock incredulousness.

"Now, if I was trying to distract you, I'd be asking you what you thought about the article featuring my sister and Rhett. Or how my dad is taking yours to that car auction in the new year as he prepares to buy his first classic, despite your mom's opinion. Or if that web designer got back to you. Those would be the direction I'd go if distracting you was my aim."

She shakes her head and raises her brows at me for a few silent seconds. Then, just as I had expected, I knew that last point was going to bate her.

"Well, if you really wanna know, he got back to me and sent me a mockup of what he thinks it should look like based on my list of requirements and ideal layout."

Her excitement is contagious, and it helps bank the nerves that have started simmering to the surface. Just ahead of us I can see a rest stop and know it's the perfect place for us to stop. I have to bite my lip to stop myself from laughing when I see the confusion on Ruby's face.

"Umm... okay, are we just taking a little break from

driving or something?" she asks, looking around, trying to decipher what's going on and where exactly we are.

"Not exactly. I need you to put this on," I tell her as I reach into my jacket pocket and take out the sapphire blue satin blindfold.

One of her brows raises slightly.

"As much as I love the direction your thoughts are going, right now things are staying PG, and I just want to keep the surprise up. But we can for sure revisit whatever ideas you got floating later on," I tease, giving her a quick wink.

"I know. Well, I thought it wouldn't be something kinky. But given that you have not indicated what the surprise is you can't really blame my mind for running through all possibilities."

"Well, the quicker you get the blindfold on, the closer you'll be to finding out."

Once her eyes are fully covered, I turn the engine on and continue on our way. I keep her distracted by chatting about our Christmas plans.

Pulling up to a stop, I take a second to swallow down the lump in my throat. Until now, I've just been so preoccupied with trying to make sure everything worked out just right that I haven't really thought about the magnitude of it all.

"Hold on a second. I'll come round and get the door for you," I tell her before getting out, walking round, and helping her out of the car.

Lacing my fingers with hers, I guide her up the path. I can feel a slight tremor in our linked fingers and at first, I think it's her excitement. Only to realize it's me.

"Careful here. There are two steps. Yeah, that's the first, then the next one. Perfect. There you go."

With my free hand, I grip the key out of my pocket and open the door. Keeping my hand on her shoulder, I stand behind her and take the blindfold off. My heart is pounding so fast, I can feel it in my mouth.

"What... Roman, what's going on?" she asks, turning around slowly. Her eyes are wide as she looks around. "What are we doing here? How? What? Where's the realtor?"

Taking her hand, I lead her further into the house that seemed to all over again, until we reach the open brick fireplace in the living room.

"There is no realtor. Not anymore."

Ruby's mouth opens, but no sound comes out.

"I bought the dream house."

Her gasp echoes around the empty room.

I take a quick, steadying breath before continuing. "After my accident, I wasn't really paying attention too much that was going on. You know that better than anyone. Anyway, after they found out I'd never be able to play pro anymore, my team met with my agent and not only let me keep my signing bonus, but added a little extra. I guess it was like a consolation or a kind gesture given everything that happened. In addition to that, I've been saving pretty well the last few years to ensure I'd be able to buy whenever I was ready. I just never had a reason to. Not until now."

The golden hue of her eyes looks like they are glowing right now.

"Ruby, I have made so many mistakes in my life. There have been countless hours I've sat, got angry and frustrated, wishing I'd have done things differently. But the biggest regret I have ever had, the biggest mistake in my life, was letting you go. Not being strong or brave enough to get up, dig deep, and fight. Fight for you. Fight for us. Living my life without you hasn't been one that's been worth living. I'd prefer to relive that accident a million times over than growing old without you."

Tears begin to stream down her face, and her hand claps my arm tightly.

"Oh, Roman," she says, her words choked as her lips tremble.

Squeezing her hand, I get down on one knee.

"I want to wake up next to you every single day. I want to watch you build and conquer your business. I want to lay with you on the couch as you watch your favorite shows while the rain falls outside. Take you to flea markets and do challenges and treasure hunts. I want us to be here, watching our children open their presents on Christmas morning right beside this very fireplace. *Volim te.* I hope I pronounced that right. I've been asking your mom for help with that."

She laughs and nods as tears roll down her cheeks.

"I fucked up before, but I won't make the same mistakes again," I vow. "I love you more than anything in this world. I need you, because without you, I'm not whole. So, Ruby... will you marry me? Will you let me prove to you each and every single day just how lucky I am to have you forever and always?"

Sobs echo around us as she cries out, her tear-filled eyes widen as she frantically nods her head.

"Yes. Yes, of course, a million times. Yes, I'll marry you."

I catch her in my arms and honestly have never felt joy like this. Snatching her onto my bent knee, I take the ring box from my jacket pocket and open it.

"Oh, Roman, it's beautiful," she sobs.

Sliding the white gold, sapphire diamond, halo ring onto her finger feels like I've just turned the key to the door to paradise. Grabbing my face with both hands, she captures me into a kiss. One I will never forget for the rest of my life.

Clutching her to me, I wrap her legs around my waist and stand. Walking us towards the kitchen island, our lips never breaking contact as I carry her in my arms and place her on the counter. Pouring every ounce of love, appreciation, gratitude, and happiness into our kiss. Reaching up I gently grasp her hair, trailing my mouth along her cupid bow, and around her mouth.

"I love you so much. I just can't believe this."

Her brows arch and her cheeks flush into an even deeper hue of red and I can see the shock and disbelief on her face.

"How did you do it? How did you get the house and pull all this off? I've been with you for most of the time. I just... how?"

I excitedly beam at the bewilderment in her tone.

"After your mom spoke about it at dinner, I called her the next morning and asked if she could get me the contact details of the relator. The minute she sent me the number I called and told them I'd be paying cash and would do it at the asking price, on the condition that we can get it sorted as soon as possible."

"Damn, that's why she's been so over the moon. I thought she was just being overly excited about me moving back."

Both of us laugh.

"I also had to tell Serena since I needed her to go over contracts and help with the legal stuff. Especially as I wanted it completed so fast. I guess times like this it's useful having a sister who's a lawyer."

"I'm just so... I'm speechless."

"I meant what I said. I want us to live our lives together. Make our choices and plans as one. So if you don't want us living here, or are not ready for us to move in together just yet, we don't have to. We can use this as our personal getaway. We can look at other places together if you prefer. I don't mind. As long as I'm with you, that's all that matters."

"Are you insane?" she exclaims, her eyes going as wide as they can and she lets out a gasp. "Of course I want us to live here. I want everything you described. I want rainy days on the couch. I want us to have children and watch them grow here. I want Christmas mornings by the fire as they see what Santa left. I want birthday parties and family barbecues by the lake. I want it all. And there is no other person in this world I want to have that future with besides you. Roman. It's always been you."

My heart has never felt so full and I want to drink in this moment so I can remember this feeling until my dying breath.

Lifting her off the counter, I seize her, wrapping her into my arms. Spinning her around, silencing her squeals with a kiss. Knowing and vowing that I will love her until my dying day. Our lives have always been entangled, but I know to the depths of my soul, that the path of our future will be the greatest journey we ever make.

Ruby

Ouch. Despite the rest of my body wanting to stay asleep, my full and slightly sore boobs demand I wake up. Pulling myself up only intensifies the pain. The bed is empty beside me and looking over at the bassinet, I see that's empty too.

I quickly put my robe on and head to the bathroom. Just as it does every morning, the view from the widow above the large roll top bath takes my breath away just as much now as it did when we first moved in. I can't believe it'll be an entire year next week. We were both so eager to move in. With the help of both our families, we moved in just two days after Christmas.

Our plan was to take our time and decorate one room at a time, with the goal of spending about a year doing it up, then have our wedding. Though those plans changed on New Year's Eve when I went to take a sip of champagne and seconds later was running to the bathroom and throwing up.

Two days, and about eight positive tests later, we found out we would need to adjust our plans as we were pregnant.

And three months ago the greatest blessing, Dylan Cameron Parker, entered the world weighing seven and a half pounds, looking just like his daddy.

Even just thinking about him still brings a level of love I never could have imagined.

Finishing up in the bathroom, I head downstairs to find the two men that have my whole heart.

"Oh, you're awake," Roman says, stretched out on the couch with our sleeping angel on his bare chest. The sight sends warmth deep into my heart.

"Not by choice. He's due a feed. That's what woke me."

Walking round the sofa, I first kiss Dylan, then Roman.

"I wanted you to have a sleep in day. He woke at around five and we chilled down here for a bit. Then he fell asleep. He woke up hungry, but I wanted you to get some more sleep, so I gave him the bottle you pumped."

To say Roman has taken well to fatherhood is an understatement. I honestly couldn't even have dreamed of him to be as amazing as he has been. I'm the luckiest woman in the world.

"What's going through your head? I wanna know what you're thinking about that's put that smile on your face."

He stole my heart back in high school. Now, lying with our son, he's the reason my capacity for love has grown.

"You. I was thinking about you and how amazing you've been. And how lucky I am."

"I will always do everything I can to show you how much I love you. How much I love you and Dylan. Forever and always, Ruby."

"Forever and always."

Acknowledgments

This story started singing to me after my first draft of Beyond Expectations, yet I didn't start writing it for quite some time. I won't lie, I was a little nervous to write a second chance romance, as there can be a lot of judgement and stigma with them. And with some, I do personally understand it. Yet there is a part of me that recognizes that sometimes in life we meet the right people, but the unexpected hurdles that get thrown at us, can sometimes break something before it can truly bloom.

That is why, when Roman and Ruby's voices were talking to me louder and louder I knew I needed to tell their story.

As always there is no way I'd be able to get any of my stories written and published if it wasn't for the amazing help and support from those around me.

First I'd like to thank my editor, Sarah Baker @Wordemporium for helping me whip these characters into shape. For encouraging me to delve deeper and not shy away or listen to those loud shouts of self-doubt I regularly have in my head.

Another huge shout out I'd like to make is to Kerri Doyle, my proofreader. Sorry for those long voice notes and rambles and helping clear up my UK English terminology and fitting it into my US characters and world.

As always there is no one I would ever want to make my covers other than Samantha at SamanthaDesigns. Not only are you a so amazing with turning my ideas into beautiful masterpieces, but you've also truly become an amazing friend.

My next shout out goes to my PA, Natasha JPA. Girl, I don't even know where to begin. This one has been an adventure, it's been nail-biting, stressful and filled with breakdowns and worries, but you've always been there to help me through, supported me, and continue to remind me not only why I started writing, but also what it means to me. Thank you. The US tour is going to be insane!

Wrapping up my thanks I'd like to do quick mentions of appreciation to my parents, my kids and Rowena. You all mean so much to me and I honestly wouldn't be able to carry on this wild ride of being an author if it wasn't for your love and support.

And of course, I cannot thank my readers enough. Thank you. Your support, love and appreciation mean more to me than you'll ever know. I still pinch myself that so many of you have taken a chance on little old me and made my dreams come true and read my book. Thank you!!

I can't wait to share the next few releases I've got lined up so keep an eye out.

Also by Natasha Allen

Decisions and Destiny Series

Beyond Expectations

Entangled Paths

Book 3 - Coming Soon

The Pursuit of Pleasure Series

The Perfect Stranger

Enticing Choices

Heady Desires

Searing Need

Lasting Impression

The Pursuit of Pleasure

About the Author

Natasha Allen is a contemporary romance author born and raised in London, now based in East Sussex.

Inspired by the works of Sylvia Day and Kennedy Ryan, she loves to write about diverse and interracial relationships.

When she's not crafting steamy love stories, Natasha can be found lost in a good book.

With a focus on diversity, Natasha strives to create inclusive and relatable love stories that reflect the world around us.

Keep an eye out for her upcoming releases, as she continues to enchant readers with her heartfelt tales of love and desire.

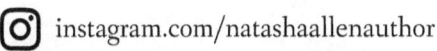 instagram.com/natashaallenauthor

 amazon.com/author/UK